Grace Livingston Hill

*America's Best–Loved
Storyteller*

AMORELLE

BA
PUBLISHING

Print ISBN 978-1-62029-389-8

eBook Editions:
Adobe Digital Edition (.epub) 978-1-62416-048-6
Kindle and MobiPocket Edition (.prc) 978-1-62416-047-9

Cover design: Faceout Studio, www.faceoutstudio.com

Published by Barbour Publishing, Inc., P.O. Box 719, Uhrichsville, Ohio 44683, www.barbourbooks.com

Our mission is to publish and distribute inspirational products offering exceptional value and biblical encouragement to the masses.

 Member of the
Evangelical Christian
Publishers Association

Printed in the United States of America.

Grace Livingston Hill

Chapter 1

Late 1920s

The minister sat in his study beside his desk, thoughtfully reading over a carbon copy of a letter written in his own characterful script.

His strong, kindly, spiritual face wore a troubled look as he considered each word earnestly, a shade of anxiety in his tired eyes, his firm lips set almost sternly. He wore the look of one who was going over once more a momentous decision to make sure he was right.

The hand that held the paper was fragile, and the flesh of his face was almost transparent from recent illness, but there was nothing fragile about his expression. Although a man of a natural sweetness and tenderness, he looked now like one girded for battle, and the reading of the letter might have been the polishing of his sword.

Presently he laid the letter on the desk and bowed his head

upon his folded hands over it, as if in prayer.

That was not the first time he had prayed over that letter. He was a man of prayer and never made a momentous decision without resorting to his Guide. The letter had been written through prayer and after long consideration. A moment later he lifted his head, and the strong, gentle face wore a look of peace. He opened a drawer of his desk, took out a large manila envelope, put the letter into it among some other papers, and replaced it in the drawer, closing the drawer carefully.

Just then, Amorelle came hurrying down the stairs and entered the room with a worried look toward the clock. Her delicate face was a flowerlike replica of her father's. She had the same mixture of sweetness and strength in her glance and the firm set of her lips.

"Father dear," she said tenderly, a little reproachfully, "do you realize that it is almost eight o'clock and you are supposed to be in bed at half past seven? You know the doctor was very particular about it this first time you are downstairs. You are more tired than you know."

"Yes, I know, dear, but I can't go for a few minutes yet. I am expecting a caller, and he ought to be here any minute now. He was to come not later than eight o'clock."

"Oh, Father!" said Amorelle in distress. "You mustn't see callers tonight! You promised me and you promised the doctor that you would absolutely drop the parishional work until you were really strong again. You know the church does not want you to have any burdens to keep you from a quick recovery."

"This is not parishional work, Daughter. This is a very

important matter of business that has been causing me great perplexity and anxiety. It will not take five minutes to transact and then I will retire at once. I have not time now, but I will explain it to you later. I wrote and asked this man to come tonight, and it will distress me greatly if he does not come. Believe me, child, it will do me more harm than good for me not to see him. It will take very little time and then I can rest in peace. It is something that must be attended to at once."

There was something in his quiet voice of authority, in the steady look of his keen blue eyes, that held Amorelle from protesting further. She stood, troubled, in the doorway, wondering whether she ought to call the doctor and get her father to bed in spite of his insistence. But while she hesitated the doorbell rang.

"There he is now," said the minister, rising, his clerical dignity upon him like a garment. "Won't you let him in, dear? It is Mr. Pike. Lemuel Pike."

"Oh, Father! Lemuel Pike! How could he possibly be connected with anything important enough to risk your health? He is a sucker, that's what he is, a selfish sucker! Everybody says so! He just wants to bleed you, borrow money or something. He always has made you look troubled every time he has called. Please, *please*, Father, let me tell him you are not well enough yet to see him."

Amorelle's voice was full of distress.

"No, Amorelle, I must see him. This matter is most important to me. You do not understand. I will explain when he is gone. Will you open the door or must I go myself?"

There was a look of determination on her father's face that Amorelle knew well, a look she had learned to obey during the years, and she turned swiftly to open the door.

"I can't let you stay but five minutes," she said in a low voice, but pleasantly enough, to the tall, thin visitor who stood on the porch. "This is Father's first day downstairs, and he ought to have been in bed half an hour ago."

Amorelle wondered why it always annoyed her that this man's eyes were set so close together.

"Your father sent for me!" said Lemuel Pike coldly. And he strode past her into the study, closing the door behind him.

Amorelle looked anxiously after him then hovered around the hall and parlor, not far from the study door. For some unexplained reason, she felt uneasy about this meeting. Her father seemed tired and worn. That transparent look in his face frightened her. She eyed the clock and listened for the slightest sound from the study but heard only a low murmur of voices now and then.

She went from one window to another, looking at the clock all the while. At last when the parlor clock had ticked out ten minutes after eight, she went to the study door and grasped the knob firmly, at the same time tapping lightly with her fingertips on the door, and then swinging it wide open.

"Father dear!" she said with a very good imitation of his own firmness. "I really must send you to bed at once or I shall have to call the doctor. You know I had very definite orders from him that I dare not disobey."

She had a swift vision of the two men standing facing one

another, her father with a bunch of bills in his hand and Mr. Pike holding a slip of paper. Had Lemuel Pike been borrowing money from Father, now when they were having such heavy expenses?

She gave the caller a quick, suspicious glance, and Lemuel Pike returned a malignant glance to her, deliberately folded the slip of paper, and put it into his pocket.

But when she glanced at her father again, he seemed astonishingly relieved and was answering her meekly enough, "Yes, dear, we are just done."

Lemuel paused with his fingers still at his pocket.

"You don't think you would be willing to rewrite this, leaving out that objectionable phrase, Mr. Dean?" he asked, looking away from Amorelle and giving the minister a meaningful glance.

"No, Mr. Pike, I have thought the matter over carefully, and I feel that it is written as it should be."

Lemuel passed from the room without even a good night. At the front door he paused and gave a swift look back. Something made Amorelle turn back also. She saw her father bent over, groping on the floor for something. As they both looked, he turned back the corner of the rug and seemed to be feeling around.

"Don't do that, Father!" she called sharply, fearsomely. "I'll find whatever you have dropped in just a minute. You are exerting yourself too much!"

The close-set eyes of Lemuel gave another swift glance back. The minister seemed to be poking something under the rug and smoothing the rug back again.

"I've found it," he said a bit breathlessly, slowly straightening up. "It was just my desk key that I dropped."

But Lemuel's look lingered thoughtfully, almost suspiciously, on him as he stepped reluctantly from the manse, leaving behind him that which he loved dearer than his life. Amorelle caught his glance. She never had liked Lemuel Pike. She felt that he was almost criminal now in coming to bother her father when he was just recovering from a serious illness. He ought to have known better even if her father did send for him. It was very likely that Lemuel had asked to come or else her father would surely never have sent for him at a time like this. She could remember that, for a number of years, every time her father had been to see Lemuel Pike, he had returned with distress in his eyes and had sat for long periods, looking off thoughtfully into space, with troubled brow and deep-drawn sighs.

Amorelle closed the front door forcefully and hurried back into the study. She found her father had sunken back into his big armchair, where he had been sitting most of the day, a bright look in his eyes but unutterable weariness on his white face.

"Well, it'll be all right now, little girl!" he said in a weak voice, with a faint smile on his pale lips. "I was so afraid I would leave you without—" The last words were almost a whisper, a gasp. Amorelle looked at him in consternation.

"Sit still," she said gently, trying to keep the fright from her voice. "I'll get you some hot milk before you try to go upstairs."

She hurried into the kitchen, hoping Hannah was still there, but Hannah had gone out to visit her sick sister for a while, and Amorelle had to heat the milk herself. When she came back with it, her father's eyes were closed, and there was a strange stillness about his figure that frightened her. She tried to force a spoonful of the hot milk between his lips, but the lips did not respond.

Frantically she ran to the telephone and called the doctor, rushed to the medicine cabinet, and brought smelling salts, but before she heard the doctor's step at the door, inexperienced as she was, she was sure that her beloved father had left her.

They carried the precious form up to his room and laid it upon his bed. The doctor worked over him for hours, but the minister did not come back from the other world to which he had passed so swiftly and easily.

Kind friends came quickly in response to the doctor's call. They wore startled faces and spoke gently to the minister's white-faced daughter. They offered sympathy and comfort and wept because they had loved the minister. They tried to take Amorelle away to their homes—several of them tried—but the girl sat, white and silent, and shook her head. She even smiled at one dear woman.

"I couldn't leave him!" she said. "Please don't ask me."

"But you cannot do anything more for him. He would want you to come away, I am sure," urged the woman.

Amorelle shook her head.

"No. He wouldn't," she answered softly. "He would know how I would feel. He would know I would want to be here till the end. He knew he must go soon, even if he got well from this attack, and he often talked it over with me. Please, I could not go away."

So they let her alone at last, all but a kind neighbor who insisted upon staying through the night. They were very kind people and were deeply shocked that the man who had brought them comfort and sympathy in all their distresses, who had borne with their whimsicalitites and criticisms and bickerings and strife, had slipped away so quietly without warning. They had not supposed his illness was serious. He had not wanted them to know. So they were sincere in their deep sorrow and tender with the young daughter left thus, alone in the world.

The next morning the city newspapers told the story. Her father's face looking earnestly at her from the printed column with a notice of his death and a brief account of his life was like a blow to Amorelle. How had they known so soon? It seemed almost an intrusion, yet afterward when she summoned courage to read what they had printed, her heart throbbed with pride that he was rated so highly. Her quiet, unobtrusive father who had never sought honors was yet honored by those who had sometimes ignored him in his lifetime.

Then there came letters—flocks of them, troops of them. All the brother ministers in the vicinity wrote, telling how they honored him. Some of the names she recognized as those who had opposed him in presbytery in some move for deeper spirituality, who had playfully laughed at him as being a little fanatical. Yet they honored him now. She could read the sincere appreciation of his strong, true character even between the polite phrases that they felt it incumbent upon them to write.

Telegrams of sympathy poured down upon her from men high in office in his denomination, from college presidents, from scholars, and especially from several great spiritual leaders. It almost overwhelmed her and brought sudden tears of joy to her eyes. Not that it mattered what the great of the earth thought about him, but yet it comforted her that his worth and integrity had been recognized by his contemporaries.

The strange days before the funeral dragged by relentlessly; sad decisions to be made, terrible questions cropping up that seemed so out of place at a time like this and yet were a part of the whole cruel business of dying.

There came a message the second day after her father's death from her uncle Enoch, her father's brother.

I mourn with you in your great loss which is also my own. Deeply regret an injury to my knee will prevent my being with you at the funeral. We want you to plan to come at once to us and make your home here at least for the present. Let us know when to expect you.

Uncle Enoch

Amorelle looked at the message with a sad little smile and thought how pleased her father would be that this message had come. He was very fond of his brother, though they had been separated for years. But he had been sure that Uncle Enoch would stand by her when the shock of his death should come.

She put the message away in her bureau drawer. It was good to know that there was a place to go, but there was an unknown quantity to deal with in the shape of a strange new step-aunt and cousin whom she had never seen, a recent second marriage after

Uncle Enoch had been a widower for years. She shrank from the unfamiliar contact. Aunt Clara, in her few brief messages, had impressed her as a worldly woman, perhaps a selfish one. However, that was a question that would have to be dealt with afterward. So she laid the message out of sight and tried to put it out of mind while she went alone with God through the hard days that were before her.

There were many who came to offer loving sympathy, but of course it was hard to meet even the ones whom she and her father had always loved. Again and again she had to retreat to her room and kneel beside her bed for strength to go on. It would be so much easier if she could have died, too, she thought.

There were kindly, well-meant offers to do shopping for her. Shopping! What would one want of shopping now? What did anything matter now, with her world gone into twilight? "No thank you, no shopping," she said sadly, trying to keep the astonishment out of her voice.

"But surely you'll want a black dress and hat!" they said.

"Oh, no," she said quickly, "my father did not like the idea of putting on black because a dear one had gone to heaven. He would not want me to dress in black for him. I'll just wear this brown dress and hat. He liked them, and they're almost new. Oh, I'd rather not think about clothes now, if you please!"

They shook their heads sadly and said she was odd. Of course her father had been a little bit odd, too. But a young girl, one would think she would want to look like other people.

She did not choose the notables and the great of his

denomination to conduct the service. She rather chose a plain, obscure man who had been his closest friend in that area, a man who would speak about the coming of the Lord Jesus when He will bring with Him the dead in Christ. She wanted a joyous note in the service, and she asked for his favorite song to be sung. The officials in the church had to plan a few extra items in the service to get in all the dignitaries their church pride demanded for a minister who had served their congregation these many years. Amorelle submitted to their wishes, for she did not wish to argue, but she did not like these things. She knew her father would not have liked them. But she also knew he would not oppose anything so nonessential.

So at last the service was over, and his tired, overworked body was laid to rest under the shadow of the church he had served for over twenty-five years; and Amorelle went back to the manse, which kind, skillful hands had made so immaculate and so desolate. A home that was no longer a home. A home with the heart of home gone forever from this earth.

Hannah prepared a nice little supper and tried to make the dining room look cheerful. There were delicate dishes sent in by loving friends and neighbors, but they could not tempt her appetite. Life had become a vast blank. She tried to grasp at the hope and help that her father's advice had left her in the precious days while he was yet with her, when he tried to prepare her for this blank, but somehow her mind was numb. Perhaps she would be able sometime again to think and reason with herself, but as yet there was only one thing her father had taught her that she could remember and grasp, and that was that God was her refuge and strength. She couldn't see the refuge, she couldn't feel the strength, but she knew it was there, and she trusted in it.

But Hannah was suddenly sent for to attend her sister who had developed pneumonia. She went away, expecting the same neighbors who had stayed the night before to come again to be with Amorelle, but they, in turn, understood someone else was to be there. And so the girl was left alone in the house that seemed so silent and empty, and for the first time since her father's death, she was absolutely by herself.

She was secretly relieved not to be under watchful eyes. Everyone had been so kind, and there had been someone continually with her. There had been no chance even to weep. Indeed she had scarcely shed a tear. So now, knowing that she was all alone, she went up to her room in the darkness and flung herself across her bed, letting her desolation sweep over her.

Then for the first time the tears had their way, breaking in a healing flood over her exhausted young soul.

It seemed a long time that she lay there, sobbing into her pillow, feeling that all the waves and billows of life had gone over her and left her alone, forgotten on the shores of life. And then like a faraway echo of her dear father's voice, there came to her words that he had so often of late repeated to her when they were sitting together at twilight, or when he was lying on his bed during his illness.

Fear thou not; for I am with thee: be not dismayed; for I am thy God. . . . I the LORD thy God will hold thy right hand, saying unto thee, Fear not; I will help thee.

And so, resting on the promises that she knew would never fail her, she sank to sleep at last.

It was bright morning when she woke, a trifle later than usual. She had been aroused by the sound of footsteps coming up the path to the house. Had Hannah come back? She sprang up quickly, flung on some garments, and rushed downstairs.

Chapter 2

Amorelle unlocked the front door of the manse, threw it open, and the spring sunshine flooded in and fell across the hall floor. It startled her to see that the sun could shine brightly in a world that had become so dark to her. It was almost like a blow, that sunshine going on just as if nothing had happened.

But Amorelle had no time to consider, for Mrs. Brisbane stood on the front porch, a plate covered with a napkin in her hand, her eager little gimlet eyes boring into the girl's consciousness uncomfortably.

"Good morning. Am'relle," she said, stepping into the hall with assurance. "I just thought I'd run over and see how you got through the night. Did you sleep much? I don't believe you did. You look kinda peaked."

"Oh, I'm all right, thank you, Mrs. Brisbane," said Amorelle, summoning a wan smile. "Yes, I think I slept some."

"Well, I suppose you're not to be blamed for grieving. Your pa certainly was a good man, but you've got your own life to live, you know, and it don't do to give way to one's feelings. Your pa certainly wouldn't have wanted you to do that. He was a sensible man, a very sensible man. I always said that about him, even though he didn't have very good health recently. And then you've got to think of his gain, you know. He's passed to his reward, and you wouldn't want to bring him back, you know, into this world of sin and misery."

Amorelle's lip quivered suddenly, and she caught her breath in a quick way that was almost like a sob as Mrs. Brisbane's pious tone swept ruthlessly over her sensitive consciousness. Then she set her lips in a firm, controlled line.

"Won't you sit down, Mrs. Brisbane," she said politely, motioning toward the shabby manse parlor. "It was very kind of you to come and inquire. But I'm quite all right, thank you."

"Well, I always said you were a brave girl," said the caller, giving her another searching glance as if still hoping to find some evidence of weakness. "Yes, I'll sit down for just a minute, but I can't stay. I'm putting up crab apples today, and I must get at it. But I just thought I'd run over and see if you were all right, and I brought you just a taste of hot biscuits I made for breakfast this morning. Have you had your breakfast yet?"

"Oh, that's very nice of you, Mrs. Brisbane," said Amorelle, trying to make her voice sound steady. "No, I haven't had my breakfast yet. I didn't seem to feel hungry. But perhaps this will help me to eat."

She took the little plate offered graciously and lifted one

corner of the napkin, trying to look interested.

"Oh, they smell delicious! You do make such wonderful biscuits always. It was very kind of you to think of me."

"Well, I didn't think Hannah would likely bother to make anything hot for your breakfast, so I thought I'd just run over with these," said Mrs. Brisbane with a gratified tone to her voice. "Hannah never was one to make hot breads much, was she? Has she got your breakfast ready? Why don't you call her to put these where they'll keep hot till you sit down?"

"Why, Hannah isn't here this morning, Mrs. Brisbane. Her sister was taken very sick last night with pneumonia and they came for Hannah to nurse her!"

"And she went off like that and left you all alone in the house! The first night after a funeral! Well, upon my word! And who stayed with you?"

"Oh, I didn't need anybody to stay with me," smiled Amorelle wanly. "I wasn't afraid."

"Well, but that wasn't hardly respectable!" said Mrs. Brisbane indignantly. "I'm surprised at Hannah!"

"Oh, Hannah wasn't to blame," said Amorelle. "She was distressed about leaving me, but I told her there were plenty of people I could call upon, and she mustn't think of such a thing as waiting a minute. But I really was all right, Mrs. Brisbane. I rather wanted to be alone and quiet just for a little."

"Well, it isn't good for you, and it mustn't happen again. You'll just come over to our house to sleep tonight. I won't hear to anything else."

"You are very kind," murmured Amorelle with a troubled

look in her eyes. "I'm not just sure what I'm going to do yet. I appreciate your invitation, but I think perhaps Hannah may be back tonight. She thought her sister from Barlow might be over to take her place. It really isn't worthwhile for me to bother anybody else. I'm just as well off here, and I'll be having plenty to do."

Mrs. Brisbane's sharp eyes went around the room surprisingly.

"Yes, I suppose there will be plenty to do, but you'll hardly know how to go about it, will you? Didn't I hear your father had a brother?"

"Yes, Uncle Enoch. He lives in the West."

"Strange he wasn't here at the funeral." The sharp eyes searched the girl's sensitive face.

"Why, he had a sprained knee," explained the girl, "and wasn't able to travel. He telegraphed. He said I was to come on and visit them for a while."

"H'm!" said the caller. "He has a family then. One would have supposed some of them would have come to the funeral. His only brother! It would only have been decent."

"Well, you see, Aunt Clara is Uncle Enoch's second wife. We don't know her very well. I don't suppose she would have thought it necessary. My Aunt Jean, Uncle Enoch's first wife, died over ten years ago."

"Weren't there any children?"

"Aunt Clara has a daughter, by her first husband. She's a girl about my age."

"H'm! That don't sound so good for you. Didn't your Aunt Clara write, too, inviting you?"

"Not yet," said Amorelle wearily. "She's scarcely had time."

"Well, are you intending to go?"

"Oh, I'm not sure what I'll do," said the girl, passing a frail hand over her eyes. "You know I really haven't had time to think anything about it."

"It's an awful pity you couldn't just stay here," said the visitor, looking around the room speculatively. "If they should get a young minister, and he should be unmarried, it might be just natural for him to take to you, and then you could just stay here and the manse would be all furnished. It would be a real godsend to a poor, young minister."

"Oh mercy! Mrs. Brisbane, please don't talk like that!" said Amorelle desperately.

"Why, why shouldn't I, child? It would be a perfectly natural thing for a young minister to marry a minister's daughter, and so economical, too—save moving and buying furniture. I heard some folks talking down at the Ladies' Aid the other day, the day your father died. They said if anything happened to him, they thought we ought to have a young minister next time. A change was a good thing. And some of them mentioned that Mr. Cole that's been holding evangelistic services over at Claxton Center. They do say he's open for a church, and he's real spiritual for a young man. Of course, he's lame in one leg, but you wouldn't mind a little thing like that. Only some said they thought he was already engaged. Only, of course, engaged isn't married, and there's many a slip."

"Oh, Mrs. Brisbane! Please," pleaded Amorelle. "Please don't say such things, even in fun."

"Why, I don't see why you feel like that!" said the woman, looking at the girl's troubled face in astonishment. "I'm only suggesting it would be awfully convenient if things would fall out that way. You know you'd really be a lot happier if you were married. That's a girl's natural lot, and there's nothing to be ashamed of about it. I said last night to Mr. Brisbane that it's a pity some well-fixed bachelor here in the town didn't come forward and marry you. At a time like this, you being all broke up this way, it wouldn't be necessary to be formal and wait a long time. It would only be kind to get things settled up for you. I said to Mr. Brisbane, I said, 'And I presume they would, only Amorelle's always been so choosey, never really going with any of the young men, just good friends with all.' It really wasn't called for, Amorelle. You weren't the minister, and you had your own life to live. I always said it wasn't right you shouldn't have had any beaux. Your father ought to have had more forethought."

Amorelle fairly quailed before this avalanche of opinion. But when her caller reached the point of criticizing her beloved father so recently separated from her, her eyes flashed indignantly.

"Mrs. Brisbane," she said with a gentle dignity, "that's enough! Too much! I don't want to get married! And I don't want to hear about it now, either."

"Oh now, Amorelle, don't be foolish! You've got your future to consider, and there's nothing immodest in a girl discussing the possibilities of her marriage. I'm only being kind to you, saying what your own mother might say if she were here. And I say that if some well-fixed young man should come forward and offer to marry you, I think you should accept him. I think the whole parish would bear me out in feeling that way. And there's plenty here could do it, too. There's Carson Emmons. His wife's been dead a good year and he's had seven different housekeepers. It really would be to his advantage to get a good wife. You'd make a good mother for his poor little, peaked twins, and you'd run his house much more economically than any housekeeper. And see how well you'd be fixed. A nice two-story house on the edge of town and a new car and everything!"

"Oh, Mrs. Brisbane!" Amorelle's face was the picture of disgust, but it was no hindrance to the voluble woman.

"No, now, Amorelle, don't be so modest. It's perfectly right what I'm telling you. I haven't a bit of doubt that if Carson Emmons thought you'd accept him, he'd come running. He just needs some good mother to talk to him, and I wouldn't mind being the one!"

"Mrs. Brisbane!" There was horror in Amorelle's tone now.

"No, I wouldn't!" went on the caller, now thoroughly started on a campaign for the good of her minister's orphaned daughter. Mrs. Brisbane loved to set the world right. She felt she had a gift at that sort of thing. "And there's several other in our church and community that I could suggest, too. There's Mr. Merchant! A big house and grounds, a good business, and he a nice, kind bachelor! His wife would have everything easy. Of course he's a bit older than you are, but what are years in a case like that where people are well fixed? Of course his mother is living yet, but she's just on the edge of the grave, so to speak, and it wouldn't be long till you had everything just as you wanted it. I know Mr. Merchant real well. I wouldn't mind putting a bug in his ear."

"Listen, Mrs. Brisbane," said Amorelle, whirling around from the window where she had been staring blindly out, trying to conquer her temper, "if you ever dared say a word like that to any man, I should be so angry I would never want to see you again. I feel as if I could never hold up my head and go around the town again after you have made such suggestions."

"Oh, now don't be silly, Amorelle! I wouldn't say anything you would mind. I'd just kid 'em along. You know me. Why, child, there's plenty in town would just jump at the chance to marry you, and that would settle all your troubles in no time and just fix you for life. There's that Johnny Brewster! A clean, fine fellow, everybody says. Got a nice grocery business going, doing well. He owns the building, and there's a nice little apartment over it you could live in. Course Johnny's young, but I guess at that he isn't more'n a year or two younger than you are, and he's real well and hearty and sensible. Only thing, he hasn't been to college, but you've got learning enough for two, and anyway, in your position you can't afford to stop on a little thing like that!"

Amorelle dropped into a chair weakly and looked at her caller helplessly, on the verge of hysterical laughter. How could she stop that awful tongue? She felt so humiliated it seemed as if she never could hold up her head again. But the clattery tongue went right on.

"And then there's Mr. Pike! He really needs to get married! His hair is beginning to get thin on the top. And they do say he's got plenty of money stowed away!"

Amorelle suddenly rose from the chair, her face white with anger, trembling from head to foot.

"Mrs. Brisbane," she said, "we will please talk about something else. I do not wish to hear anything more about marriage! I do not intend to marry anybody at present, and particularly not any of those men you have mentioned. You may intend kindness, but you make me very angry, and if you say another such word I shall go out of the house and leave you by yourself."

"Hoighty toighty!" laughed Mrs. Brisbane. "A tempest in a teapot! I thought they said you were such a good Christian! Well, if you're so set against marrying, what are you going to do? You might teach school, but all the positions in town are filled for another year, and you wouldn't stand a chance out of your own county where you are known. It takes a lot of pull today to get in anywhere. You might teach music, I suppose," she said with a speculative glance at the old upright piano, "only public opinion wouldn't back you in taking pupils away from Miss Rucker, now that she's lost her leg and couldn't very well do anything else."

"Really, Mrs. Brisbane, I don't think you need worry about me. I shall find my place somewhere," said Amorelle, trying to steady her voice.

"Well, I think it's our call to worry about you," said Mrs. Brisbane virtuously. "You're our pastor's daughter, and of course we feel we must see you into some safe harbor. What are you going to do about your furniture? You can't take that to your uncle's with you. It would cost too much to ship it so far. I suppose you'll have to sell it. The ladies were talking about it the other day. They seemed to think it might be possible for them to buy a few things from you. Mrs. Woods spoke about that walnut bedroom set up in the front room. They were talking about furnishing a couple of the rooms in the manse. You know it used to be quite the thing to have a manse ready furnished. They spoke about your father's library. His books likely would be a great help to a young minister just out of seminary. I think some of the Ladies' Aid are coming in this afternoon—no, I believe it's tomorrow they're coming—to put a price on the things they are willing to buy for the manse. Of course they couldn't give much, but you'd want to help out with your father's old church, and it would really be a blessing to you to get things off your hands. Especially a lot of theological books."

Amorelle gave a cold, startled look at her caller.

"Oh, I couldn't give up the books," she said with decision. "I wouldn't part with them for anything."

"For heaven's sake, why not?" demanded the woman calmly. "That's foolish, Amorelle. What could you do with a lot of books, carting them over the country? Your uncle certainly wouldn't want to pay cartage for them, and you haven't any way to pay storage."

"I haven't made my plans yet, Mrs. Brisbane," said Amorelle with reserve. "There will be a way for everything."

"Well, of course you haven't had much time to plan with your father scarcely cold in his grave yet," assented the woman calmly, "but that's why I came in this morning to say we are willing and glad to help. I don't suppose you've got any money, have you?"

The color swept up into the girl's pale cheeks and over her white forehead into her hair. Her sweet dignity was astonishing.

"I think—I'll manage—Mrs. Brisbane! We haven't any debts, at least."

"Well, that's one good thing; your father always was honest, if he wasn't very provident. It does seem as if out of his salary, with only you to keep, he might have put by a tidy sum. I've known ministers with less than he had to have managed a good, big life insurance, or bonds or something. But then your father never had his mind much on the things of this world, and I suppose in a way that's a credit to him, but somehow it doesn't help out in paying bills. How about the undertaker? Are you figuring to pay him or were you expecting the church to pay that?"

"Certainly I shall pay it!" said Amorelle. She felt cold and numb now to her fingertips.

"Well, that's good if you can do that. Of course the church expects to do something. I don't know just what. I heard the men talking at prayer meeting the other night. They might give you a month's salary if there aren't too many bills left to be paid. That's what the people did for the widow of Reverend Salisbury over at Greenwich last winter. One month's salary clear! But then, you know your father was sick a good two months, and they had to get fill-in preachers as well as pay him. You've got to think of that, you know."

"I'm not expecting anything from the church, Mrs. Brisbane. I would much rather they didn't do anything for me. I'll be all right."

"Oh well, they'll do something. I don't know what it'll be. But it'll be something nice, of course. Our church always does the right thing, and they really thought an awful lot of your father. Of course if they decide to buy your things, why that'll count some. It's the Ladies' Aid really that's thinking of them."

"Mrs. Brisbane, I wish you would ask them not to worry about me." Amorelle was trying to speak pleasantly, almost cheerily. "There really isn't any need for anybody to worry about me. I shall soon have my plans made now and get my things out of the manse."

"Well, yes, of course you wouldn't want to hold up the work of getting ready the place for the next minister," admitted Mrs. Brisbane, rising with a deprecatory look around. "The paint looks pretty well worn off the doors and window sills, doesn't it? Wasn't that just painted last season? Seems as if it ought to have lasted longer than that, doesn't it? What kind of soap do you use?"

Amorelle's desperation was suddenly relieved by the sharp ring of the manse doorbell.

"Mercy! Who's that?" said Mrs. Brisbane, whirling around to peer out from behind the faded, old chenille curtain, through the glass at the side of the front door. "Oh, it's Mrs. Spicer. She's got something in a covered dish. It's likely one of her Spanish omelettes. She thinks everybody appreciates them as much as she does. For my part I think an omelette ought to be eaten piping hot off the skillet and not steam in a dish all the way across the road. Well, Amorelle, I'll just slip out through the kitchen door. I really haven't time to stop and talk. Mrs. Spicer is so long winded. I'll just slip those biscuits onto another plate as I go through and save you the trouble of bringing back the plate and napkin. Good-bye, child! I'll be over to help you bright and early tomorrow. Don't you worry about one thing. I'm going to have you right on my mind all the time!"

Mrs. Brisbane timed her sentence exactly to make the last syllable audible in the hall before the front door opened and she vanished into the dining room, where she slid her biscuits upon a china plate from the corner cupboard, gave an appraising glance around at the immaculate room, and hurried on through, missing not one thing in the kitchen as she unbolted the back door.

Mrs. Spicer was a thin, little old lady with water-faded eyes, crumpled parchment skin, and the palsy. She wore a small perennial shoulder shawl of Scotch plaid, and there was a pitiful shake to her head as she spoke. She held in her shaking hands a covered silver dish, and there was a gentle whine in her voice.

"Oh, good morning, Amorelle"—she quivered—"You poor little lonely thing. I've just been having you on my heart all night!" Her voice quavered into a sob, and the tears rained down wetly as she managed a feeble little arm around the girl's reluctant neck and drew her into a damp embrace.

Amorelle wondered, as she struggled against the over-powering gloom, why it displeased her so to have this dear, little old lady weep. It was wicked of her, of course, to resent other people crying for her.

"It's very dear of you to think of me," she said, trying to speak cheerily. "Won't you come in and sit down?"

The old lady tottered gently in and sank into the upholstered chair by the door, almost upsetting the steaming dish she carried.

Amorelle rescued the dish.

"Shall I set this down for you?' she asked pleasantly.

"Why, yes, if you will. It's just some of my Spanish omelette. Most folks like it, and I thought it would be tasty for your breakfast. That is if I'm not too late? You haven't eaten your breakfast yet, have you?"

"Oh, no, Mrs. Spicer, I slept late this morning. That's very kind of you to think of me."

"Well, I've just been bearing you on my heart all night," said the good woman, letting loose the tears again. "I expect you didn't sleep a mite all night. I expect you just cried your heart out!"

"No, Mrs. Spicer," said Amorelle quietly. "I didn't cry much. Of course I'm going to miss my father desperately, but we talked about his going to heaven. He didn't want me to grieve. He wanted me to think of the time when we shall all be together again. By and by. He wanted me to be brave and trust God and live out whatever God had for me to do. Of course it's terribly hard, but I'm glad for him, joyously glad. You know he suffered greatly those last few months."

Amorelle brushed away a bright tear and tried to smile into the watery old eyes, and the old lady stared at her in wonder.

"Well, it's very wonderful if you can feel that way," she murmured, "but weak human flesh falters. Death is such a final thing! And you and your father were always so close. I know you must feel it intensely."

She got out a black-bordered handkerchief and wiped her eyes.

"One doesn't get over those things! I always say death is so final, so inevitable. I grieve as much today over my sainted husband as

I did the day he died, and that's nearly twenty years ago."

"Yes, it's very hard to face," said Amorelle with a quiver of her lip, "but I promised Father I wouldn't give up to grief and I'm going to try to keep my promise. You know, when you realize that the Lord Jesus has conquered death, there is no more terror in it. The parting is hard, but we who believe do not have to sorrow as others who have no hope. We'll all be at home together someday. Mrs. Spicer, there are sometimes things harder to face than death."

The old lady stared uncomprehendingly at her.

"Yes, I suppose it is so," she assented with a sniff. "But I have always felt keenly the fact that I didn't have a home of my own. It was through no fault of Mr. Spicer's, either. It was all through the machinations of a man who borrowed money from him under false pretenses. A man who lives right here in this village. He was a mere boy when it happened, but he was a slick one. He's old now, but he's still slick. His name is Pike. I'm sure I hope others will be saved from his grasp. And you, Amorelle, poor child, you haven't any home either, have you? Oh, if I had a home of my own I'd invite you right home to live with me as long as you would stay. But you know it's not the same when you're living in your son-in-law's house. You don't feel free. But, poor child, what will you do?"

"I'm not sure yet," said Amorelle reservedly. "My uncle has invited me to come to him. I haven't got my bearings yet, but I'll know soon, and I'll let you know my plans before I go away anyway. I certainly do appreciate your kind thought of me. Now, would you like me to empty this pretty dish right away? You may need if for the next meal."

"Well, if you don't mind," said Mrs. Spicer, rising reluctantly. "Nobody knows I brought that silver dish. They might miss it."

Amorelle slipped the sinking omelette into another dish and hurried back to her caller, who was standing in the hall now, looking back into the study where the door stood open.

"And that was your father's study!" said Mrs. Spicer with a sob in her voice. "Oh, I can see him sitting there in his big chair at the desk now. Such a holy man he was!"

"Yes," said the tortured daughter with an attempt at a smile. "But it's beautiful to think of him in heaven now with his Lord. That's the way he wanted me to think about him."

She held her head high and winked back the tears that wanted to come, steadily holding her lips from trembling.

"Well, if you can feel that way I suppose it's a good thing!" sighed the widow, wiping her eyes. "But somehow poor, weak human nature must grieve!" And she wiped another torrent of tears away.

When Mrs. Spicer had gone, Amorelle locked the door and pulled down the little shade that guarded the glass from curious visitors. Then she walked quickly back to her father's empty study, her hands clenched at her sides, her head thrown back, her eyelids pressing back the hot tears that kept crowding for admission.

"Oh!" she said aloud in an agonized voice. "How am I going to stand it? There will be so many of them! How can I bear it? Even the nice ones we have loved will be so hard, *so hard* to bear! Oh!"

But in a moment more she opened her eyes, shaking off the tears, and looked around. Her father's bookcase with his beloved books stood just before her. And they wanted her to part with them! A look of fierce resolve came into her face. Perhaps before the day was over they would be down upon her, suggesting what she should do with her beloved, shabby old possessions! And if she had not some definite plan, they would overrule her. She was sure of it! Those kind, benevolent, dear, nosey people would insist on running her affairs. Just because she was so young they would think it was their business to engineer every move she made. She thought of Mrs. Brisbane's suggestions with a shudder. No, she must lose no time in getting a plan and acting upon it.

She cast another wild look around her at her father's beautiful desk—the gift of a beloved old friend—his chair, his books, and then she whirled around and ran upstairs.

There was just one person in the whole parish of whom she was willing to ask advice, and that was Miss Lavinia Landon. She would go to her quickly before anyone could hinder.

Chapter 3

Miss Landon was one of the humblest of the parishioners. She was a maiden lady who had lived in a little shingled cottage behind tall lilac trees that had been growing for many years till they almost hid the modest dwelling from the street. She did plain sewing, and some that wasn't so plain, and now and then some fine embroidery, and nobody thought much about her except when they wanted some work done. She lived over in Glenellen, a good mile and a half from Rivington where the church and manse were located, but all her life she had been faithful in attendance at church whenever the weather made it possible for her to get there. She was wisehearted and loyal, and Amorelle's mother had been very fond of her.

Amorelle did not stop to dress up. She put on her hat and hurried out the kitchen door, not even giving a glance to the tasty breakfast that had been brought to her. She had no desire for food. She locked the back door and went out through the little alley behind the garden. She did not want to meet any more kind parishioners yet. She felt that she could not endure any more condolences from anybody until she had talked with Miss Lavinia. She would understand.

She hurried along the alleyway for two blocks to avoid her neighbors. If she met any, they would be sure to ask where she was going so early in the morning.

Her feet sped rapidly across the street and took the river road to Glenellen. It was not a hard walk and was pleasant all the way, but this morning Amorelle's heart was very heavy, and when she raised her eyes to notice the scenery, which she usually loved, it was only to wonder that all things could be so lovely when her dear father was gone from her. It seemed to her a cataclysmic occurrence that ought to affect all nature.

Her heart was beating fast as she hurried along the road. She was trying to put into words just what her heart was feeling, trying to formulate her errand, yet what she was really going for was a smile of understanding. She felt like a little girl rushing to a friendly, loving lap to hide her face and cry therein.

So she was almost breathless from her hasty pace when at last she reached the picket fence and swung the gate open on its big chain. The old weight dangled just as it used to dangle and clank when she was a little girl and used to swing on the gate and eat a rosy apple while her mother talked with Miss Landon.

But the door swung wide before she had time to knock, for the frail, little old lady who sat sewing in the window behind the old lilac bushes had seen her coming down the road and was ready for her with loving arms to gather her in.

"My dear," she said, holding the girl off for a loving smile and then pushing her gently into a waiting rocker. "I've been thinking of you. I'm glad you have come."

Then suddenly Amorelle, who had gone like a soldier through all the hard hours since her father had died, who had borne the grilling services in the church and at the grave with a sweet calm that astounded the whole parish and had met all condolences without giving way, put her face in her hands and began to weep till her whole frail young body shook with her sobs.

"That's right, dear," said Miss Landon, lifting off the girl's hat and smoothing back her brown hair. "Just you cry it out, child. I'll get you a sip and a bite when you're done, for I doubt you've had any breakfast."

Softly she slipped away and let Amorelle cry, and presently she brought a dainty tray. A glass of water with a tinkle of ice; a fragrant cup of coffee; thin, delicate slices of toasted muffins; a fragment of the breast of a chicken.

She set the tray down and lifted the girl's chin in her hand and gently passed a clean, cool, comforting wet washcloth over her face.

"Now, little girl, you'll feel better," she said tenderly. "See if you can't eat a bite and drink a sip of coffee. It will give you strength to talk."

So Amorelle, with an apologetic smile, thanked her and tasted the coffee.

"I guess this was what I needed," she said sorrowfully. "I'm sorry! I didn't mean to cry!"

"Dear heart! Cry all you want to. Just come here whenever you want to cry and I'll quite understand."

So gradually Amorelle grew calm, ate the tempting breakfast, and little by little Miss Landon drew from her all that was in her heart to say. Before long she had told about her two visitors that morning.

"Job's comforters!" smiled the old seamstress. "Well, dearie, don't take them too seriously. But it must have got on your nerves to have it hammered right into you that way. But Mrs. Brisbane at least *thinks* she is kind hearted. You mustn't mind her. Now, dearie, how can I help you? What is it that's troubling you most?"

"Oh, I don't know," said Amorelle catching her breath. "I guess I just needed your heartening smile. It's good to look into your eyes and know you aren't going to try to marry me off to anybody in town nor insist on buying my most precious things."

They laughed together a minute and then the old lady said, "Well, now, let's see just what you ought to do. Had you decided anything, or do you just want me to let you alone and not bother you?"

"Oh no, you couldn't bother me!" said the girl, trying to smile. "I've got to have some advice. That's what I came for. I knew your advice would be right. You see, I suppose I've got to go to my uncle's, at least for a time. Father said some time ago that when he was gone he hoped Uncle Enoch would invite me to come there, and he has, at least briefly by telegram. I suppose there will be a letter. I'm not specially anxious to go, but I guess I ought to for a while anyway. It would have pleased Father.

But I never thought at all about my furniture and Father's dear books. I couldn't part with the books. We've read so many of them together—" she said with quivering lip, "and yet I couldn't exactly land on relatives with a lot of furniture and books."

"Of course you couldn't," said Miss Landon briskly, "and you wouldn't want to take even the books there until you were sure you were going to stay. It might make needless expense. I'll tell you what to do. Why don't you just bring them here and put them in my kitchen chamber? It's a great big, dry, empty room that is never used, and you could store things there as many years as you wanted to and it wouldn't cost you a cent. Then, if you finally decide to marry any of the Brisbane suggestions or anybody else, or if you should want to come back to Glenellen and set up housekeeping sometime, why, it would be an easy matter to move your things."

"Oh, but Miss Landon, I couldn't let you do that for me, not without paying a little something at least," said the girl. "I'm sure I could pay just a little. Perhaps I can get something to do somewhere to earn something. And I'm going to sell some of the things, of course. Perhaps I'll just let the Ladies' Aid have what they want."

"No, you won't," said the old lady decidedly. "You just sell them on your own hook, anything you don't want to keep. Tubs and the gas stove and a lot of junk that's always cluttering around any house. You'd get a little something from them. If I were you, I'd stop at Abe Neatherby's second-hand place on your way back and ask him to come up and look at what you don't want to keep. Then you'll have yourself in hand. The Ladies'

Aid is all well enough, only I know who runs things like that—Mrs. Brisbane and Mrs. Ferguson. And they would skin the eye teeth off an angel. The rest of the women are lambs, but they wouldn't interfere in a matter of that sort, for Mrs. Ferguson has always run the financial part of the Ladies' Aid, and always will as long as she lives. I'd just love to see you get the better of her."

Amorelle smiled sadly.

"Well, I don't want to be mean," she said gently, "but I do hate to have those two women talking over Mother and Father's things."

"Of course!" said Miss Landon brightly. "Well, now you just run home and begin to pack up. Have somebody in to help you move trunks and boxes. I'd come myself and help you only I've promised these curtains by tomorrow noon, and it's going to keep me hustling."

"Oh, I don't need help," said Amorelle. "You've helped me wonderfully already. I didn't know how to keep any of my things without storing them, and I knew that was awfully expensive. But I can't consent to let you do this for me unless you'll get some benefit out of it yourself. Couldn't you use a few of Mother's chairs and her sofa perhaps, or some of the tables and beds? I'd feel so happy to think of some of them being in use."

"Why, yes of course," said Miss Landon looking around. "I'd be pleased as punch to have that lovely sofa and chairs in my front room. I've never been able to replace some of the furniture I had to sell when Mother was sick, and the front room has nothing but a pine table and three cane-seat chairs. You can put your parlor things in there, and Sundays I'll enjoy them, sit on first one and then another and think of you. And sometimes when I have a very high-class customer, I'll take them in there just to show I know what's what in the way of a parlor."

Amorelle laughed in spite of the tears that suddenly sprang to her eyes, and then went and threw her arms around the little old lady and kissed her.

"You're so dear," she said.

"So are you," returned Miss Landon, winking back the tears that came into her own eyes. "I wish you were my niece. I'd like to have you come and live with me. If I only could get back some of the money I had in that bank that closed its doors I'd have you here in no time, uncle or no uncle."

"Oh, you dear Aunt Lavinia! I couldn't do that, of course, but I love you for suggesting it. But aren't you ever going to get any of your money back at all?"

"Well, I don't know. I might and then again I mightn't, but I just can't count on it. But, child, you must remember this: if things don't go well with you, you're always welcome to come to me, and we'll make out somehow. I just love you like my own."

Amorelle came away comforted at last, with a happy little feeling that there *was* a haven for her if everything else should fail. It was good to know there was a refuge, even if she knew she never would let herself seek it unless she had money enough to be a help and not a hindrance to this hard-working woman.

But as Amorelle went in the back gate and unlocked the kitchen door of the manse, she heard the front door bell ringing violently, and she wondered if some of her tormentors had already arrived.

In trepidation Amorelle hurried through to the front door and opened it to find Johnny Brewster standing there, red and embarrassed, his big hands revolving his straw hat nervously, his red curls newly wet and slicked back, a spruce dark blue coat buttoned over the old brown sweater he usually wore on weekdays. His grocery truck was parked halfway down the street on the other side.

Ordinarily Amorelle was very good friends with Johnny. He had been an eager member of the Christian Endeavor under her leadership, a willing helper at all Sunday school picnics, church socials, and the like, and an ardent lover of her father. She had always had a pleasant word and a smile for him, and he had always seemed to admire her respectfully from afar, never by word or look presuming to offer her personal attention. But now, as he stood there fumbling his hat and looking at her out of oddly frightened eyes, their relationship seemed somehow to have changed. With a horrible memory of Mrs. Brisbane and her ill-timed suggestions, the girl began to quake with strange premonition.

"I— You—" began Johnny awkwardly. "That is, may I come in a minute? Are you very busy, Miss Amorelle?"

He had always called her Miss Amorelle. It had been the outward sign of his recognition of the difference between them in class and education.

"Oh, why come right in, Johnny!" she said, trying to make her voice sound bright and natural. "Sit down, won't you?"

Ordinarily Johnny would have breezed in respectfully and remained standing while he told his errand. This time, however, he strode into the parlor and sat down on the edge of the first chair that presented itself, twiddling his hat wildly as if the motion of it would help him keep his equilibrium.

Amorelle looked at him with trouble in her eyes and dropped weakly in the big chair opposite him, trying to disarm her fears. Probably he had only come to offer her sympathy and didn't know what to say, poor lad. Oh, was everybody in the parish going to come? How could she stand such long-drawn-out, sorrowful kindness?

Johnny's good, honest face flushed painfully as he lifted anguished eyes to her gaze and plunged wildly in.

"I wanted ta come and tell ya how sorry I am fer ya, Miss Amorelle!" he began. "I sure did love your father. He sure was a great preacher!"

Amorelle drew a breath of relief and smiled.

"Oh, thank you, Johnny. I do appreciate your sympathy," she said. "And Father was always very fond of you. He was proud of the splendid Christian stand you took among your friends."

The young man flushed with pleasure, and then he looked wildly around the room as if clutching for another sentence to help him through and began again.

"That was why," he said earnestly, "that was why I wanted ta come—at least I dared ta come—that is I come ta offer ya my sympathy—that is my—help. That is, anything I cud do fer ya."

"Oh, you are very kind, Johnny," said Amorelle, looking at him with puzzled eyes.

"No, it ain't kindness!" he blurted out embarrassedly. "I've always thought an awful lot of ya. That is, I've always thought ya were wonderful. But I never dreamed—that is, I never wouldda presumed—and I don't know as you'd consider it now, Miss Amorelle, an' ef ya wouldn't it's all right with me. That is, I mean no offense. I know I'm not in any way fit fer ya, only I'd like ta take care of ya ef you'd let me. And somehow I thought ef you wouldn't mind we ud get married, an' then I cud see ya didn't have things so hard. I got a real good business going now, an' I cud afford ta hire help an' you wouldn't havta work. And I'd take real good care of ya an' see ya had things just as ya wanted 'em, as far as I was able, an' ya wouldn't need ta have anything more ta do with me than ya wanted. I'd try not ta stick around too much, ya know. But I'd be powerful proud of ya— I know I'm not in your class—"

He lifted miserable, shamed eyes to her white face now, as if to implore her not to think too ill of him, and suddenly she bowed her head in her cold hands and began to laugh and cry together, her whole body trembling and shaking with her mirthful sobs.

Johnny stood across the room, twirling his hat, his own face gone white now, his honest, blue eyes filled with distress, his soul racked with compunction. He longed to do something to comfort her, yet he would not lay so much as one of his strong, rough fingers on her sweet bowed head.

In a moment more she had control of herself and lifted her face, wet with tears, yet a smile trembled through.

"Oh, Johnny, *dear!*" she said earnestly. "Please forgive me! I wasn't laughing at you, I'm just all upset; and I do appreciate your great offer. It's the biggest thing a man could do for a woman.

And it's beautiful, what you have said to me. I'll never forget it! But, Johnny, you and I are *friends*, not lovers. There's no question of marrying between us."

"Oh, I know I'm not of your class—!" he broke forth again in a troubled voice.

"No, Johnny, it's not a matter of class between us. It's just that God hasn't put us into that relationship to each other, Johnny." She looked at him keenly. "Whenever did such a thing come into your head? You never had such an idea before, did you?"

"Well, no," said Johnny, getting red again. "I—I. . .just thought of it this morning. I thought I was well fixed— And I thought I'd like ta make things easy fer ya—"

"Johnny, has Mrs. Brisbane been into the store this morning? Has she been talking to you about me?"

Johnny's honest eyes met hers and then dropped sheepishly.

"Well, yes," he owned uncomfortably. "She was in. She did mention ya, but I—"

Amorelle was suddenly seized with that uncontrollable desire to laugh and cry again, but she mastered it.

"Now look here, Johnny," she said earnestly. "You're my friend and I want to keep you so, and you've got to help me. Mrs. Brisbane was over here this morning suggesting all sorts of wild things to me, even suggesting different people in the town I could marry. And I was simply furious at her, but I never dreamed she'd go out and tell the people! Oh, Johnny, I'm so ashamed and troubled! Johnny, I don't *want* to get married! I don't want to marry *anyone*. I'm going out West to live with my uncle's family, and I want to get away from here quietly and decently and not have people talking about me. Won't you help me, Johnny? Won't you help me to put down such ideas and go away like any quiet, decent person? I can't marry you, Johnny, and I hope you won't feel bad. I'm sure you'll be glad someday I said no. But I do want your help. Won't you help me? Won't you be like a good, friendly brother to me?"

"I sure will!" said Johnny earnestly. "What could I do? How should I go about it?"

Amorelle looked wildly around her and, through the open doorway, caught a glimpse of her father's bookcase in the library opposite.

"Well, if you could help me get a few things packed and moved, I'd be so grateful. I want to get Father's books put away in boxes and some of my precious things moved away to the house of a friend, over near the Glen, who is going to keep them for me. You see, I think some of the ladies have an idea of trying to buy Father's books and furniture for the manse, and I couldn't part with them. I'd like to get them all put out of sight before anybody can come and suggest anything about it and make an embarrassing situation for me. Mrs. Brisbane said some of the Ladies' Aid were talking about it."

"Sure I'll help, Miss Amorelle," said Johnny in his old breezy tone. "I'll be glad ta beat that bunch of old cats to it! I sure will! Whaddya wantta do first? The books? Say, I gotta lotta good strong, empty boxes over ta the store. They're clean and nice. I can bring 'em over at noon, and we can get those books into 'em in no time and nail 'em up. Then when I take the run over ta the Glen, I ken deliver 'em, and when anybody come around wanting 'em, they'll be *gone*, see?"

"Oh, Johnny, that would be wonderful," said Amorelle. "But I couldn't take you all that time away from your store. If I just had the boxes, I could pack them and get a truck to take all my things over at once."

"No sense in wasting truck hire," said Johnny. "Ef I'm your brother, why not let me cart 'em? I run over that way twice a day anyway, and my truck is good and strong. I can get quite a load in every time I go, and before you know it they'll all be gone!"

"But some of them are heavy; I'm afraid you couldn't manage them alone."

"Aw, whaddya mean manage? Besides, Tod often goes out on the truck with me, and we'll take the heavy things at night after dark. Then I'll leave Tod over at his home on the way back. That's all fixed now; that's what I'm going ta do. And you don't know how glad I am you'll let me be of some real help. But say, Amorelle, you won't lay it up against me that I asked you that other? I know it was sorta presuming, but I'd a ben glad ta do it ef you felt it was the right thing."

Johnny was all eagerness now, wistfulness. His big, earnest blue eyes searched her face tensely. He was calling her Amorelle just as if he'd always done it, and he didn't even realize it.

"Why, of course not, Johnny. That was really a wonderful thing for you to propose," said Amorelle gently. "That is the highest honor a man may offer a woman. Only you know, too, Johnny, that you are young, a year or two younger than I am, and that you have friends of your own that probably have been occupying that place in your thoughts, and I hope you'll be very happy someday in that snug little house over your store. I'll love the girl you will choose. But you and I are just friends, and today you've come to be more like a brother, too, and I'm glad. I'm just going to call upon you to help me in my need and be real happy in the asking. Father loved you, and he'd be glad that you're helping me. So don't say anything more about presuming, please, and let's be glad in our friendship."

"Well, now that's settled," he said in a relieved tone. "Just let me take a look at those books to see about how many boxes we can use, and I'll bring 'em over when I go to my lunch."

Johnny stumped away, whistling happily, slamming the manse door behind him. And Amorelle retired to her father's big chair to laugh over the strange, embarrassed proposal of marriage and to grind her teeth over Mrs. Brisbane and wonder if the woman could possibly have dared to talk of marriage to the other men whom she had suggested. Oh, how terrible! How humiliating! And there was nothing, *nothing*, she could do to stop it. Her mind ran over the list of available bachelors her caller had mentioned, and she shuddered.

Then suddenly she looked around her. There was just one thing she could do, and that was to get out of Rivington as soon as possible. She must get packed up in a hurry and moved before anybody realized what she was doing. Oh, if only Mrs. Loomis Rivington was at home, she would be able to stop all this nonsense and take her under her watchful eye!

But the Rivingtons were in Europe. They would write lovely, kind letters and probably send her a present of some sort and great sympathy when they knew of her father's death; but they could not protect her from the village gossips and the church meddlemakers. Strange that the two most loved members of her father's church should be from the opposite walks of life. The Rivingtons were old settlers, rich and influential. The town was named for them. Old Judge Rivington had been her father's closest friend and adviser until his death some five or six years before. The younger Loomis-Rivingtons were like him in their friendliness and generosity. And strangely they and Lavinia Landon had the same sympathetic, comforting ways with them. But the Rivingtons were in Europe and Lavinia Landon was not a person of influence. There was nobody to help her. Just nobody! A little dry sob broke in her throat.

Then suddenly there came a thought of her father's tender smile and his voice as he had said to her not long ago, "There is *always God*, little girl, and He loves you more than anyone could."

Ah! She had been forgetting.

She lifted her eyes to the little silver-and-blue card that hung on the wall above her father's desk and read the familiar words: "The eternal God is thy refuge, and underneath are the everlasting arms!" And for a moment, she bowed her head on her father's desk and prayed in her heart for the help she needed. Then she sprang up and went to work.

Chapter 4

Amorelle got a dust cloth and went swiftly around the rooms taking down the beloved old pictures, thankful that she had a place to put them out of the way for a while and that she did not have to decide which to keep and which to give away or sell. There was room in Miss Lavinia's kitchen chamber to stow them all away.

There were not a great many pictures, and it took only a few minutes before they were standing face to the wall in a compact bunch, ready for Johnny any time he should demand a load.

Next she went through the little parlor gathering out a few books and papers, a few vases and ornaments that would need to be packed carefully in her bureau drawers. She came back from carrying them upstairs and looked around, trying to banish the memory of the flower-banked casket that had stood over in the bay window only yesterday, trying to keep back the tears.

Ah! Pain and sweetness and love and parting. How they were mingled. But she must not stop to think. She must go on and get things done. It would all be easier, perhaps, if she would just goad herself with the thought that she must get as much done as possible, irrevocably, before the Ladies' Aid should descend upon her.

She looked around the parlor again, removed a couple of chairs that she did not care to keep, a little table that she never had liked and that had no special associations. There was nothing left now but the couch; the chairs that belonged to it that had been her mother's; a fine, old inlaid table; a small bookcase with glass doors; and the old piano. She eyed the latter with a troubled glance. It wasn't a very good one and had seen long service. Some parishioner moving away had given it to her when she was a child, just beginning music lessons. It wasn't valuable. She couldn't, of course, take it with her, and it would be expensive to move it to Glenellen. Besides, she had to have money to get to Uncle Enoch's. There would be other expenses, too. She must not be dependent upon what the parish would offer to do for her. If they did anything, let it be a surprise, an extra, but she must be independent and pay for everything, though she knew her small bank account had been sadly depleted in the last few sad days. She must get together all she could.

So she deliberately went to the telephone and called up the mother of a small member of her Sunday school class who had told her only a few days before that her daddy was going to get her a piano.

"Mrs. Wayne, this is Amorelle Dean. I'm calling about my

piano. Tessy told me you were going to get one, and I wondered if you would care to consider a second-hand one to start with, and then when she is getting on a little farther, you might be able to trade it on a new one? You see, I'm having to break up my home here, and I can't very well take my piano with me. Of course it's not new, and I wouldn't expect to get much for it. But I thought it ought to bring at least thirty-five dollars. I thought I'd let you know first before I told anyone else."

The outcome of that conversation was that Mrs. Wayne promised to run right around and see the piano, and presently she arrived eagerly with Tessy by the hand and her husband trailing behind.

Mr. Wayne did try to reduce the price, but Amorelle was firm.

"I'm sorry, Mr. Wayne, but I just felt it wasn't worthwhile to part with it for less than that, and I've got to have money to get things settled up here."

The Waynes consulted together in the hall and finally decided to take the piano and said they would send for it around five o'clock that afternoon.

After they were gone, Amorelle went over to the old piano and laid her hands lovingly on its ivory keys. It was like parting from another friend. Perhaps she ought not to have done it. And yet she knew it had been right. She must have money. She slid down to the stool and let her fingers wander softly over the keys, playing an old hymn or two that her father used to love, playing the first little piece her mother taught her when she was a child.

Then suddenly the doorbell sounded out sharply through the house, and she closed the piano quickly and went to the door, hoping nobody had heard her soft music. The parish would think it dreadful of her to be playing the piano the day after her father's funeral.

But it was only Johnny, with his honest face beaming and two boxes on his shoulder.

"I couldn't raise anybody at the back door," he said with a grin, "so I hadta come around here, but I got the truck in the alleyway, and ef you want I should take anything out to Miss Lavinia's I can just sneak 'em out the back door an' nobody'll notice. Now, where do we get the first books from?"

"Oh, I can pack the boxes," said the girl eagerly. "What nice boxes!"

"Naw, you better let me pack 'em. I'm usedta packing, see, an' besides, books are too heavy for your little hands to handle."

So Amorelle opened her father's bookcase and they went to work, Amorelle flicking a duster whenever she got a chance, though Hannah had always kept her minister's study well dusted and they didn't really need it. But Johnny worked fast and skillfully, and the two boxes were tightly filled in no time. Johnny fished out a handful of nails from one pocket and a hammer from the other and nailed the tops on with strong, firm blows. Then he went out to his truck for another box. At last Amorelle gazed at the empty shelves with a sad satisfaction. Now there could be no question about anybody trying to buy her father's library, the most precious treasure she owned.

Johnny promised to be back again at dark for another load,

and Amorelle went into the house to get a bite of lunch. But somehow Mrs. Brisbane's biscuits didn't attract. It seemed as if they would stick in her throat. She swept them and the shriveled Spanish omelette into the garbage pail and found herself a glass of milk and some bread and butter. She didn't want to be reminded of Mrs. Brisbane while she ate.

A letter came from her aunt, special delivery, and Amorelle read it gloomily while she finished her meager lunch. It somehow sounded alien and uncordial, but perhaps it wasn't meant that way. It read:

My dear niece:

Your uncle wants me to write and second his invitation given by telegraph yesterday. He wants you to come and spend the winter with us, and of course we shall be glad to make a place for you in our home while you look around and see what you want to do.

We are not having any second maid this winter, so you will fit in very nicely and won't need to feel that you are on charity. Of course, my daughter, Louise, is going out a good deal socially this winter as it is her first winter out of school, and I don't want her to feel bound too much by home duties, so I shall expect you to do a good many of the duties that she has always looked after, just as an older daughter would do in a home. And, of course, as you haven't any friends here you won't mind staying in when it is necessary.

Your uncle wanted me to say how sorry he was that he couldn't come on to the funeral and to help you settle up things. But I guess you won't have much to do. Of course, you won't need to bring anything but your trunk. Your uncle said you better get a second-hand man in and let him give you a price on everything and dispose of it all at once; that will be the easiest. Of course, I don't suppose you have anything of such value that you would be likely to be cheated.

We thought you'd probably get here around the end of the week. Send us a line to say on what train to expect you. You'll have to get off at the Westside Station and take a taxi to the house. You might have difficulty in finding it if you tried to take the trolley.

So unless we hear to the contrary, we shall expect you by Friday afternoon at the latest. Your uncle's knee is somewhat better, but he isn't able to be out yet. We hope you'll get along all right.

Yours affectionately,
Aunt Clara

Amorelle drew a deep breath when she had read this and gave a little involuntary shiver. Did she only imagine it or was that letter really cold and heartless? However, it was Uncle Enoch who was father's brother and who had sent the first invitation. Father had wanted her to go to Uncle Enoch and she was going. She would try and not think about it till she got there. If it proved uncomfortable she didn't have to stay. She could get a job somewhere and get out. To that end she must get all the money she could from the goods with which she was willing to part. She looked speculatively at the old sideboard and dining room table.

She remembered that her mother had always called them ugly. She herself had never liked them. Perhaps even the small sum they would probably bring would be more profitable to her than keeping them. It wasn't likely she would set up housekeeping and need them. If she did, it would likely be in a little apartment with no dining room. She resolved to sell them if she could. There were no tender memories connected with them as there were with the old rosewood sofa and chairs.

She went around for a few minutes, mentally deciding what to sell in the kitchen and dining room. She must keep her mother's wedding china, of course, but the kitchenware could be cheaply replaced when needed. Strange how quickly chattels assembled themselves into three classes—those to be kept, those to be sold, and those to be given away.

She was upstairs, packing away table linen, bedding, and towels in the walnut bureau drawers, with bits of cherished bric-a-brac in between, when the doorbell again rang sharply through the silent house.

She cast a quick glance at the clock. It couldn't be the man for the piano for it was only four o'clock. She hurried down with a little nervous tremor in her heart. Would Mrs. Brisbane and Mrs. Ferguson come so soon? She had hoped to get more things out of sight before they arrived.

But when she opened the front door her heart sank, for there stood pale-faced, weak-chinned Carson Emmons—the widower of a year whom Mrs. Brisbane had recommended that morning as a possible husband for her—and by either hand he held a sallow little twin. Oh could it be that Mrs. Brisbane had dared to talk to him? Her heart failed her, and her knees grew weak. She stared at the man, and he smiled affably and essayed to come in. Of course she couldn't turn him out. But she felt suddenly as if she might be going to faint! What kind of dreadful meeting was this to be?

"Shake hands with Miss Dean, Annabel, Amelia," admonished the father suavely, and each apathetic twin stuck forth a bony little hand and surveyed her coldly, almost reluctantly, she felt.

"Won't you sit down?" said Amorelle, trying to make her shaking voice sound pleasant and casual.

The widower sat down, and the twins drifted into awkward positions on the edges of two chairs and stared around the room.

"It may seem a little soon for us to call," said the man in some embarrassment. "My excuse is that my business is such that it may be of advantage to us both to transact it soon."

Amorelle gave him a cold look and tried to keep her lips from shaking.

"Yes?" she managed to say steadily.

"You see, I have thought," he began again, looking at her with appraising eyes as if he had never quite noticed her before, "that is, it has been suggested to me that on account of my children I should marry again, rather than try to get along any longer with housekeepers, which are most unsatisfactory."

He paused an instant and looked significantly at Amorelle as though expecting some help from her, but Amorelle sat fixing him with a frozen stare, her whole being up in arms at the awful thing she was being made to endure. She felt chocked with indignation when she thought of Mrs. Brisbane.

"And," said the man, with a quality in his voice that sounded as if he felt he was getting on very well with his difficult speech, even without her help, "when I looked around I felt there was no one who would be better fitted than you to take the place of my sainted wife and bring up my children. In short, Miss Dean, though it may seem a little out of place so soon after a funeral and perhaps a trifle abrupt, I have come to ask you to marry me. I trust you will pardon my haste. It seemed best to come to the point at once and save both you and me trouble. You will be wanting to move out of here soon, and it would save much trouble and expense to move your things right to my house."

He cast an interested glance at the rosewood sofa and chairs and, smiling confidently, awaited an answer.

Amorelle looked at his weak chin, at the sparse yellow moustache that surmounted his fulsome upper lip, at the two prominent front teeth that held in the weak under lip and chin, and barely restrained a shudder.

"I was sure you would understand why I am so precipitate," he added confidently.

Amorelle summoned her voice at last, out of a dry and convulsive throat.

"I quite understand, Mr. Emmons." Her voice sounded dead and far away to her own ears. "But I am not thinking of getting married at present, and when I do it will not be for reasons of convenience."

The man edged out on his chair and spoke with a trifle more color to his voice.

"Oh, but I assure you that is not the only reason I wish to

urge," he said, looking at her as one might admire a new piece of furniture or an automobile one had decided to purchase. "I have always admired you exceedingly. Why, even when my wife was living we used to speak of you always in the highest terms. She felt that you were a young woman of great promise, and it was for your Christian character and your ability that I have admired you. In fact, when this matter first came to my attention, my heart went out to you at once as one whom I could not only admire and respect but also become very fond of. And I can assure you that my children have the same feeling. Amelia, Annabel, speak up and tell Miss Dean how much you think of her."

Suddenly the two pale, inanimate twins arose as one man and spoke in concert in monotonous, well-drilled tones. "We like you, Miss Dean, and we want you to come and be our mother. We promise you we will be good, obedient children and try to please you."

The twins came to an abrupt halt, swaying on their bony little legs and looking timidly toward their father for approval, as if they had just recited a piece and wondered what to do next.

Amorelle had a sudden desire to laugh, yes, and to cry, too. Was it possible she was going to become hysterical?

"That's very sweet of you," she said, trying to smile at the two frightened little girls, "but it's quite impossible. I hope you'll find a nice mother somewhere whom you will like even more and be very happy."

Then she turned toward the father quickly.

"Mr. Emmons, I certainly thank you for your appreciation,

but I'll have to refuse. I have other plans, and I do not want to marry anyone."

The widower gasped slightly and stared at her out of unbelieving eyes.

"But, but—" he said, edging a little farther forward in his chair. "You do not understand. I'm sure you do not understand. I'm very well fixed and my business is growing. In a little while I should be able to offer my wife almost anything she wants. Indeed, even now I would be willing to get you a small car of your own and would allow you a private bank account as well as an allowance with which to run the house. I—"

But Amorelle broke in upon his remarks.

"No, not for a car of my own nor a private bank account nor anything you could offer me, Mr. Emmons. I wouldn't marry you now or ever. I'm sorry if I'm disappointing you, but I just couldn't ever marry you."

But Carson Emmons, in spite of his weak chin, was not in the habit of easily giving up anything he had set out to get, and he simply settled down doggedly to business and proceeded to argue his case, inch by inch, moment by moment, until Amorelle's lips became a thin, firm line of adamant, and her eyes grew frantic with aversion and horror.

Suddenly she glanced up at the quiet little clock on the mantel and saw that it was ten minutes to five. In ten minutes the piano movers would be here. Must they find this ridiculous person still nagging her to marry him? She looked at him in despair. How could she get rid of him?

Just then he arose and came toward her with a motion

almost as if he intended to go down on his knees to implore her to yield to his proposal; and the round-eyed twins sat watching him, fascinated.

Amorelle sprang to her feet and backed off away from him.

"Oh, Mr. Emmons," she cried anxiously, "please, please don't say any more! I cannot marry you. I do not want to marry anyone. Really, you are only making it hard for us both. And, Mr. Emmons, I'm sorry to seem rude, but a moving van is coming at five to take some of my things away, and I'm not quite ready for them yet. Would you excuse me now?"

The pale young man paused and stared at her dumbfounded. Could it be that she was really refusing him finally?

"And you really mean that there is no hope for me?" he said reproachfully. "You would leave these two little motherless girls to grow up under the care of servants? What am I to do?"

Amorelle looked at him desperately.

"The little girls are not my responsibility, Mr. Emmons. God has not put it into my heart to marry you nor to look after them. If you would get down on your knees to Him instead of to me, perhaps He would show you what you are to do. But once and for all, no, Mr. Emmons, I cannot marry you, and I wish you would please go and say no more about it." She was shaken between hilarious laughter and furious tears.

The small, pale blue eyes narrowed almost to the point of indignation, and a baffled look came over the weak face.

"I don't suppose you realize in the least what you are giving up," he said, speaking as sternly as a weak-faced man could speak. "You have not seen the addition I have recently made to my house, nor the handsome furniture I bought shortly before my wife's death. I will go now, but I would like to come after you tomorrow in my car and take you over to my place and let you see how I am fixed before you give your final decision."

"I shall be busy all day tomorrow, Mr. Emmons, and I prefer not to go to your house. I would not marry you under any consideration."

Amorelle's voice had taken on a tragic edge now, like a frightened child, and she felt that if he did not go at once she could not stand it any longer.

He regarded her morosely for a moment and then turned, and taking a twin by either hand, he marched from the door of the manse with haughty mien, down the steps, and out to his car.

Amorelle closed the door quickly, locked it, and fled upstairs. Oh, how much more of this torture had she yet to endure? Would that terrible woman speak to *all* those men she had suggested? How could she escape?

But there was little time to consider. A large moving van was rumbling up to the door.

Amorelle gave a frightened glance from the window and, seeing the van, hurried down.

When the piano was gone, she looked around the room pitifully. Already the place seemed to have taken on an alien look. The home of her childhood was going fast. In another day or two, all would be changed. In another week she would be gone; sooner, if she could get ready. Well it could not be too soon, if she was going to have many more such callers as she had this afternoon.

She set to work again frantically; Johnny would be coming for a load soon after dark.

When Johnny arrived, backing up his truck in the alley, she had the bureau packed and ready to go.

"I'm taking two loads tonight," he said. "Mebbe three, I'll see. We wantta get away with as much as possible before the angry mob arrives!" And he laughed cheerily.

Johnny and Tod hustled things out of the room and stowed them away in the truck, which seemed to hold an amazing amount, and did it all so breezily that Amorelle had no time to feel sorrowful. One minute they were there, the next they were gone, and suddenly she looked around the little parlor that looked so amazingly large and unfamiliar now and found it empty.

She went and sat down on the stairs and tried to stop that sinking feeling that came over her. True, she hadn't eaten much that day, but she didn't want to eat. She passed her hands over her tired eyes and then remembered that Johnny and Tod would soon be back for another load and she must get some old quilts to put around the furniture to keep it from getting scratched.

When Johnny came back, he brought a pail of barley soup and a covered dish containing a generous piece of custard pie.

"Miss Landon says you're to eat that right away," ordered Johnny. "It's good. She gave us some, too. That's why we were so long. Now, can we get that bedroom set?"

Amorelle was very tired when the last load was gone. She had eaten the soup and custard pie with relish, and now she desired nothing so much as to drop into bed and go to sleep.

But just as she was locking the front door, she heard footsteps outside and the bell pealed through the house once more. For an instant she looked wildly around her with the idea of turning off the light and stealing away without opening the door, but she knew she could not do that. It might be almost any of the congregation, and she must not hurt the feelings of people who had loved her father and been good to her for years.

So she girded her heart for whatever might be coming and opened the door, and there stood Mr. Merchant, the third of Mrs. Brisbane's matrimonial suggestions, his big, kindly face beaming genially at her from the dim light of the porch.

Amorelle felt her knees beginning to sag under her. Could she go through another proposal tonight? Wasn't there some way she could get out of it, excuse herself and say she had to go somewhere immediately? But no, he would only offer to go with her, and she really was too tired to go anywhere. While she tried wildly to think of some excuse, Mr. Merchant stepped in and took off his hat, greeting her delightedly as if his errand was a real pleasure to himself.

In a husky, tired little voice, Amorelle offered him a seat in the dining room, explaining that the parlor furniture had all been sent to storage.

"Oh well, now, now," said the caller, looking around and blinking at the empty room. "Why, you really are torn up here, aren't you? Why, I didn't come any too soon, did I?"

Amorelle sat down in a chair on the opposite side of the table and gripped her cold, young hands together in her lap. She felt a constriction in her throat and a terrible desire to cry again.

She looked at the caller with haggard eyes and waited for him to make known his errand.

"Of course I want first to express my sympathy, Miss Dean, in your great bereavement," he began, resting pleased eyes on her face. "Your father was a good man. The salt of the earth. This church will search long to find another as good. The church has been truly blessed in having his ministry through so many years, and blessed also in having you, his daughter, to help him. You have been a great example to the young in this town!"

Amorelle listened to his words wearily, noticing the gray around his temples, the sagging lines around his mouth. She had always thought of him as a pleasant, harmless, elderly man. But now with the thought of him as a possible suitor, he suddenly seemed very old and tiresome, utterly obnoxious in such a role. If she could only think of some way to keep him from saying what she dreaded. She had a desire to get up and run down to the cellar or out the back door and leave him by himself—but of course she could not treat a respected member of the church that way, and she tried to make her voice pleasant and polite as she answered.

"Thank you, Mr. Merchant. My father always appreciated your friendship."

"Well, that's nice to know, but I want you to understand that for a long time I have looked upon you as a most worthy and capable young woman. I—this is— Well, you know—I—"

Amorelle in a panic broke in upon his careful speech.

"That's kind of you, Mr. Merchant. And how is your mother? Is she suffering as much this fall?"

"Oh, my mother? Yes, my mother. Well, I was coming to her. Yes, I'm sorry to say she is suffering a great deal, but she knows her time is short now, and she is resigned."

"Oh, I'm so sorry!" said Amorelle, hoping against hope that she might be able to switch the conversation away from herself.

"Well, as I was saying," resumed the caller, "she knows that her time is short, and perhaps that is the reason she is so willing that I should make some change in my life at this time. Perhaps you are not aware, Miss Dean, that when my mother was taken so ill, her one obsession seemed to be a dread that I would leave her, or perhaps marry and bring someone home who would not be congenial to her."

"Oh, poor thing," said Amorelle, trying to make her voice sound sympathetic and not hysterical.

"Yes, that is the way I felt," said the man, beaming upon her. "I am glad you feel that way about her, too. It makes me feel that I am right in my conclusions. And so, as I was saying—"

Amorelle caught her breath desperately, but the man went steadily on.

"I promised my mother that I would never leave her while she lived, and that I would never marry without her complete agreement in my choice. So the years have passed happily and I have not been moved to choose a mate for myself until— well—I might say, quite recently."

He paused to smile at the girl, but Amorelle was struggling with a wave of anger. This, of course, was going to be some more of Mrs. Brisbane's meddling! How outrageous!

"To make it more definite, it was this very morning that I

got to thinking about you and what an excellent wife you would make in every way, and how alone you must be now, and how opportune it would be for you at this time if a home could be offered to you. After casting about in my mind a time, I went and had a talk with my mother, and I found her most agreeable to the idea. She felt that you would be a most suitable wife for me, and she seems quite eager to have the marriage consummated at once. She says that she will be able to help you, teach and advise you in so many ways before she is taken from us, and she desires that no time shall be lost—"

Suddenly Amorelle arose with protest in her eyes, her face very white.

"Please, please, Mr. Merchant, don't say any more—" she began earnestly, but the man lifted a restraining hand.

"Just a minute, Miss Dean. I would like to finish, if you please!"

There was a slight note of hauteur, almost offense, in his voice.

Amorelle dropped into her chair again, a hopeless look in her eyes. What would it be like to be married to a man who insisted upon finishing all his elaborate sentences with a smile like that on his face?

"And so, as I was saying," he went on, looking steadily at the impatient girl, "she insists that we lose no time. In brief, Miss Dean, while I fully realize that you may feel it is a little soon after your recent sorrow, I have come here to offer you my hand and heart in marriage, and to suggest that the ceremony be performed at once, so that you can come immediately to your husband's home for refuge. I shall have a right then to stand between you and the world. I feel that under the circumstances haste is quite justified. I feel that your father would quite approve and be glad to have me take you over and protect you. Now, what do you say?"

He finished with a complacent smile and looked at Amorelle to have his suggestion ratified.

"I shall have to say no, Mr. Merchant," said Amorelle with her mouth in a little firm line. "I do not wish to get married."

"Oh, but my dear, you are not going to disappoint me, after I have waited all these years for the right one to come and the right time to ask you."

"It won't be a great disappointment if you only thought of it this morning, Mr. Merchant." Amorelle tried to smile and make light of the matter.

"Oh, but you mistake me, Miss Dean. I have often sat in church and watched you at the organ and thought what an ideal woman you were. I have dreamed about you, thought about having the sunshine of your smile always in my home. I have admired you beyond any woman I have seen in years. I feel sure we should grow very fond of one another. I feel that you are quite queen of my heart."

He laid his hand on his heart and bowed low in an old-time courtly way that suddenly gave Amorelle that inane desire again to burst out laughing. She restrained herself, however, and felt a touch of pity for him. Poor soul, he had never had any youth of his own and now he was making a snatch at hers; and from horror, her feeling turned to sadness.

"No, Mr. Merchant," she said, shaking her head earnestly. "You have made a mistake. I am nothing but a child compared to you. I don't want to be unkind or ungrateful for all the nice things you have said, but I must speak frankly if you insist on talking any more about this. I have always looked upon you as my father's friend, not mine. I would never feel that you were a suitable person for me to marry, even if I wanted to marry anybody. There is far too great a difference in our ages. I don't want to hurt you, but I can remember when you used to buy me dolls and fur bunnies for Christmas and Easter."

She tried to smile. But the complacent smile did not fade from the man's face.

"That is to me but one more advantage," he answered. "I feel that I know you thoroughly, and you know me. We shall the more easily adjust ourselves to one another. And it may surprise you that the very fact of your youth was the thing that most recommended you to my mother as suitable. She felt that you being young would be the more pliable and easy to be trained by her than an older woman. You satisfy my mother fully, Miss Dean."

"But I don't care to marry your mother, Mr. Merchant. I think we need say no more." And Amorelle arose.

Yet still he lingered, unable to grasp the fact that she had really, definitely refused him. Even when he stood reluctantly at last upon the doorstep saying good-night, he turned back to say, "Well, if after thinking it over you change your mind, please feel perfectly free to let me know. I shall be anxiously awaiting a word from you, and I shall not consider that this is final. Good-night!"

He was gone at last, and Amorelle closed and locked the door firmly, snapped out the hall light, and walked back into the kitchen where she paused in the dark, clenched her hands, and stamped her foot angrily.

"Oh, that *woman!*" she said between shut teeth. "That woman! And to think I'm helpless! I can't do a thing about it!"

Then after a pause, she said aloud again, "Well, thank goodness there's only Mr. Pike left, and I'll take care that he never gets in the house while I'm here. If I see him I'll run away, or go upstairs and lock myself in!"

She said it with determination, and then a sudden horror came to her. Perhaps the woman would think up some more bachelors to add to her list. What a thought!

Eventually Amorelle went up to bed and, kneeling, tried to commit herself to her heavenly Father, tried to put aside her anger and worry and just trust herself in the only hands that could protect her. But after she lay down to rest, it was long before she could get to sleep in spite of her weariness. As her mind threshed over and over the scenes through which she had passed that day, she wondered anxiously what trying things were to be her portion for the morrow.

"Oh, I'm not trusting God the way Father taught me to do." She sighed wearily as she turned over for what seemed like the thousandth time and wished for day.

Amorelle did not know that, though she had carefully drawn down all the shades in the lower floor to protect herself from prying eyes, she had gone upstairs and left two lights burning—one in the kitchen and the other in the study—

without in the least realizing that she had done so. If she had not been so distraught, she would never have been so careless. But the fact that the lights were burning saved her from one more unwelcome visitor who was not yet aware that Hannah the faithful was still nursing her sister, and that the minister's orphaned daughter was alone in the manse again that night.

Chapter 5

Johnny brought two barrels on his first round in the morning and left them in the dining room for Amorelle to pack the china she wanted to keep. She went straight to work, carefully wrapping each delicate cup and plate of her mother's wedding china and stuffing in the straw and wood shavings that Johnny had provided. Dear Johnny! Good Johnny! If all the would-be lovers took their rebuffs as pleasantly and helpfully as Johnny had done, life would have less perplexities and problems for her.

She worked rapidly to get done. The sooner she got out of the town, the sooner such exciting episodes as had filled yesterday would be over.

When the last bit of her mother's china was packed, she flew around getting together articles she wished to sell. This proved to be a trying matter to decide just what to keep and what to sell. But the man arrived in the midst of it and settled several troublesome problems by offering more than she expected for some things and refusing to take others. She was agreeably surprised, when he had gone the rounds from cellar to attic and set down the articles with the prices that he was willing to give, to find that it all amounted to a little over fifty dollars. Her heart grew somewhat lighter as she ate her lunch. She would surely be able to pay all her indebtedness and have enough left for a ticket to her uncle's.

But her lunch hour was cut short by callers again, and with trepidation she saw Mrs. Ferguson's firm, uncompromising countenance through the front door glass as she went to answer the bell.

There were three ladies standing on the porch—Mrs. Ferguson, Mrs. Woods, and Mrs. Brisbane. The representatives of the Ladies' Aid had arrived. Like a soldier girding on armor, she lifted her heart for help from above and went forward to let them in.

"I'm rather torn up here," she apologized with a faint smile. "I'll take you into the study. I guess that is the least unsettled."

"Torn up?" said Mrs. Ferguson in her deep bass voice, casting a swift, scrutinizing glance into the empty parlor. "Why, not torn up already?"

"There wasn't any point in waiting," said the girl, trying to speak cheerfully. "It was easier to go right to work. It had to be done!"

"But, my dear!" reproached the deep voice, fixing her with hard eyes through double lenses. "You should not have gone ahead without advice. You are very young, and it is our place to see that you do the wisest thing. I thought I sent word to you through Mrs. Brisbane that we were coming for that purpose. I don't understand why you had to be in such a hurry. Of course, I had to have a little time to consult with some of the other members of the Society."

"Mrs. Brisbane spoke of your coming," said Amorelle with a sweet dignity, "but I didn't want to be a trouble to anyone. I didn't want you to feel that I was a burden you had to carry. I'm quite able to see to things, and Father and I talked some things over together, too. Come into the study, won't you? I'll bring in a couple of dining room chairs and we can all be comfortable."

But the self-appointed committee stood immovable.

"But what have you done with your parlor furniture?" demanded the deep voice of the general, looking hard around the little, empty parlor, as if expecting to find it hidden in some of the empty corners.

"I have sent it away to a friend of Mother's who is going to keep it for me until I know just where I am to be permanently," said Amorelle sweetly.

"But my dear! You should not have done that!" said the chairman of the committee. "We have been considering buying it for the ladies' parlor in the church, unless the Society should decide to partly furnish the manse for a very young minister who may be called, in which case, of course, it could stay right here. And Mrs. Woods also has been thinking of buying it herself for her east room. She wanted to look at it carefully and see if it was really in as good repair as she remembered it. What a pity you should have sent it away and made us all the trouble and expense of bringing it back again. I hope it has not gone far. Mrs. Brisbane, didn't you make her understand that we were coming here for that purpose?"

"I certainly did!" said Mrs. Brisbane with set lips.

"But I had no intention of selling that furniture, Mrs. Ferguson. It was old and very precious, a part of my mother's possessions that had been in the family for generations. I would not sell it under any considerations. I'm sorry you are disappointed."

"But can you afford to keep for sentimental reasons, my dear, anything that would bring you money at this time?"

Amorelle merely smiled.

"I think so," she answered quietly. "Will you step into the study, Mrs. Ferguson?"

"Well, you're a very silly child!" said Mrs. Ferguson, following her with her chin in the air. "We shall have to talk of that later."

"But Amorelle," protested Mrs. Woods, suddenly entering into the conversation, "you really don't understand what you are doing, I suppose. I was willing to pay quite a little. I had thought of offering you fifteen dollars for that sofa and perhaps two and a half apiece for the chairs. I might even be willing to make it twenty-five for the sofa and five apiece for the chairs if I found them in justifiable condition for the investment."

"I'm sorry to disappoint you, Mrs. Woods, but Father told me never to let those pieces go under a thousand dollars, as they are very rare. But personally I wouldn't sell them at any price. Not if I hadn't a cent in the world left, and I'm not quite down to starvation yet."

All three ladies gasped.

"How ridiculous!" snorted Mrs. Woods, her face growing red with disappointment. "I've heard that you had an unbalanced judgment, and I begin to think it is true."

But Mrs. Ferguson diverted attention now in her deep, throaty voice.

"Oh, and yes, there's the desk, Amorelle. Now, I'll tell you, we had thought if we bought a number of your things from you that, being as the desk was given to your father by the church, you would want to leave it here in the manse as a donation from him."

"Oh, but it wasn't given to him by the church, Mrs. Ferguson!" said Amorelle quickly. "It was a personal gift from Judge Rivington."

"I beg your pardon, Amorelle. I was not so informed. You have probably forgotten. I was told that the church came here as a surprise party and brought the desk with them on the occasion of some anniversary."

"I am sorry to have to contradict you, Mrs. Ferguson," said Amorelle. "The church did give us a surprise party and brought a little desk light for Father. It was on his fiftieth birthday. But the desk was given privately about two months before that. Have you never seen the inscription? Here, let me show you."

"Inscription?" said Mrs. Ferguson. "If there was an inscription, why, of course it was given by the church."

Amorelle went to the desk and drew out the upper right-hand drawer.

"There it is, Mrs. Ferguson. You can read it for yourself," she said, lifting a pile of writing paper and revealing a silver plate set deep in the wood and engraved in clear script.

Mrs. Ferguson leaned over and brought her severe gaze to bear upon the words.

To my beloved friend and pastor,
Rev. John Anderson Dean,
In loving recognition of the
spiritual help and comfort
I have derived from his teaching of the Bible,
and from personal association with
his beautiful Christlike life.
from
Reaver Rathbone Rivington

Mrs. Ferguson read it through twice, carefully weighing each word with a hope that she might find a loophole to bear her out in her statements.

"Well," she said straightening up, "that is most extraordinary! I certainly was informed— Just when was that plate put in there?"

She fixed Amorelle with a gimlet stare.

A wave of scarlet swept over Amorelle's white face and her eyes suddenly flashed angrily.

"I'm sure I don't know," she said haughtily. "It was in there when the desk came to the house, and it happened to be on the anniversary of Father's wedding day, so I can tell you the date of the arrival. If you doubt my word you might write to Mrs. Loomis Rivington. She and her husband came along with Judge Rivington when he presented it to Father."

"Oh, no, I don't doubt your word, of course," said Mrs. Ferguson, "but it does seem strange! But even so, Amorelle, Judge Rivington was a member of our church, and in a way that desk was a gift from the church, you know, and I thought it would be so appropriate for you to present it to the church study or the manse study. We could of course pay you for it, if you felt you could not afford to give it entirely. I suppose you'll have to sell it. It's a handsome thing and ought to bring you in something, and of course you could not use it yourself, a man's desk!"

"No, Mrs. Ferguson, I couldn't sell it. Father gave it to me. He spoke about it. He wouldn't have liked me to give it away even if I were willing. It is one of the precious things that I want to keep always. Besides, I don't think the Rivingtons would like it either."

"Well, you're a strange girl!" said Mrs. Ferguson, setting her lips disagreeably. "Well, now about your father's library. We'll buy that anyway. Why— What have you done with his books? I thought we'd just buy the bookcase and all as it was! We were going to put a memorial plate on it and put it in the church study for the use of all ministers, you know, and it would serve as a memorial for your father."

"I'm sorry to disappoint you," said Amorelle in a weary little voice, "but I couldn't really think of parting with my father's books."

"But my dear child!" exclaimed the woman aggressively, as if this was entirely too much to stand. "A theological library! What could a girl possibly do with a theological library?"

"You don't understand, Mrs. Ferguson," said Amorelle gently. "It is not just that to me, although a theological library is to me the most interesting kind of library there could be. But, you know, almost every one of those books I have read aloud with my father. We have talked them over for days at a time, and they have grown precious to me. I could not think of giving them up! Besides, Father and I went without something to save the money for almost every one. You know each of the books has an individuality to me. They are almost like people, friends of my father's and mine."

"Well, upon my word!" boomed the deep voice. "I never heard of such sentimentality! Fancy! Just books! And some of them very valuable books indeed, I suppose; that is, to the proper person. You certainly have been brought up most unpractically."

"I always said a man wasn't a proper person to bring up a girl, anyway," put in Mrs. Brisbane.

"Well, it's too late to consider that now, of course," said Mrs. Ferguson, "but I certainly wish we had come over yesterday morning. It is really going to be quite awkward, after the whole Society had such a time deciding what they would do about it, and Mrs. Skelly starting things off finally with that five-dollar donation. A good many people are going to be disappointed, and after so many of them being so generous, too. Well, Amorelle, how about your piano? Or are you attached to that, too?"

"No, Mrs. Ferguson, that is sold," smiled Amorelle feebly. It seemed as if her nerves were being extracted one at a time and she had to smile to the last. She wondered if she could hold out.

"Sold! Oh, what a pity! Not definitely, I hope. Well, you

probably have been cheated on that. I suppose you got a mere pittance. Why, Amorelle, we were prepared to offer you twenty-five dollars for the piano, and that's more than you could have gotten at the piano store for it. We inquired before we came."

"But I got thirty-five for it, Mrs. Ferguson," said Amorelle quietly.

The lady stared.

"You don't mean it? Well, it certainly must have been somebody who was no judge of instruments who paid that. Well, what is there left, Amorelle, that you are willing to part with? We came here to help you out but it seems you didn't need us."

"Thank you for your kind intention," said the girl gravely, "but I expected to have to make my own arrangements, of course. I don't really believe there is anything that is worthwhile. I have disposed of all the things I did not wish to keep. I was anxious to get everything settled. I understood that the manse might be wanted soon. I am hoping to have everything out of the way and the house pretty well cleaned by the first of next week, perhaps sooner if Hannah is able to help me."

"It seems to me you are in a great hurry," said Mrs. Woods offendedly. "I supposed we would be in plenty of time. By the way, didn't you have a walnut bedroom set? I was prepared to pay a good price for that if I found it what I remembered it to be."

"I'm sorry, Mrs. Woods, but my walnut bedroom set is not for sale!"

"Oh! Indeed! Well, it really doesn't seem necessary for us to stay any longer, does it?"

"Won't you sit down for a little while?" asked Amorelle

wistfully. She could not bear that even these women, unpleasant though they had been, should leave in a huff. They were members of her father's church. It seemed a desecration to fight over his precious books and desk.

"Well, no, I think not," said Mrs. Ferguson. "I really left very important matters to come here to do what I supposed was a kindness, but it seems it was not needed. Now, if there is anything more I can do, perhaps you will suggest it, Amorelle."

"Oh," said the girl, almost ready to burst into tears, "I just want your kindly thought. I don't need to bother you with the other things, but I do appreciate your love of my father, and your intention to help, even though I didn't need it. I know I'm young and I'm quite liable to make mistakes, but you see, most of these matters I had talked over with Father, and they were practically settled before he went. But I know he would appreciate your thoughtfulness for me."

Then suddenly her eyes rested on Mrs. Brisbane, and a quick, startled remembrance of all the mortification that mistaken woman had brought upon her hardened the smile which she had tried to muster.

"Well, I've had you on my mind right along!" responded Mrs. Brisbane with a look of satisfaction.

They filed out presently, after a few expressions of sympathy, but there was in their manner a crestfallen look of offense—if those two things can be combined—that was almost amusing.

"For all the world like three wet hens that had just had a bucket of cold water frowned over 'em an' lost out in gettin' the worm!" spoke out Hannah, just behind her as Amorelle closed the door after her callers.

Amorelle turned with a start.

"Oh, Hannah!" she said, dropping weakly on the stairs. "When did you come in? How you startled me!"

"H'm! I come in jes ez the doorbell done rung!" responded the faithful old servant. "I made out ta go ta the door, but you got there fust. I just stuck around in the kicchem an' lissum good. They all jes' like three old animals come snoopin' round, tryin' to get things for theirselves. That big one name Ferguson with the man voice, she like n'elefant; that Woods woman somepin' like a chipmunk chatterin' away; and that Brisbane, she like one of these ferrets. There just ain't nothin' she don't know. You ain't gwine let 'em browbeat you, is you, honey? You ain't gwine give in an' let um have any your nice old things?"

"Oh, no, Hannah!" said Amorelle, laughing. "I've sold what I don't want and I'm keeping the rest. I think I made them understand."

"Yes, you was right firm in your words, honey. I was proud of you. But now, honey, what you gwine do? I'se back now an' I'se ready ta he'p. Sorry I hedta leave you just then, but I couldn't he'p it nohow. I knowed you'd understand. But my other sister come from up the state now, an' I'here ta stay, an' the fust thing I'se gwine do is get you a nice mess o'vittles. I bet you ain't et sence I lef'."

"Oh, yes I have, Hannah! I've been all right. But I'm glad you've got back. It's lonesome, nights especially. And there'll be a good deal to do getting the house cleaned. I want to get out as soon as possible. The things that I'm keeping will all be taken tonight and tomorrow, and the things I'm selling will be taken whenever I am ready to let them go. I've saved a few things for you I knew you liked."

"That's jis' like you, honey-sweet!" said the servant gratefully.

Hannah walked through the rooms, her arms akimbo, and surveyed the destruction, ending with a tremendous sigh.

"Well it do make me feel sad," she said, "but I'm glad you was brae an' started right in. Who all's got your pre-anna?"

"Little Tessy Wayne!"

"H'm! Well, I 'spose you kin get a better one someday. It was powerful scratched up sence the las' time they young folks borrahed it ta take over ta the church fer that shebang they had last Easter. You done kep' the parlor furnitoor? H'm! Well, we'll get to wuk good an' early tamorrah. Mebbe I'll get in a fe licks tonight yet. Now le's see what we got ta make supper of. I brang along a steak. That big butcher down ta the corner sent it. He said you needed ta be fed up, an' when I passed Janders' fruit store, they called me in an' said ta bring this here basket of fruit down. Got grapes an' pears an' apples an' a big honeydew mellum, an' he gimme a bag with a shellin' of peas an' three ears of lovely corn. I'll whip up some tea biscuits an' we'll have supper soon. You go lay down an' fergit them three pizenmouthed wimmen awhile, an' I'll jest pout things in shape out here in the kitchen."

"Oh, but I was just going to wash some windows," said Amorelle. "I don't want to lie down now. I'm not tired since you've come."

"Wash windows—a lot, you will!" said the old woman. "That's no job fer you. I'll do the cleanin'. That's what I'm here fer. Al you gotta do from now on is boss! And say, here comes some more wimmen folks. You better skitter upstairs and lay down, an' I'll say you're needin' rest."

"Oh, but I can't treat the church people that way!" said Amorelle in dismay. "Who is it, I wonder?"

"Looks like that old Mrs. Ritter's got a crazy son, an' the nice body that lives acrost fum her; Mrs. Crosby, ain't it?"

"Oh, I must see them. They are dear!" said the girl, remembering with a pang the last time she and her father had called up in their neighborhood.

So Hannah slid some chairs from the dining room into the parlor while Amorelle opened the door and ushered in the ladies.

The two callers were plain and loving. They brought no sharp words and bartered for none of the manse's furnishings. They brought only sweet sympathy and offers of help. They brought humble invitations to stay with them indefinitely. The ice and anger began to melt around the troubled girl's heart.

It did not prove to be a very good afternoon for work so far as Amorelle was concerned, for it seemed as if everybody selected that day to come and see her. All the dear, tenderhearted people who had loved her father; the plain, the substantial, the truly consecrated people of the church. They came in little groups, one overlapping the other, and they kept coming until a little after five o'clock.

They did not come to see what they could buy, nor to question her curiously; they came to offer love and help and sympathy, and Amorelle's heart was cheered and her spirit strengthened.

One and all were dismayed at the dismantled appearance of the parlor that had once been such a cheery place to come, and they mourned that she had decided to leave them. For Amorelle told them all that she was going to visit her uncle for a time, probably all winter at least.

When the last one had gone, Hannah put her head in at the door.

"Your dinner's all ready. You better come git it befo' the next batch o' folks comes."

Amorelle ate her dinner with a better appetite than she had had for several days, and before she was through, Johnny Brewster breezed in.

"Gonta take that desk now. Gotta chance fer a coupla extras to help move it up them stairs over ta the Glen. Is't ready ta go now? Got an old quilt ur somethin' I ken lash over the top so it won't get scratched? Better lock the drawers. No, I don't need ta take 'em out. It ain't too heavy fer four of us. We're goin' up in Sam Owen's big truck. He's goin' out that way."

When the desk and its swivel chair were gone, Amorelle had a wave of desolation sweep over her. But old Hannah wisely called her to consult about what should be done next, and before everything was settled, more callers had arrived. Mr. and Mrs. Tremstead, old dependables of her father's, came to ask her to spend a week with them, or longer if she chose. They tucked in her hand an unostentatious envelope containing a crisp ten-dollar bill and gave her a deep look of love when they left. Mr. and Mrs. Farley and their little girl came to tell her how her father's prayers had borne them up during sorrow and illness and loss. The three Hooker sisters brought a little snapshot they had taken of the church and her father standing on the steps the last day he preached there, just before his final illness. Sweet little Mrs. Brant, who had always quietly helped her pastor pray out the troubles in the congregation, came too. It thrilled her heart to remember what her beloved father had been, and when she closed the door on the last caller around half past ten, her eyes were shining and her head was up bravely. She felt comforted for the hard things that had gone before.

But as she drew her bedroom shade down, she noticed a tall, thin figure standing across the road in the shadow, as if he watched the house. Who could it be? He didn't look like a policeman. He looked like— Oh, could that be Mr. Pike? Had he perhaps been watching for a chance to call? The last man on Mrs. Brisbane's list of possible lovers! She snapped her light out quickly at the thought that he might even yet venture to come and began swiftly to undress in the dark.

Chapter 6

Sometime in the night, Amorelle awakened sharply with the impression of a sudden, stealthy noise.

Hannah was sleeping in her room at the back end of the hall and sometimes snored. But the noise had not come from the direction of Hannah's room. It seemed, rather, to be downstairs. Amorelle listened, her senses bewildered at first. She couldn't quite analyze the sound. She was not sure but it was part of a dream.

No! There it was again, a stealthy movement like someone sliding along on the floor. It sounded down in her father's study. She lay rigid, listening. Yes, there it was again! It was certainly not her imagination. Perhaps it was a mouse. But a mouse would never make that sound!

Softly she rose on one elbow, staring toward the open door into the hall. Her room was at the front of the house, and from her door, she could look down the stairwell and see halfway across her father's study.

Noiselessly she folded back the blankets, swung her feet to the floor, and reached for her flashlight that lay on the little bedside table close at hand. She stole cautiously to the door. A wraith could have gone no more silently. She steadied herself for an instant, with her hand on the doorframe, and peered down into the darkness of the hall.

There was a tiny speck of light moving around like a will-o'-the-wisp! It danced over the floor in an ordered manner—up a few inches, down the next few inches—as if the place was being searched. Once it showed a bit of fabric in a fold, as if the rug had been turned back. Then it danced away a few inches farther back, touching the bare floor for a little way.

Amorelle's heart was in her throat. She tried to think what to do and stood paralyzed, looking around her. Was she really awake, or dreaming? She gripped the doorframe to make sure, and then the light danced around and swept the open doorway where she could see distinctly a form bending and holding a small pocket flashlight, a spot of light gushing here and there on the floor.

Amorelle had never been a girl of fears, but she stood breathlessly leaning against the doorway, studying the crouching form. Who was it, and what could he be looking for under her father's study rug?

It seemed several minutes that she stood there, her finger on the switch of the big flashlight. Should she turn it down on the intruder and get a view of his face? But perhaps he carried a gun and the light would give him a good target.

Well, must she stand there and let him prowl through the house? She cast around in her mind for a weapon that would frighten him away quickly without making him realize just where she was. She might drop something over the stair railing that would startle him. Would that be better than making an outcry? There was a telephone extension across the hall in what had been her father's room, but could she get across there, open the door, and telephone before he would hear her and flee—or perhaps come running up the stairs and smother her?

To be sure there was Hannah down at the end of the hall, but Hannah was sound asleep and wouldn't be any help in an emergency like this. Hannah would likely be scared.

Amorelle didn't realize that she was herself trembling like a leaf.

Then suddenly her bare foot came in contact with a cold metallic surface just beyond her door, and she remembered that Hannah had said she was going to begin on the upstairs windows the first thing in the morning and had brought up the scrub bucket, soap dish, scrubbing brush, ammonia bottle, and bundle of chamois and rags and dumped them by her door. What better weapons could she have wherewith to frighten a burglar? Oh, if she could only see what he was like before he fled! It was so strange what he could be doing! Why should he want to search around in front of the fireplace and bookcase? Then suddenly the prowler turned and flashed his own light for an instant full into his own face, and Amorelle's heart stood still with unbelief. Pike! Mr. Pike! There couldn't be another slick

Uriah-Heepish face like that! What could Mr. Pike be doing down in the study? He certainly wouldn't come to propose marriage at this time of night!

Like a flash, her fear of him disappeared and left only indignation. Whatever he was doing, he had no right.

Impulsively she stooped with silent, swift movement and felt for the handle of the big galvanized bucket.

Amorelle was unaware that Hannah, thinking her young lady might wish to sleep late in the morning and not wishing to disturb her by turning on the bathroom spigot, had drawn a goodly portion of water in the bucket before she retired to her bed. So when the bucket was lifted hastily, it proved to be heavier than anticipated. But Amorelle in her excitement swung it high over the banister, and water and all, it sailed over, just grazing the stair rail below, swashing out in a well-aimed stream toward the astonished burglar. It crashed into the hall almost beside him, where the rest of the water splashed up in a geyser-like torrent into his face and over his hands and feet.

The little spotlight on the floor of the study went black; there was a spluttering gasp, and Amorelle, now really frightened at what she had done, reached down for the saucer containing the big bar of kitchen soap and the scrubbing brush that lay beside it, and dashed them wildly after the bucket. Then she touched the switch of her flashlight and, shielding herself behind the doorjamb, poured its light in a great flood down upon her victim.

Just for an instant she had a vision of a wild-eyed Pike— yes, there was no mistaking Pike's long, thin nose and eyes set too close together—and then he faded out of the picture. And

Amorelle had sense enough to turn off her light and retreat toward her window, her heart beating so wildly she could hardly breathe.

But then suddenly things began to happen in another part of the house. There was a sound of clatter in Hannah's room; the falling of some heavy object; heavy, bare feet moving hastily. And downstairs, there was a sound of stealthy feet, too frightened to be wary, moving hurriedly in the direction of the kitchen and the back door, feet that came into several sudden contacts with objects not reckoned on in the pathway.

Amorelle ventured out to listen again, her flashlight grasped tight in her hand but not lit.

Now Hannah had been down in the cellar that afternoon, after hearing the account of Mrs. Brisbane's visit the day before and her remarks about the paint being worn off the windowsills, and she had discovered several pails containing small portions of leftover paint, most of them dried to the bottom. But among them she had found a gallon can half full of white paint with an inch or so of water over its surface, put there to keep it for future use. This, with a stiff paint brush in another can of water, she had brought upstairs to her room, intending, in the small hours of the morning before Amorelle should be awake, to stir up that paint to useable consistency and work over that brush with warm water and soap and two inches of turpentine she had found in a bottle until it was fit to touch up the bare places in the interior paint.

And Hannah had waked up some seconds before Amorelle and had been standing in capacious flannel nightgown and floppy nightcap at her door, listening, when Amorelle flung her bombardments over the stair rail and stabbed the darkness of the hall with her flashlight.

Hannah heard the groping, hurried footsteps downstairs. She knew exactly which way the intruder was moving, and she prepared her ambush hurriedly. By the time the burglar had reached the back door and was about to dash wildly for freedom over the back fence, she was standing at her window just over the back steps with the half gallon of thick white paint mingled with water held at just the perfect angle for action when the precise moment should arrive.

The burglar was in his stocking feet and had not time to retrieve his shoes before his hasty exit. He stubbed his toe on the edge of a hole in the kitchen linoleum, which did not help matters for him. But as he arrived on the step of the kitchen and the cool evening air greeted his heated brow, something else descended upon him. A long, cold stream of water and white paint came dashing over him, trickling down his neck, filling his hair—for his hat had dropped off in the kitchen when he stubbed his toe—and streaming over his quivering, frightened face.

Moreover Hannah let out a yell such as is not often heard on a summer evening when right-minded folks are all abed and asleep.

"Help! Help! Murder! Robbers!" she shouted, and was about to add "Fire!" to the list when she heard a policeman's whistle far up to the next block and changed the word to "Police! Help! He's getting away."

Over the fence went Mr. Pike, hatless and shoeless, dripping, gasping, choking with the paint deluge, leaving a well-defined set of fingerprints and footprints down the garden walk, over the back fence, and a long way down the back alley.

Windows were thrown up all along the street behind the alley; heads were thrust out; cries of "What is it? Police! Help!" and presently the police were on the spot with whistles, and a motorcycle was tearing down the street.

While down the shadowy side of the alley, blinded by paint, stealthily crept the former intruder, pausing only long enough behind a dark hedge to tear off the telltale socks and stuff them in his pocket before he fled by devious ways to refuge in his own lair.

Amorelle came hurriedly back to Hannah's room and laid a quiet hand on the excited woman's arm.

"Don't yell anymore, Hannah! He's gone! I'll turn on the lights and go down to speak to the police."

The doorbell was ringing now, and Amorelle, in her little, dark robe that had seen so much service during the nights of her father's illness, hurried down, with Hannah in a flaming flower creation of the vintage of "Mother Hubbard" days sweeping protectingly down behind her.

Amorelle told briefly of her awakening and what she had seen, except that brief instant of recognition. The time might have to come for that, too, but if possible she must prevent that man's name from being connected with hers.

Then it seemed that the house was full of policemen, though in reality there were only two, the rest having followed the white footsteps down the back alley. But Hannah triumphantly led the representatives of the law to the scene of her coup and gave a voluble description of all that occurred from her point of view. Then they went down again to the minister's study, examined the turned-back rug, threw their mysterious powder here and there trying to get fingerprints.

It was a weird, mysterious business, and to the girl standing shivering in the hall, it all seemed so futile.

She wondered idly what Lemuel Pike could possibly have wanted there in the little, bare study. What could there be that would make it worth his while to risk breaking into a house? She recalled his last words to her father about some objectionable phrase that he wanted rewritten. Could he possibly have come to find a paper? No, that did not make good sense. If he had been borrowing money, as she had decided must have been the case, what possible value could any other paper have? Her weary brain refused to think it out.

She recalled the matter of the desk key, which her father had been searching for just as Lemuel went out the door. Perhaps he thought it might still be around there somewhere. Perhaps he did not notice in the darkness that the desk was gone, and he hoped to find the key and unlock the drawer and discover the receipt that her father would undoubtedly have taken if he loaned the man money. That was it! That sounded plausible. Well, what did it matter! Her father wouldn't likely have loaned such a man a very large sum, and, anyway, she would rather lose the money than get her name mixed up with Lemuel Pike, especially since Mrs. Brisbane's foolish interference with her affairs. It only meant that she must hasten her departure from the town.

Eventually the house settled to rest again, Hannah insisting upon bringing her mattress and casting it down before Amorelle's door.

The night went on; the police searched. They traced the footsteps to the street where Lemuel Pike lived, but there they ended at the foot of a tree. They searched the tree with their flashlights. They even climbed up and explored every branch, but there seemed no possible clue. The street was a perfectly respectable one. There was no apparent reason why any dweller in that street should be suspected of being a house-breaker. Little did they dream that up that very tree Lemuel Pike had disappeared not a half hour before they halted under it, and that he had often disappeared in that very same way after some questionable night excursion. The well-placed trees with their thick foliage told no tale of a man if he cultivated the habits of a squirrel and swung himself silently from branch to branch, straight into his own second-story window. And so that particular night raid, like many others, remained a mystery for the morning papers, much to the relief of the minister's sad young daughter.

Thereafter, to get done and get away from the town, in spite of all its kindly folk who would gladly have detained her and done for her, became an obsession with Amorelle Dean.

Johnny Brewster came over early that next morning to see if there was anything he could do and heard the whole tale with embellishment from Hannah. Before he left he had arranged to bring his gun and sleep on a cot in the kitchen as long as

Amorelle remained, and before night she had several offers of
protectors.

Well, at least, thought the girl, as she went about the
harrowing work of breaking up the only home she had known
since she was born, *there's one of Mrs. Brisbane's suitors that will
be out of the running now. Lemuel Pike will never dare to come and
propose marriage.*

But she did not know Lemuel Pike.

Late that afternoon there came a letter written in a neat
bank clerk's hand, on most correct stationery, and full of high-
sounding phrases. It read:

My dear Miss Dean:

*It has occurred to me that you and I are both in the same
sad condition, alone in the world without kith or kin.*

*Who would have dreamed when I called upon your
sainted father such a few short days ago, to give him a
little contribution for the missionary cause, that he would
be so soon called to his reward? Ah, life is ever thus. The
unexpected comes and we, how ill prepared! This is what
I said when my own sainted mother passed on, and I say
it now to you.*

*But we must not mourn. Our loss is their gain. Life is
stern, and we must live out our days.*

*And so, my dear Miss Dean, I come to you with a
proposition that may benefit both our sad hearts. I have
long entertained a fondness for you in my heart. You of all
the girls I know have been for years my ideal. Yet I dared*

not harbor any dreams. I had my mother to care for while she lived, for she was strangely dependent upon me. And when she was gone I perceived that you had your now sainted father as a sacred trust and could not leave him.

But now that he is gone I feel that the way is clear for me to confess my love to you—

Amorelle read so far and then, jumping to her feet, tore the letter in half and in half again. Taking a match from the brass safe on the mantel, she set fire to it and watched it burn in the empty grate till it shriveled to a crisp. One sentence that she had not read till then stood clearly out above the hated signature of Lemuel Pike before the flame died out. She could not help but read it.

I feel you need my trained mind and expert skill to help you manage your estate—

"Oh!" gasped Amorelle and laughed aloud. "Oh! How very, very funny. Estate! Oh, Father dear, if you could only be here for just a minute to laugh with me."

Then the last flicker died out and she poked the crisp black flakes down through the ash damper out of sight. At least that would be one thing the town should not know. Not unless Lemuel told it himself. Oh, how had he dared write that letter after what he had done? Could it be possible that she had been mistaken in his identity last night?

But if it was Lemuel, what had he been after? Was there

some hidden reason why he wanted to marry her, something he had failed to find that he thought he could get only by marrying her? Estate? Estate! Ridiculous! There was no estate. And if there had been, *he* would never have known about her father's private affairs. It must be he imagined it. She would put the whole thing out of her mind. It was too preposterous even to remember. Oh, would these terrible days never end and let her get away from such abnormal happenings?

Perhaps it was the receipt of this letter more than any other phase of the question that made her decide to accept her uncle's invitation at once, just as soon as she could possibly get away. She had a strange uneasiness about Lemuel Pike. What might he not do next?

So that night she wrote her uncle and aunt, addressing the letter to both of them and setting a definite time for her arrival.

Chapter 7

When the manse was thoroughly cleaned, everything sold or stored or packed, and she herself ready to leave, it appeared that the church had arranged a farewell reception for her. They didn't call it that. They said it was just a quiet little gathering of her friends to say good-bye, but they were so insistent about it that she could not in decency refuse to stay a couple of days longer.

She went around in a fever of dread lest she should encounter Lemuel Pike, but some of the dear church friends kept her so busy coming to dinner and breakfast and tea and staying all night that there was no chance, and she was well guarded.

He did appear on the fringes at the farewell party and did his best to get near her. But she was so surrounded that he had no word with her in private, and no one noticed that she did not respond to his salutation as he passed her in the throng. She was cold and hot and frightened when she caught his eye across the room and turned away as if she had not seen him, but she kept continually envisioning him with his flashlight poking under the study carpet and wondered how he had the nerve to be present. Was it just another bit of evidence to prove him innocent in case anyone had suspected him?

But she saw it in his cold blue eyes that he meant to manage that night somehow to ask her about the letter he had written her, and she was in a panic to prevent it.

At the last she managed to slip away with Miss Landon, out to where Johnny was waiting in the street to take them home, for she was staying with Miss Landon this last night. She drew a deep breath as she sunk into the backseat with her friend and saw Johnny spring to the wheel. Then, just when she thought all was safe, she heard that snaky voice from the sidewalk.

"Miss Dean! Just a minute, please! I want to ask you if you got my letter, and if I can see you sometime tomorrow morning about the matter of which I wrote?"

The words were unmistakable and clear, but Johnny had already heard the low-spoken, imploring words *Let's go* from the shadow of the backseat, and speeding his motor unmercifully in low and second gear, he roared away, leaving Lemuel Pike's last words to float harmlessly on the idle breeze. Johnny's car rattled at a good pace down past the manse and out toward Glenellen by a roundabout way, just as if he were taking Amorelle to one of the houses on the hill to stay all night. Lemuel Pike might be clever, but Johnny Brewster was clever, too.

The ladies of the church had given Amorelle a charming little platinum wristwatch, and the church fathers had given her two hundred dollars, or a month's salary they called it. The church had also voted to put up a handsome stone, suitably inscribed, over her father's grave and a bronze tablet at one side of the pulpit. There were sketches of the memorials lying on a table in one of the classrooms at the farewell gathering, and the members slipped in critically and came out proudly. Most of them considered that they had done very well by their departed pastor and his daughter.

Amorelle was grateful and knew her father would have been pleased at what they had done for her. But he would not have cared for the elaborate monument, nor the honor to himself. Still it was gratifying that they had cared to do it, even though there was much of church pride in the act.

The next morning, quite early, the sweet old seamstress arose and prepared a sumptuous breakfast for her departing guest, put up a tempting lunch because Amorelle was going in a second-class car and could not afford diners, and then kissed her good-bye, assuring her again that if her uncle's home was not all that was to be desired she was to come right back to her and they would manage together. Then Johnny Brewster, wearing his Sunday coat and a collar and necktie, drew up in the grocery truck, put her baggage in behind, and took her down to the 5:57 train. Johnny was cheery and a little solemn as he drove along. But before he reached the station, he had managed to inform his passenger that he had "asked" his girl the night before and that everything was "okay," and in some mysterious way, he seemed to think that his good fortune was due to Amorelle's friendship.

"I guess you kind of give me courage," he said shyly.

Dear Johnny! She tried to tell him how much he had helped her, and she saw him actually brushing a hasty tear away as he drew up at the station in the pearly mist of the September morning.

"Well, say, ya know you ben an awful help ta me!" said Johnny eagerly. "And your dad, well, he kind of gave me the right start in life. No tellin' what I mighta ben ef I hadn't turned Christian when he got hold of me, ya know! And say, I talked to Dorothy last night and we agreed that ef you ever needed a home or friends that you was ta come right ta us. Of course we can't have it grand, not for a while yet, but you'll always be welcome. I've told Dorothy how grand you was, and she says she just loves you."

Hannah loomed out of the mists of the morning and kissed and cried over her dear young lady and told Amorelle if she ever got a home of her own, she was to send for her, and she would work just for her board. Hannah had brought a whole sheet of hot cinnamon buns that she had stayed up half the night to bake. They were tied in a bulky paper package.

So it was not unmourned that Amorelle started on her way into a new life.

And presently, just before the train, came several others—the senior elder of the church and his sweet old wife; the superintendent of the Sunday school; three girls from her own Sunday school class, giggling and weeping alternately; and lastly a group from the Christian Endeavor Society who bunched themselves together as the train swept in sight and began to sing "God be with you till we meet again," to the edification of the sleepy travelers on the early train.

Amorelle had packed so that she had only a small suitcase to carry, but almost everybody that came down to see her off had brought flowers or fruit or candy. She was embarrassed with her riches. Johnny gathered his arms full, helped her on board, and stowed all the offerings in an empty seat. Amorelle presently found herself ensconced like a princess among her possessions, moving quickly away from the familiar home station with its blur of loving faces and waving handkerchiefs.

"When life's perils thick confound you, put His arms unfailing around you—" rang out the song from the Christian Endeavor, and suddenly Amorelle, who had gone bravely through all the farewells, anxious only to have them over, felt a lump in her throat and the smarting tears in her eyes, felt a great wave of loneliness and homesickness, and wondered why she had not managed somehow to stay in that dear hometown.

She stared blinking out into the flying fields, trying to recognize each landmark, grudgingly letting them pass like precious things she might never see again. There was the little brown house where the blacksmith lived and plied his trade in the open shed nearby. She remembered the first time her father took her there when she was a little girl and she had watched the sparks fly from the anvil as the hammer beat the molten iron, while her father talked of another world to the grim old blacksmith who couldn't see that there was a God because so many of His followers were untrue. There was the road where they used to walk in spring when the dogwood trees were in bloom, the road that wound up the hill and into the woods. There was the little weatherbeaten house where old Grandma Duff used to live. They always carried jelly and oranges to her when she was sick. And there was the country schoolhouse where Father used to hold services evenings sometimes, and she always went along to play the funny cabinet organ and help with the singing. That meant five miles off, out into the strange world alone. She hid her face against the windowpane and struggled with those tears. She must not let one get through, or there would come a torrent, right here on the train, before a lot of round-eyed children in the seat in front of her who were staring at her with all their eyes.

In another half hour she would be in the city station and have to change to the western express, and there were all those gifts, a whole seatful, to be disposed of somehow. What should she do with them? She couldn't possibly carry them alone. To summon a porter and arrive in a second-class car with them would make her ridiculous for the whole journey. Yet she couldn't throw any of these love tokens away. Even if she were sure that it would never get back to the dear souls who brought them, she could not bring herself to be so untrue.

So she began to sort them out—the roses from the goldenrod and chrysanthemums, the gladioli from the asters and salvia—choosing a flower from each tenderly with a thought of the giver, laying them flat in a magazine to press. Those she would keep to remember her friends by. The large package of hot cinnamon buns she reduced by more than half by bestowing them upon the staring children, who fell upon them ravenously, evidently having had no breakfast as yet.

There were little gifts in pink tissue paper, tied with ribbon—a lace collar, several pretty handkerchiefs, an embroidered dressing case, and a pair of soft, lovely gloves. Those she slipped into her suitcase, strapping the magazine with its pressed flowers on the outside smoothly. Finally, just as the train was sliding into the city station, she asked the children if they would like the rest of her flowers, and they snatched at them eagerly. Perhaps their mother might regret it later when she marshaled her five sticky children looking like an animated flower garden, but at least she smiled her thanks now upon Amorelle.

So Amorelle gathered up what was left of literature, candy, and cinnamon buns, massed them in an amazingly small compass, picked up her suitcase, and smiled good-bye to the smiling children. They were waving and shouting noisily their farewells and already beginning to quarrel over who had the most roses.

Started at last on her long journey, she watched her way out of the city until the countryside appeared again, and then she put her head back and closed her eyes. She was tired, so *tired*. Would she ever be rested? Would she ever be interested in life again?

Over and over again she went back through the experiences of the past sad week. Sorrow and humor and tenderness. Stupidity and interference and kindness. What a jumble! And those pitiful proposals of marriage. What a travesty! To think that Mrs. Brisbane had dared—for she must have done it! There couldn't be a coincidence like that. Every one she had mentioned had come and proposed! No, there was one missing; the young minister she had spoken of who was rumored to be engaged. There was no telling but Mrs. Brisbane would even yet hound him on, get him unengaged, and send him after her!

Marriage! What would marriage be with one whom Mrs. Brisbane selected? There were so many married people that did not seem at all happy. Marriage was a big chance. Yet her father and mother had been wonderfully happy. She could remember the days when her mother was living and how home seemed like a little heaven. How her father adored and tenderly cared for her mother, and how her mother was always planning some little surprise for Father, or trying to save him in some way. True married love must be like that, always joyful sacrifice for one another. But love like that would be rare. She told herself she had never seen a man that she could care for in that way, as her mother had cared for her father.

She had asked her father once, not long ago, how a girl could know she truly loved a man enough to marry him and if there were rules to guide one in such a situation. He had given her a curious, tender look and told her she would know it beyond a doubt if she was ever really in love. If there was any question about love, there was no question!

Then he had talked quietly on, almost as if he had been her mother.

"Of course a Christian would first ask, 'Is he a Christian? Does he know and love my Lord? If not, we could have no true marriage unless I became untrue to my Lord!' 'Can two walk together except they be agreed?' There is no point of disagreement worse than between believers and unbelievers."

He had paused to let her consider that a moment and then gone on to say that even between believers there could be no true marriage without love. Love that forgives faults and failings and loves on in spite of them. He spoke of the love of Christ to the church and how God used the earthly love of man and woman in marriage as a picture of His love for the church.

They had talked that over for some time before he went on to speak of other things.

"It is not usually a wise thing for two people to come together in marriage who are from different ranks in life, different standards of refinement, culture, education. One needs a super love to overcome the differences. Little acts of refinement or the lack of them can grate upon tired nerves and become a great separator. I do not say that it is *never* right for two who have such differences to marry, but I say it is a perilous experiment for which one needs almost infinite love and special divine grace to keep the love under such circumstances."

The daughter sat with closed eyes, considering what her father had said and wondering idly if the time would ever come when she would be weighing and measuring this question in the light of her father's advice with any special person in mind. She could imagine that life could be very beautiful with such love and the right person, but it all seemed too utopian ever to happen to her. She meant to keep a level head and try to make a place in the world for herself.

She settled this question with a sad little sigh and sat up determinedly, looking out at the new landscape. She hadn't been on a journey in several years, not since she was sent as a delegate to a Sunday school convention just before she went to college. Her college had been in the nearby city so that had not taken her far. If she stayed indefinitely with her uncle, it might be a long time before she went on another journey. She must make the most of this while it lasted. She sighed again, thinking what a delight it would be to watch every mile of the way if her father were only where she could write about it all to him. How he loved her descriptions of people and places and things. But now, no one cared.

But she steadily kept herself looking out the window, watching everything just as if she were going to write about it to someone. It seemed the only way to keep from thinking sad thoughts that brought undesired tears.

She ate her delicious lunch when noontime came, sampled some of her candy, shared some of it with a shy little girl and her weary mother across the aisle, and found plenty left in the lunchbox for her dinner. But when darkness began to come down and obscure the landscape, her brave spirit faltered. She felt that she must stretch out on a bed and sleep in spite of the price it would cost, so she found her way to a sleeper and, fortunately, secured a berth.

It was late when she awoke the next morning. She had missed many of the sights which would have interested her, but she felt more rested than she had for a week. When she had dressed, she explored her lunchbox and found a sandwich and a large, juicy pear left for breakfast.

The train was due to arrive at her uncle's city at three o'clock that afternoon, and Amorelle, more cheerful than the night before, began to take an interest in the new landscape around her. She went to the dining car at lunchtime and began to feel herself part of a new world.

As her destination drew nearer, she tried to fancy how the strange relatives would look and act. She had not seen even her uncle since she was a very little girl. It was good to think of having some relatives. She made a lot of resolves about making them love her, and she tried to hope they were all going to be glad to see her. She wondered if they were Christians. She knew her father had been troubled about his brother. He had said he was immersed in business and never wrote on such topics but that he was a church member. Amorelle wondered if it would be any easier to live in the same house with people who were not Christians than it would be to be married to them.

As it drew near three o'clock, she got out her aunt's letter and read the directions over carefully, though she almost knew them by heart. But when she landed in the strange station with many people jostling by her and the noise of the big city outside, she felt very much alone and wished someone had seen fit to meet her.

Seated in the taxi, she found her heart beating wildly. She felt she had come a long way from the girl she had been yesterday. It seemed as if her father had been dead a year and she had been growing up very fast. When she looked up at the somewhat pretentious house at which the taxi stopped, her heart almost failed her. Just for an instant she wanted to turn back, go somewhere else and get a job, support herself, and write her uncle she had changed her mind. Why hadn't she thought before that that was the thing to do?

But the driver was opening the door and waiting for his fare, and of course someone might see her out of the window. Now she was here, she must go in. She steadied herself with the thought that, of course, she could make an excuse and go away in a day or two if she found things unpleasant. And then with an upward cry for help, she got out of the cab and went up the steps of the house.

While she waited for the door to be opened, she glanced around curiously. It was a pleasant neighborhood. There was shrubbery in front of the house, partially hiding it from the street. The wide porch was covered with matting of an orange and black pattern, and there were bright orange cushions on the chairs and couch and swing that hung from the ceiling on chains. The tables and other furniture were lacquered black. Scattered around lavishly were bright magazines, with startling pictures of movie stars in sketchy bathing suits. A book with silver and black covers entitled *Her Scarlet Sin* lay open face-down on the black wicker table. Beside it a cloisonné ashtray held several cigarette stumps and plenty of ashes.

Amorelle turned from a thoughtful contemplation of the scene to see that the door was opening and a maid, obviously finishing the adjustment of her hastily donned cap and apron, stood looking at her curiously.

"Is this where Mr. Enoch Dean lives?" Amorelle asked with a frightened wish that the girl would say no and she might yet turn and flee.

But the girl nodded.

"You're Miss Dean, aren't you? Well, you're to go right upstairs to the third story, the middle room, not the front room—that's the sewing room. You'll find it right at the top of the stairs. Ms. Dean is gone to a bridge party and Miss Louise, she's at the country club. They said fer you ta make yerself at home."

Amorelle stepped into the hall with a feeling as if cold water had been suddenly thrown in her face and yet a relief that she would not have to face the formidable strange aunt and cousin right at once.

"Is—my uncle—able to see me?" she asked, hesitantly pausing on the first step of the stairs.

The maid was already untying her apron and unpinning her cap and did not stop in the action as she answered.

"Oh, him? He's down at the office. He don't get home till six any night."

"Oh, but I thought he had been in an accident," said the girl, puzzled. "I thought he had hurt his knee."

"Oh, he did, last week, but he ain't missed a day at the office yet. Ef he wanted to *she* wouldn't let him anyway. You got a trunk coming, ain't you?"

"Yes," said Amorelle, feeling more of a stranger than ever. "Here is my check. Had I better leave it with you? Will they bring the trunk up to my room?"

"Not n'less you pay him an extra quarter. It's fifty cents fer the second floor, seventy-five fer the third. Of course you could unpack it and lug it up yerself ef you wanted to."

Amorelle coldly handed the maid the seventy-five cents and plodded up the two flights of stairs. When she reached the little middle room with its one high dormer window, its ugly collection of heterogeneous furniture, she closed her door, sat down in a shaky rocking chair with her elbows on its arms, and buried her face in her hands. What a home to come to! She thought of the dear little manse in Rivington with its tasteful arrangement of fine old furniture; she thought of her own dainty bedroom; she remembered the loving faces at the station when she had left, even dear old Hannah in her plaid gingham, and the world seemed very black. She wondered why she had ever come here.

It was a good thing that her trunk arrived just then—she had started it a full day ahead of herself—else she might have fallen into utter despair, so prone are these spirits of ours to be affected by our surroundings. But the trunk demanded immediate attention. She had asked the expressman to unstrap it for her, and at once she became more cheerful as she caught sight of her own things lying on the top, just as she had placed them a couple of days before.

She took out her father's picture and placed it on her bureau, the beautiful picture that the kind-hearted photographer, a member of their church, had had enlarged and framed for her a Christmas ago. What comfort it was that she had that picture now. She remembered that Johnny Brewster had said he wished he had a copy of that picture, and she thought to herself that she would write and get one finished and framed for him. Johnny hadn't taken a cent for all the moving and help he had given her. But that was one thing she could do for him, and she must see to it at once. How good Johnny had been to her! A brother could not have done better, at least in the ways he understood her need.

There was an ugly bureau of golden oak in the room and a maple chiffonier. They were not decorative, but they provided plenty of room for putting away garments. There was also a rather shallow closet containing six hooks and three wire hangers. However, it was more interesting and less disheartening to dispose of her garments than to sit and wonder why she had come, and she went to work trying to forget her cold welcome and the dismalness of the little room. At least it was her own. She would not have to share it with any disagreeable cousin, the dread of which had been one of the bugbears of her way there. There was a bathroom down the hall. She would probably have to share it with that grumpy maid, but there might be worse things than that. At least she looked clean.

About half past five, she thought she heard a car drive up to the house and opened her door to see if any of the family had arrived.

She had dressed herself in a pretty silk of brown with Persian red that her father had always liked, and she was questioning within herself just what etiquette required of a guest who had arrived during the absence of family. Should she rush down and try to be quietly glad to see them, or should she wait for them to come to her? Of course her own feeling was to await developments, but maybe that was not the Christian attitude. They were relatives, and there might have been plenty of excuses for their not having planned a more cordial greeting. Besides, it was all pride anyway. She must put those thoughts aside and try to be natural.

But just as she reached this conclusion, she heard voices.

"Oh, so she's come, has she? Oh heck, Clara, she's *come*! Now isn't that awkward with Sam Bemis coming to dinner, and very likely Anne and Tommy and George Horton will be in for the evening!"

It was a young voice that was talking, but who was she speaking to as Clara? Not her mother, surely! But yes, that must be it, for an older, bored voice replied, "Oh, for sweet pity's sake, Louise, don't worry me now! I'm tired to death! I can't see what difference it makes about this particular night. If your stepfather insists on having her here all winter, why, there isn't anything we can do about it. Just act as you would anyway."

"Oh heck!" said the younger voice. "Does she have to come down to dinner?"

"Certainly! I suppose she does. You know you couldn't get away with a thing like that. It'll just have to be understood that she belongs to the family. She won't likely want to be very social just after a funeral! Louie, dear, go tell Ida not to disturb her yet awhile. I want to get a nap before dinner. I'm simply passing out. Tell her to call your cousin when dinner is ready and not before, do you understand?"

"That's a help!" said a relieved younger voice. "Clara, you certainly are a cherub when it comes to in-laws. I'm simply dying for a smoke and a hot bath before I dress. I was afraid you were going to make me the goat, and I simply wouldn't stand for that!"

Amorelle shut her door softly and went and sat down on her bed, staring off at the ugly flowered wallpaper, her heart sinking lower and lower. Was this what she was up against for the winter? What could she do about it? What would her father want her to do?

Chapter 8

Ida did not take the trouble to call her even when she heard a silver chime ring out, which surely must be the dinner signal. She hesitated at the door, wondering what she ought to do. Her own wish in the matter would be to remain where she was until summoned even if it took all night. But she had spent some time on her knees, inquiring her way through this difficult path that lay before her, and a spirit of meekness had come upon her through heavenly converse, which shone sweetly in her quiet face and made her anxious to do the thing that would the least provoke. So far as was in her, she was determined to try out this unknown world and see if she could win its inhabitants. Or, failing in that, at least to leave a Christian witness behind her if she had to go.

So now she paused at the head of the stairs and heard a clatter of voices downstairs. It might be only one girl and one young man, but they were conversing loudly. Then she heard a door open on the floor below and a man's slow step going downstairs.

The young voices did not pause for more than "Hello" as the elder man arrived among them but chattered and laughed on. And then she heard another door open on the second floor and a woman's step, the rustle of a skirt, a waft of perfume, and she knew her aunt was coming out. Now was her time, and she sped down her flight and met the imperious lady of the house, just advancing from her room to the head of the lower flight of stairs.

"Is—this—Aunt Clara?" she asked, shyly lifting her eyes to meet hard, calculating gray ones that surveyed her coldly.

"Oh, it's *you*, is it?" said the woman, not offering any warmer salute. "Ida said you had come. Did you have any trouble in finding your way?" She put her hand on the balustrade and advanced one foot to the top step of the stairs.

"Oh no," said Amorelle quietly, wishing she had stayed in her room, "no trouble at all."

"Well, you may as well come right down to dinner," said the aunt, launching her heavy body on the downward way and indicating by a casual motion of her free hand that Amorelle might follow her if she chose.

Amorelle, struggling to keep her meekness, followed.

At the foot of the stairs, the rest of the party was grouped. An elderly, sad-eyed man with a cane, somewhat apart from the young people, leaned back against a heavy mulberry curtain, which draped the wide doorway to the dining room, as if he had no part in the activity that was about to occur. There was something half-familiar in the lines of his face, though when she tried to find it, there seemed only dullness and indifference, a disappointing likeness to something precious.

The two young people turned and stared at her rudely. There was something half-belligerent about the girl's look, but there was a supercilious sneer on the young man's face, mingled with something like surprise and an unexpected interest when he saw her.

"Mr. Dean," said the wife as she arrived heavily on the first floor, "your niece is here!" She gave a half wave of her hand toward Amorelle and stepped at once into the dining room.

Amorelle thought she saw a brief gleam of interest in the silent man's eyes as he looked up and said "Ah!" and she stepped quickly to his side and put out her hand. Her impulse would have been to give him a warm little-girl kiss; but he showed no sign that this would have been welcome, and she seemed to feel the eyes of the two young people scorching her back with contempt.

But her uncle took her hand, slowly, in both of his own, and held it warmly, looking down into her eyes with something like hunger for an instant.

"Oh, you look like your mother!" he said in a half-hesitant voice. "You have eyes like hers! I'm—glad you have come!" Then he dropped her hand suddenly, as if he felt he had forgotten himself and held it too long already, and a peevish voice from the dining room showed he was right.

"Come, Mr. Dean, are you going to stand out there in the hall

all evening sentimentalizing? Don't you know you are holding us all up and the dinner is getting cold?"

A sensitive flush went over the man's face and Amorelle felt for him, almost as if he had been her father. That sensitive look was like her father.

He hurried in instantly and went to his seat at the head of the table. Amorelle all too soon came to see that it was one of the few places in this household where he took the actual head.

His wife was already standing grimly at her own chair, looking reproachfully at him until he was in place. Then she turned hard eyes on the new arrival.

"*You* may sit there!" She indicated the seat at her left. "I'm sure I don't know what to call you. You have a simply impossible name. I've never been able to pronounce it or remember it."

Amorelle tried to summon a pleasant smile.

"It is an odd name, isn't it? It was my mother's maiden name, you know, Amorelle!"

"Absurd!" said the older woman. "I shall never be able to pronounce it in all the world. So unpractical, something like a fairy tale. Haven't you a middle name?"

"No," said Amorelle gravely.

"We'll have to find something. Just plain Jane would be better than that fancy thing. Well, shall we sit down, Mr. Dean?"

They sat down, and Uncle Enoch bowed his head and mumbled and hurried an inaudible grace while the others maintained a half-amused silence, with heads scarcely even inclined toward a respectful angle.

"So absurd in this day and age," gurgled Aunt Clara with

an embarrassed smile toward the grinning youth who was their guest. "It's an old custom in Mr. Dean's family, and he can't seem to get over it," she explained.

Amorelle flashed a quick look of sympathy toward her uncle before she remembered that every glance was being watched by the lynx-eyed Louise who sat opposite her. It would not be a politic move, for either herself or Uncle Enoch, for her to be ranged with him against them all on this first night of her arrival, before she even knew them. And what was to be gained by it? So she dropped her eyes to her lap for the time being until they stopped noticing her. Later, when the talk was going more freely between Louise, her mother, and her guest, she could venture to study this other girl who was her cousin.

She wasn't really pretty, Amorelle decided; her mouth was too selfish for that and her black eyes too small, but she was smart looking. Her hair was very black and slicked close to her head, bobbed of course, and licked out sharply on the artificial pallor of her sallow cheeks. Her ears were showing and carried long, sparkling earrings. She was wearing a bright red satin dress, cut exceedingly low in the back and with no sleeves. Amorelle studied her curiously. She was not familiar with low backs except in fashion magazines. Her world did not wear them, though of course she knew they existed. One did not wear low-backed dresses to a prayer meeting, or even to a church social, in Rivington. She realized that her plain brown crepe was not in a class with this new cousin's apparel. Even Aunt Clara was wearing a low-cut black lace dress, and her stout white arms were bare to the shoulder. Amorelle realized that she must look like a little brown sparrow next to her aunt and cousin.

But it was presently borne in upon her that neither aunt nor cousin was aware now of her existence. At least they had the air of trying to forget that she was there. And presently when she raised her eyes to her uncle, who had been addressing himself to his fruit cup, she found his eyes upon her furtively, and she flashed him a real smile without getting caught at it by the others.

"Did you have a comfortable journey?" he suddenly asked her in a low tone, under cover of the hilarious laughter over one of the young man's jokes.

"Quite comfortable, thank you," she answered with another warm look that thanked him for the friendly little question.

"What did you say, Mr. Dean?" demanded the querulous tone of Aunt Clara, stopping in the midst of her flattering laughter.

"Oh, nothing!" said the man of the house quickly. "I was just asking Amorelle about her journey."

"Oh, you seem to have mastered her name quickly enough, though I'm sure you haven't heard it in years!" she sneered politely. "Well, don't you think it would be better form if you spoke loud enough for everybody to hear? I hate to be thinking someone is speaking to me and I have not known it."

The man flashed her a bitter look. It struck Amorelle that he looked so much older than her father had, though she knew he was almost five years younger.

"Will you ring for some bread and butter to be brought?" he suddenly demanded and looked down at his plate again.

"Oh, Enoch, don't you know this is *dinner*? We don't eat bread and butter with *dinner*!" snickered Louise amusedly.

"Do you *really* mean that you want *bread* at *dinner*time, Mr. Dean?" asked his wife disapprovingly. "You know it is not our custom to serve it in the evening."

"I *do!*" said Uncle Enoch, lifting his eyes sternly to his wife's for an instant and then dropping them to his plate again.

"But you know that *nobody*, simply *nobody*, serves bread at night with dinner," argued his wife.

"I do," said Uncle Enoch doggedly.

"And *butter?*" asked the incredulous voice.

"And *butter!*" said the determined voice.

"But I never heard of such a thing, Mr. Dean!"

"Yes," said Uncle Enoch, apparently unexpectedly, for his answer had a sudden silencing effect, "you have heard of it. You heard of it last night when I asked for it, and the night before, and the night before that, and all the nights!"

"Mr. Dean!" said Aunt Clara and subsided into dumb fury. Then in a moment she rang the bell and gave the order.

"Ida, bring Mr. Dean a piece of bread and a helping of butter."

"No, Ida, bring a plate of bread, plenty of it, and a *dish* of butter!" said Uncle Enoch. "My niece may care for some also."

"Would you really care for bread and butter at night?" asked Aunt Clara in that incredulous tone, turning to look at Amorelle curiously but much as if she were asking it of a toad that had inopportunely hopped in her way.

"Yes, thank you," said Amorelle, giving her what she hoped was a bright smile that ignored the pitiful dialogue that had just occurred.

"Oh, *really?*" That was all Aunt Clara said, but she flashed Amorelle a look of malice and later gave her husband another.

Louise ducked her head sideways toward the young man and giggled, murmuring into her napkin, "Oh, Enoch, you're just the limit!"

"That will do, Louise!" said Uncle Enoch sternly, speaking to her as if she were a child. "If you can't be respectful you can leave the table and the room!"

"Oh, yeah?" said the girl resentfully and relapsed into a sullen silence.

Amorelle was very uncomfortable during the remainder of the meal. She felt that in some mysterious way she had been the cause of the unpleasantness. But the young man was most effervescent. He told a funny story and presently had them all laughing, all but Uncle Enoch, who seemed not to have heard it, and Amorelle, who couldn't quite see the point. She wondered if Aunt Clara could. Aunt Clara was apparently laughing to encourage the young man.

It was a relief when the meal was ended.

A man, it appeared, had been waiting in the library to see Uncle Enoch. He picked up his cane from the floor and limped off. Amorelle was relieved to see that he was really lame and hadn't just made an excuse about coming to the funeral. But in the doorway, he suddenly turned back and looked at her as she rose from the chair.

"You'll—be—all right?" he asked her, under cover of the chatter of the others.

"Oh, surely!" she said brightly with a smile. It warmed her

heart to have him care and stabbed her with the consciousness that there seemed no one else to care.

The front doorbell had rung again and several more young people barged into the house noisily. They were hailed boisterously by Louise and placidly by her mother.

Amorelle hesitated on the threshold of the dining room and wondered what she ought to do next. Was she supposed to go in with the others? But no one made any move to introduce her. They were all engaged in talking, shouting almost it seemed, for each spoke louder than the other, and there was an immoderate amount of laughter about nothing. Amorelle felt utterly out of it. It was as if she had not been present. She began to feel like a ghost. Had she suddenly become invisible?

Only one young man glanced across and noticed her, tried to draw her into a laugh over something he had said. They called him George. He was big and good looking, with bold blue eyes slightly disguised by long, gorgeous, golden, curly eyelashes that added a touch of the angelic to a face that otherwise might have seemed coarse. And George lifted those bold blue eyes more than once toward Amorelle, seeking for her approval of his remarks, seeking to draw her into the general conversation.

If Amorelle had not felt so exceedingly alone there, she might have been annoyed at his informality; but as it was, she could not help a kindly feeling toward him.

Louise, however, had noted his glance, and with a supercilious look toward her new cousin, she drew George away into the living room. The rest of the young people immediately followed.

Amorelle made one step forward, hesitated, and Aunt

Clara immediately turned upon her like a detour sign in an open road.

"And you," she said, looking at Amorelle as if she were something out of place, "what are you going to do now?"

Amorelle was like a thermostat, instantly sensitive to temperature, and she knew that she was not wanted.

"I wonder if you would mind if I slipped away and went to bed?" she asked sweetly. "I find I'm rather tired with all I've been through."

"I was wondering if you wouldn't want to go to your room," said the aunt, speaking more warmly than she had yet spoken to her. "If there is anything you need, or don't know about, you can just ask Ida. I guess she gave you towels, didn't she? Well, we have breakfast at eight o'clock. At least your uncle does. I take mine in my room and don't usually come down before ten. Louise, of course, stays out all hours and sleeps as long as she pleases. Ida'll tell you how you can help around after breakfast in the dining room. Good-night. I hope you'll be comfortable!" Aunt Clara sailed placidly off into the living room and settled down to her elaborate knitting.

Amorelle fairly flew up those stairs, out of sight. Anger and desolation blazed in her face, and she didn't want anybody to see her. She dashed into her own room and locked the door, not even stopping to turn on the light. She went over to the little high window and looked out, determined not to cry; looked out on the myriad lights of a strange city in the distance and the clustering houses of a pleasant suburb close by. Down below her she could see into a lit room where people were sitting around a table, eating. They were all laughing and talking. It seemed a happy home. There were children in it and a grandmother. Across the way another lit room showed happy groups. She only, of all the world, seemed alone and sorrowful.

She stood there a long time looking out on that strange world, blinking back tears she would not shed. Then softly there came to her mind the promise her father used to repeat so often: *"I the LORD thy God will hold thy right hand, saying unto thee, Fear not; I will help thee."*

Then she turned and went to her refuge, kneeling at her bedside. If this was one of the tests that her heavenly Father had for her to go through that she might see how weak she was in herself without Him, and how great and strong He was in a time of trial, she was willing to yield herself to His will. It wasn't going to be pleasant; it was going to be greatly humiliating, but He had brought her here, and perhaps He wanted her to stay awhile. At least while she stayed, He had her by the hand and nothing really harmful could come to her. But while she stayed, she must witness for Him.

Presently she turned on the light and read her Bible. That eased her troubled spirit, and then, as she was really worn out with all the excitement and sorrow and hard work of the past few weeks, she went to bed and to sleep, hoping that the morning light would make the world seem a bit brighter.

She did not know how long she had been asleep when she was suddenly brought back to life by a loud knocking at her door and a voice calling.

"Hello, hello! Wake up! What on earth have you got your

door locked for? You don't think anybody is going to steal you, do you?"

She came suddenly awake and, sitting up, looked around her. For an instant she did not know where she was. Rivington? Glenellen? The sleeping car? Then it came to her! And that was her new cousin's nasal voice out there saying disagreeable things to her.

"Yes? What is it?" she managed to call back sleepily.

"For heaven's sake open this door!" called the voice cautiously. "I can't scream what I want."

Amorelle hurried to the door, grabbing her robe on her way.

"What is it?" she asked. "Is something the matter?"

"Plenty!" said Louise, stepping inside and drawing the door closed.

"I just got home with a crowd and found Ida had forgotten to make the sandwiches and hot cocoa I ordered. It's her night out, it seems, and she never said a word. Enoch went to bed hours ago, and Clara went out to the country club with Mrs. Salisbury just as we left. There isn't a soul to get any food for us, and of course I can't leave my guests. Can't you come down and make us some sandwiches or something? Anything that passes for food. We're simply starved!"

"Why, yes, I guess so—!" Amorelle hesitated. But perhaps this was her chance to win her way with Louise. "Yes, I'll be down in a minute as quick as I can get some clothes on!"

"Don't stop to dress. Just come in pajamas. Everybody's used to them."

"Well, I'm not," laughed Amorelle.

"Well, make it snappy. Don't wait for stockings. Our crowd hardly ever wears 'em!"

Amorelle refrained from replying to that. She was already drawing on hers.

"Where shall I find things? Will you come out and show me?"

"Mercy, no! It's a wonder they aren't hunting me now on the roof. You don't know that crowd. Just go down the back stairs and you'll find the refrigerator and pantry. Use anything you see. I'll answer for it. Get us up a good meal and make it quick, that's all I ask. I've got a coupla new fellas in tonight and I want things to be right, if you know what I mean."

"I'll do my best," promised Amorelle, swinging her dress over her head.

She waited only to get a clean apron out of the drawer and then she sped away to her task, wondering if this was a part of her testing in this strange new home to which she had come. As she went she rubbed the sleep from her eyes and cudgeled her brain to think how she could quickly make an appetizing midnight supper.

From that night on, Amorelle's status among them was established. She was chief cook and bottle washer at any hour of the day or night, and nothing more. They never by any means took her in as one of them, or even spoke to her except to demand more food, none of them except George Horton. He often hovered around her and helped, and nobody tried to stop him, because they didn't want to go near enough to any work themselves to have it supposed they knew how to do it. George Horton was pleasant and kind and joked a good deal, and she accepted his assistance as she would have that of a child who liked to hover around the kitchen.

Crisp bacon sandwiches and ginger ale was the menu she finally offered to the hilarious crowd, with tiny little sweet gherkin pickles. It wasn't perhaps the latest combination, but the cupboard was strangely bare of other things—only a teaspoonful of cocoa left in the box, not a drop of milk, either canned or otherwise, in the house.

Amorelle set George Horton to getting out the ice cubes for the glasses and opening the ginger-ale bottles while she warmed the butter, crisped the bacon, and spread thin slices the long way of the loaf, folding them together and cutting them into small sandwiches. The new combination was hailed with delight, and a shout went up, which must have made Uncle Enoch and the neighbors groan and wonder when these benighted young creatures would go home and let them sleep.

Amid much clamor of calling good-nights, of tooting of second-hand or borrowed paternal horns, much screaming of tires, the party got themselves away.

It was nearly two o'clock when Amorelle, having cleaned up the kitchen and washed the plates and glasses, crept silently up to her bed. And thus ended her first night in her uncle's household.

She wondered, as she floated off to sleep again, if it had done any good to get up in the night and try to please Louise. Louise hadn't said a word of thanks.

Chapter 9

Amorelle was downstairs at eight o'clock promptly for breakfast. She was one of those who could set herself like an alarm clock and wake on the dot.

But breakfast was fifteen minutes late. Ida was cross. She had been out all night at a relative's house and didn't get to the house till five minutes of eight.

Uncle Enoch came in looking tired and sick and careworn. He brightened when he saw Amorelle.

"You down?" he said with surprise. "I thought you would sleep late after your journey." But he seemed pleased to see her. He asked her about her father's last sickness.

"I wish you had written me sooner," he said sadly. "I would have tried to get away and see him. We used to be very close to one another."

Amorelle told him how her father had spoken of him so

lovingly several times in those last days, and how they had not thought he would be going quite so soon. The doctor had thought it might be several months if he took care of himself.

"I could have got away. I'm sure I could if I had only been insistent enough," he kept repeating sadly. "But I'm glad you're here. I'm not sure how happy you'll be! There are always so many outsiders around it doesn't seem like home anymore. Louise has so many hangers-on. She's just back from school, you know."

He kept looking earnestly at Amorelle and telling her over and over again how much she looked like her mother. "You had a lovely mother," he said earnestly.

Amorelle was happy while she was talking to him. She told herself that it was going to be worthwhile being there, even through some unpleasantness, if only to get acquainted with Uncle Enoch. And he did look like her father often. She could see the same expression hovering over his face now and then.

He seemed almost reluctant as he rose to go at last.

"Well, I've enjoyed my breakfast," he said with almost a smile. "I usually have to eat alone. You're a good girl, and you're like your father, too, I can see. I'm glad you've come."

When he was gone, Amorelle carried the dishes out, brushed up the table, and tidied around the dining room with broom and pan, which she managed to find without instructions from the sullen Ida. Then she picked up the newspaper and glanced over it.

There wasn't much in a strange newspaper to interest her, and after looking out the window a few minutes, she searched through the bookcases for something to read. But there was nothing but modern fiction of the most lurid type—books she had heard condemned by thoughtful people, books with titles that fairly leered at you, magazines of a world for which she did not care. She was suddenly appalled at the new life. How was she to get through her days? There would be that little contact with her uncle in the morning before he went to his office. Perhaps she could hope to win him out of his taciturnity and make a companion of him, but he would never take the place of her father. It was not in him.

There would be work. She could see that very plainly, and she was not afraid of work, though she rather resented the way in which it was demanded of one who came as an invited guest. However, she was willing to work. But what should she do in the intervals? There surely would be intervals, even in a day's work.

She went upstairs and made her bed, put some of her pictures and personal belongings around the room, tried to make it look cheery. Then she sat down to read her Bible and pray.

She heard a bell ring distantly, heard a tray come jingling to her aunt's door. By that time her own door was open, and she was listening for the rest of the house to awake. She didn't exactly know what to do with herself. She would have gone out to take a walk only it didn't seem quite the thing to do the first morning, and she was a guest. Or was she a guest? Was she not perhaps a servant? Well, the servant of the Lord, anyway, ready to do what was His will for her, even if it was not pleasant. At least that was the attitude she wanted to have. But somehow she could not quite bring herself to go down and ask that grumpy Ida for orders. She would wait till her aunt told her what she wanted. If she didn't make things definite pretty soon, she would ask her to.

So Amorelle sat in her room, read awhile, did a little mending, and waited until she heard Aunt Clara go downstairs. Then she hurried down after her and entered the dining room where her aunt sat at the table engaged in reading the morning mail.

The elder woman lifted her eyes and gave Amorelle a cold look.

"Oh, so here are you!" she said in an accusing tone. "I supposed you would be in the kitchen helping Ida."

Amorelle stood still, looking at her aunt.

"I beg your pardon," she said gravely. "I did what I could see needed doing around the dining room. If you will give me a list of things you would like me to be responsible for I'll be glad to attend to them."

Her aunt stared at her.

"Why didn't you ask Ida what she wanted you to do?"

The color flamed into Amorelle's pale cheeks.

"It didn't occur to me," she said calmly. "I thought you were the one to tell me what you wanted. I'm not visiting Ida. But I'm quite glad to help in any way you want me to."

Aunt Clara raised her eyebrows as high as they would go, but Amorelle gave her a pleasant look back, and eventually the eyebrows relaxed.

"Oh, very well, if you look at it that way I suppose I can write out a regular program for you. I'll see that you have it this afternoon."

There was plenty on the program when it was handed to her

at lunchtime, and studying it over at her leisure that afternoon, she found that she was expected to do a rather full day's work for an invited guest. However, after the first flame of anger died down, she was able to look at the matter more calmly, especially after she had prayed about it.

I'm here now; I came at my father's request to get acquainted with my uncle and, if possible, get him to receive the gospel of salvation. I'm not going to let a mere selfish, disagreeable aunt drive me away by a little work. I don't mind work.

So she went downstairs to survey her field of labor and get acquainted with her new duties. If possible, she meant to perform her activities as far as might be when Ida was out of the kitchen. Ida had a lofty, ugly way with her, and Amorelle wished, as far as was possible, to get along without clashes while only as long as it took to pack up again. But she knew her conscience and her promises to her father would not be satisfied with going at once, so she determined to be as cheerful as possible and do her work as unto the Lord and not as unto Ida or Aunt Clara.

When Louise sauntered down just before lunch was finished, she asked Amorelle if she wouldn't make a cake for her to take to a picnic that afternoon, and Amorelle perceived that Louise intended to make use of her also. But she made the cake.

After three or four days, it became apparent to Amorelle that she was not to be taken into the life of the household at all. That so far as Louise and Aunt Clara were concerned, she was no more to them than Ida, and that the only difference between herself and Ida was that she ate at the table with the family and Ida didn't.

It was only the breakfast hour which she had alone with her uncle that kept her from leaving at once. It was pitiful how glad Uncle Enoch was to see her in the mornings. It seemed to put a brightness into his face and a light into his eyes. He lingered a few minutes every morning talking with her and often asked questions about her father and his work. Amorelle talked on sweetly, telling little items about their everyday life, telling of her father's work and study, of his parish and how they loved him, telling tender little incidents of the church life. She loved to talk about the dear past days, and her uncle seemed to like to hear it. Gradually she was introducing him to the members of the parish one by one, and he would often surprise her with a hearty laugh over some of her character sketches. He told her one morning that it was as good as reading a novel to listen to her talk. So, more and more, Amorelle felt that she could not leave yet, no matter how disagreeable the rest of the family became.

One night when there were no guests at the table, Aunt Clara fixed her eyes on Amorelle and asked her bluntly, "Did your father leave you much money?" She never called her by name if she could help it, though Louise had gradually taken up her name after asking several times how to pronounce it.

Amorelle gave her aunt an astonished look, tried to conquer the anger that sprang up in her heart, and then, with an amused little quiver of a smile, answered, "Does any minister in a small suburban church where there are very few wealthy people ever leave much behind him when he goes?"

"Clara!" protested Uncle Enoch sternly. "That's not a proper question to ask the child."

"I don't know why," said Aunt Clara complacently, helping herself to more cream on the sliced peaches she was eating. "If she belongs to the family as you are always saying, I don't know why we shouldn't know what circumstances she is in. I think it is our right."

"It is all right, Uncle Enoch," said the girl, trying to smile. "I don't mind your knowing that I haven't very much. The last year there were very heavy expenses connected with Father's illness, but everything is paid, I'm thankful to say. There aren't any debts. That's what Father was most afraid of."

"H'm. He would be," murmured the stern-eyed man gravely. "He was always that way."

"But I don't see why he wasn't afraid of leaving his only daughter without sufficient support. I think he was criminally to blame if he didn't leave her pretty well fixed. Surely he had a life insurance, didn't he?"

"Clara, I insist that Amorelle shall not be put through an inquisition." This from Uncle Enoch.

"My father did all that he possibly could for me, Aunt Clara," said Amorelle quietly. "He gave me a good education, and I am quite able to earn my living if that should be necessary."

"Yes, but he should have had insurance!" said Aunt Clara fretfully. "A man is very much to blame not to have insurance! It shows a lack of intelligence and forethought. A girl alone in the world! To leave her dependent upon relatives who may not be really able to support her!"

A cold, angry retort came to Amorelle's lips. She gave her aunt one angry flash from her eyes, and then just in time, there came to her a phrase she had read in her Bible that morning, and whose promise she had claimed for her keeping that day: *"Unto Him that is able to keep you from falling. . ."*

She could not possibly go through such maddening scenes as this in her own strength without a fall, but He could keep her. She kept saying it over and over to herself, *"He is able to keep me from falling! He is able to keep me from falling."*

Amorelle dropped her eyes to her plate and kept her lips still. Uncle Enoch gave her one pitying look and closed his lips. Something in her sweet look seemed to make him understand. He said no more, and Aunt Clara went on moralizing on the wisdom of caring for your children. But nobody answered her, and at last she turned cold persistence on Amorelle and asked pointedly, *"Didn't* your father leave *any* insurance *at all?"*

Amorelle waited an instant before she replied, and then she lifted sweet, pained eyes and said, "Aunt Clara, please, if you don't mind, I'd rather not talk about it anymore."

"Well, really!" said Aunt Clara with a snort. "Is that the way your father brought you up to talk to your elders?"

Louise giggled offensively. But Amorelle sat quietly looking down, and presently, in spite of all that she could do, two great tears collected and dropped brightly down into her lap.

Uncle Enoch saw them and drew a long, deep sigh. Louise saw them and stared speculatively, wondering just what kind of creature this strange new cousin was that she did not make some angry retort. Aunt Clara saw them and was mightily incensed because she couldn't seem to think of anything to say to wither this girl who was in their household against *her* will, and who

it seemed had to stay here. She could see she was going to turn
Enoch Dean's heart away from any interest in her own insolent
child, and there would be money to be left to someone someday.
Perhaps not all to his wife. Somehow she must prevent such a
calamity.

But Louise sat and stared. She could see that Amorelle
was angry. She could understand that she was not the kind of
girl who was afraid to answer back or unable to think of sharp
things to say. She had already learned that Amorelle was bright
and keen. Why didn't she answer back and give Clara as good as
she had given? She was able, and she was angry. *Why* didn't she
do it? What was the secret of her life that made her strong while
yet she was simple and sweet?

Louise had always gained her victories by insolence, at least
with her mother. It had been her great weapon since babyhood.
To be sure it hadn't worked so well on Enoch, but then he was
old and odd. But this girl had her reserves and held them quietly,
without wrath, and got away with it. Actually, she was getting
away with it with Clara. Clara wasn't getting her answer at all! She
wasn't finding out what she wanted to know! Louise marveled.

Then when the two tears fell she knew there was a weakness
somewhere. Her lip began to curl in scorn, but something
arrested her thought. Was it weakness after all? Was it not the
greater strength? The girl was obviously feeling cut to the heart,
but she hadn't meant to let those tears fall. No more followed
them. She was in command again, and in a minute she looked
up, and finding Louise's eyes upon her, smiled a faint smile at
her. The strangest thing about it all was that Louise found herself

sort of smiling back again. She hadn't meant to in the least, but she had done it. It was a sort of overture of peace between them. Amorelle had recognized that Louise had seen her hurt and had not resented her gaze. Well, it was strange. This girl had something about her that Louise couldn't understand, and someday she meant to find out its secret.

The dessert came on and created a diversion. Silence settled on the table until Ida had withdrawn. Then Louise, just to prevent another ominous silence—which meant a long and tiresome altercation between her mother and her stepfather afterward—turned to him and said in a flippant tone, "Well, Enoch, when are you going to buy me a little run-about? All the rest of the girls have got fathers who buy them cars, but I have to walk or beg rides from the men! Aren't you ever going to buy me a car, Enoch?"

Louise hadn't the slightest idea that her stepfather would ever buy her a car. Her mother gasped at the very audacity of the request, but Enoch Dean looked at her gravely.

"I certainly should not consider such a thing for a minute so long as you continue to call me by my first name. It is most offensive!"

Louise stared at him in wonder. Did he mean that he would actually do big things like that for her if she acted in a way to please him? Perhaps it would be worthwhile. Could she do it and get away with it? It might be worth considering.

But the lady of the house shoved back her chair with an angry look that boded no good to her family and sailed offendedly from the room.

Amorelle vanished through the pantry door to make some arrangements for the morning, and Uncle Enoch took his cane and hobbled out.

After she went upstairs, Amorelle could hear an angry altercation going on in her uncle's room below. Poor Uncle Enoch was taking it in her place. Should she have answered her aunt minutely? She sat down and considered. Of course it was none of her business to inquire about money, but perhaps she ought to have answered more politely. The real difficulty, as Amorelle had to acknowledge to herself, was that until her aunt had asked the questions, insurance had never entered her mind. It seemed to her that several years ago she had heard her father speak of paying his insurance. He was not one who talked much about his business affairs. Once, about three years ago when he first began to be ill, he had told her that his will and important papers were in a little fireproof drawer in his desk. She had begged him not to speak of wills and wept, and he had smiled and told her not to be foolish and it was always best to look things in the face and be ready for any contingency. It came to her suddenly while her aunt was speaking that she had not thought of a will, nor of insurance.

Several months before, her father had put his bank account in their joint names, lest he should be sick and unable to sign checks. And Amorelle had taken it for granted that everything was turned over to her and there was therefore no need of a will.

She had given no thought whatever to the matter. In her haste to get away from Rivington and the consequences of Mrs. Brisbane's ill-advised activities, she had not even taken time to open the drawers of her father's desk and go through his important papers. In fact, the thought of it just then would have been so sorrowful to her that she would have avoided it even if she had had the time.

But of course there must have been papers, and now that she thought of it, she remembered he had once told her he had written out some directions for her concerning business. How careless of her not to have gone carefully through everything before she left.

However, there was probably nothing of immediate necessity. The papers were safe and would keep. She had the little key to the secret drawer. She might even send it to Miss Landon and ask her to take out the papers and send them to her—only that seemed rather silly. Her stay here was most uncertain. If things kept on this way, she simply could not endure to remain much longer. She would just wait and keep her mouth shut. Surely she had a right to refuse to talk about her father's affairs. Let them think, what was obviously the truth, that there had been scarcely anything.

Later, when she was carrying some towels to the laundry chute in the back hall, she heard her aunt come out of her uncle's library, and Louise, coming noisily up the lower stairs, confronted her mother with a peevish tone, "Ah, say, Clara! What's the use of arguing poor Enoch deaf and dumb and blind? You won't get anywhere with him, I'm telling you, not if you talk all night and then some. He's too old. And say, for Pete's sake, lay off Amorelle. The next thing you'll have her running off East again, or getting a job somewhere. She's not going to stand for you prying into her affairs, can't you see that? Let her alone, for sweet pity's sake."

Amorelle could hear a hoarse sobbing reply.

"That's a nice way for you to talk, Louise, when you know I'm doing it all for your sake! It was you that said it was poisonous for her to be here and you wouldn't stand for it. It was you who threatened to run away and marry some good-for-nothing if I didn't get rid of her somehow."

"Oh well," laughed Louise, "that was before I knew what good sandwiches she could make. She really isn't half-bad, Clara! She's a sort of a good egg. She's always willing to make things for us, and she doesn't seem to want to butt in. The only fella that's fallen for her at all is George, and he's been a pest so long I'm sick to death of him. Besides, it's convenient having her around sometimes when there's work to be done and I want to go out somewhere."

Amorelle passed softly into her room and shut the door. Sitting down in her chair, she buried her face in her hands and laughed. So, she had managed to get by with Louise as a good egg who would make sandwiches and not steal her admirers. Well, perhaps if she could weather it a little while longer, she might even win Aunt Clara.

She battled it out on her knees that night before the Lord and decided that He had not yet released her to go back to Rivington. And the possible private papers in the secret drawer of the desk grew hazy and unimportant. How did she know there were any papers?

Chapter 10

The winter came suddenly and with surprise to Amorelle, who was accustomed to the milder climate of Rivington. Deep snow settled down upon the land in a wild blizzard form and was slow in melting. More snow came before it was gone.

Amorelle got out her galoshes and enjoyed the sound of the crunching of her feet in the snow. She wished she were small and had a sled and could go skating and sledding. Louise did all these things, but the crowd didn't ask her. Once or twice George had asked her to go with them, but she always had some excuse.

She had by this time discovered two interests which kept her busy in her leisure hours and made her less lonely. One was a business school where she found she could take a short course in bookkeeping a few hours each week. The other was a wonderful Bible school with evening classes, and two of her evenings each week were thus delightfully employed. To be sure it was necessary sometimes when she went out at night for her to leave behind her well-prepared provision for a sudden supper when Louise and her crowd should come home, but a little forethought and extra work took care of that matter. As for the rest, nobody seemed to care in the least what she did with her time. Only Uncle Enoch inquired, and he seemed quite satisfied when he saw how she was enjoying herself.

"You're like your father," he would say thoughtfully. "You're going your own way and making good in it. I often wish I had gone with him when I was young." And then he would sigh wistfully.

Sometimes at their tête-à-tête breakfast she would tell him a little of her Bible lesson of the night before, and he would always listen interestedly, although he seldom made any comment. Often she had opportunity to tell him of the way of salvation, making it so very plain that he could not fail to remember and understand. And he always seemed thoughtful at such times and gentle beyond the usual.

Aunt Clara, for the most part, ignored her now, giving her cold replies whenever she asked her a question, issuing crisp commands for service, like little icicles that seemed to shiver and break as they were uttered.

Louise paid little attention to her except to ask favors when she needed something. And sometimes it was very hard to go on trying to pave Louise's way to have a good time when she was so utterly unfriendly.

But Amorelle was happy in her Bible school, which filled her heart with new joy and wonder as the old truths opened up into new meanings and made the Bible more precious than it had ever been. And this study was the more delightful to her because she knew it would have pleased her father so much.

There came letters occasionally from Glenellen and Rivington that made her homesick, but it seemed definite now that she was to remain in the West for the winter at least, and the things of the past began to drop away a little. The idea of a will and insurance and important papers were forgotten for the time.

Amorelle found some pleasant people in both her commercial and biblical classes, but she had little time to cultivate friendships, as there were always duties at the house to be done on schedule time. Except when George Horton chose to give her a few minutes of his time while she was preparing late evening suppers for the rest of the young people, she went her way, for the most part alone.

But one evening she had just come down to get ready a tray for a boisterous young crowd who had been practicing tap dancing for a Player's Club entertainment in which they were involved, and she heard them talking. George Horton was asking Louise to play an accompaniment for a solo he had been asked to sing in church Sunday evening at some special service.

Louise whirled the stool around and turned away from the piano with a shrug. Amorelle was standing in line with the door, setting down a plate of little cakes on the dining table, and saw the whole thing.

"Oh, I can't be bothered, George! Go get Amorelle!" she said petulantly. "She can play. I heard her the other day when she didn't know I was listening. She can play swell. She used to play the organ in church."

George came promptly out to Amorelle with his request, so while the others were noisily gathered around the dining table, Amorelle and George went to the living room. George had a big, deep voice with a rather nice natural tone, and he liked to sing, although he had never had much training. Probably he had never had such accompanying as Amorelle gave him either, and his voice boomed out, hushing even the tempestuous crowd in the other room. At the close they gave him a stormy applause and demanded more, and Amorelle played several other songs for him.

"Say, you're swell!" he said to her. "Why didn't I know you played? Say, Amorelle," he lowered his voice, "I like you a lot, do you know it?"

"That's nice," said Amorelle pleasantly in a matter-of-fact tone. "It's nice to have people like you."

He looked at her curiously, beaming down upon her with his good-looking smile.

"But it's more than that," he said, as if discovering something in himself that he hadn't recognized before. "You're a swell looker, do you know it? I never saw you look as pretty as you do tonight!" And then suddenly, without the least warning, he stooped and folded his arms around her, there as she sat at the piano, and put his handsome face against hers softly, as if he were trying her out, though it was done almost reverently for George. Then he laid his strong, laughing lips against hers and kissed her!

It was not a quick, light kiss. It was a lingering one with even something of exploring shyness in it, and that was strange for George. He was usually so bold. There was something tender about it, too, as if he sensed the rareness of the girl he had dared approach this way. As if the touch of his lips upon hers this first time had given him a new sense of how delicate and lovely a woman might be.

Now Amorelle had been brought up not to regard a kiss lightly. Being the minister's daughter and being sweetly serious, she had not been thrown in the way of the light and amorous ways of the world. This happened to be the first time that any man had kissed her this way, and it came upon her weary, lonely soul with a startling sweetness that was so new and unexpected that her soul was off its habitual guard. For an instant her body yielded just ever so little to his embrace, like a tired child that needed comfort, and her lips lay softly against his. Then she came to herself and sprang away from him.

"George!" she said, putting her hands to her flaming cheeks. "Oh, George, why did you do that?" There was reproach in her voice; she was almost in tears. She drew away in the corner of the room far from the hall door where no one could see her.

George came over to her, a light of discovery and possession in his eyes.

"Why shouldn't I do it, beautiful?" he asked with a love croon in his voice. "I did it because I wanted to. Because I love you."

"Oh, please, please, George, don't say any more! They will hear you! I'm afraid they saw—us!"

"What if they did, beautiful? There's nothing to be ashamed of about it. I don't care how many people know it."

"Oh, don't, George. You *mustn't* talk that way! Please, let go of my hand. You have no right—It is so silly— You never thought of such a thing a minute ago!"

"That doesn't make any difference!" he assured her delightedly. "I've thought of it now, haven't I? You're *mine*! You're my girl! Great Scott, what a looker you are with that pink in your cheeks! I don't understand why I never saw it before! What are you afraid of? Come, let's talk it out—"

"We can't talk here! Please let me go!"

"Where do you want to go?"

"Upstairs! George, you must let go of my wrist. We cannot talk about such things here. We have nothing to talk about anyway. It is all wrong, all a mistake."

"Not on your life it isn't. You're my girl and I don't intend to let you go! If you won't talk here, go get your coat and we'll go outside and walk. I want you to myself anyway. Where is your coat? Down back there in the hall closet? Here, I'll get it for you. No, don't you go sliding upstairs. If you do I'll chase you up to your room and carry you down, and I can do it, too, no kidding! You and I are having this out *right now*."

Amorelle stood trembling, frightened, trying to think what she should say to this wild, impetuous youth, the memory of that stirring kiss upon her lips, that handsome face against her own, those strong arms around her. Oh, it would be good to have a friend who really loved her. But this George was one of the wild crowd. He could not be her mate. He had only followed an impulse. She must try to make him see that. She must be kind to him. This was just one of his flirtations. He probably had a great many. Those big blue eyes and long, golden, curly lashes drew admiration from the girls. Even she had considered him unusually good looking. Oh, lovers and marriage. Would they pursue her here? Must her calm, which she was just hoping she had attained, be broken in upon by a disturbance of this sort? Maybe she would have to go away, after all, if he persisted. She must be strong. She must reason with him. *Oh God, dear God! Help me! Show me!*

George came in his bright, easy way with the coat and put it around her, enfolding her in his arms once more in spite of her shrinking, laid his face against hers again as she retreated where the others could not see her.

"George, I shall not go out with you if you persist in doing things like this," she whispered, pushing him away.

"Oh, all right!" he laughed. Then stepping back where he could look in the dining room door— "We're just going out to hunt some salted peanuts!" he explained with a big, handsome grin.

"But you're missing these sandwiches. They're great!" called one of the girls who admired him.

"That's all right. I know where they're made. I'll get some when I come back," he boasted, and with one stride he reached Amorelle's shrinking side again and took her arm as if it belonged to him.

"Now, look here, George," she said when they were safe outside the house. "You've got to stop acting this way or I shall not go a step with you nor talk to you any more."

"Won't you, beautiful?" he said, looking down laughing at

her. "Let's see. You wanted to get away where they couldn't see nor hear us. Come on!" He put his arm around her and fairly lifted her from her feet so that she was swept down the steps breathlessly and landed on the sidewalk, being carried along at his own pace. She had to make her feet follow him to keep her balance.

"George!" she protested. "George! You *must* stop! You make me ashamed!"

She found she was crying. He looked down in astonishment and saw the tears glistening on her cheeks and stopped to kiss the tears away. It was a courtship by storm, and there was something so gutsy and genuine about it that Amorelle's judgment took utter flight. What was this thing that had seized her, these kisses that seemed to thrill her in spite of herself? Was she fighting something perhaps that God had sent her and that she just did not understand?

Then suddenly he set her down upon her feet, took his arm away from around her, and drew her arm within his own. The joviality on his face changed into gravity. She had never seen George Horton so serious before.

"Now, baby," he said gently, making his voice soft and tender, "we're going to talk. You and I were meant for each other and we've just found it out. Didn't you find it out yourself when our lips touched that first time? Didn't you know it when I took you in my arms? Didn't you feel all rested and happy about it? Didn't that show you that we were meant for each other?"

Amorelle was silent, owning that somehow he had a strange influence upon her, yet not sure of anything. Warned of danger, yet afraid of throwing away something she did not quite understand, which might be godsent.

"Don't you love me, Amorelle?" he asked, looking down into her eyes with a look that glowed even in the dark. His hand was on hers, his fingers warm around her own. He seemed to have a strange power over her that made her question her own self, her own fears.

"Answer me, beautiful, don't you love me? Didn't you feel it when I did?"

The intimate clasp of her hand, from which she had not been able to withdraw because he was so strong, demanded an answer.

"I have—never—thought about you in that way," she answered in a disturbed tone.

"Ah! But you're going to now," said George earnestly. "And I've been thinking a lot about you, although I've never seen how beautiful you were till tonight because I was fooling around looking at other people, I guess. But now it's going to be you and nobody else. We're going to be engaged, and we're going to be married pretty soon."

"Oh, George! You mustn't talk that way! You mustn't!" begged Amorelle. "You aren't—we aren't—I'm not—"

"But that is all foolishness!" said George happily. "I'm going to show you. I'm a good man for you to tie up to. I'm steady and reliable. Everybody'll tell you that. I've got a good job for a young man like me. I've got money saved up. I'm able to buy a nice little home and set you up in fine style, and in a few years we'd be well off. You're saving and economical, I've noticed that. I've been watching you. I couldn't marry any girl who was a spendthrift. And I'm sure we'd get along fine! You wouldn't mind doing your own cooking, and you are a swell cook. I know I'm making no mistake about my end of the business. And we'd have grand times together. After a little we'd have a car and go places and see things, and your taking this bookkeeping is a good thing, too. You can help me out when I need extra help sometimes in the office. And now I've found out you can play for me, why it just shows how well we're suited."

She tried to stop the torrent of words but George sailed right on.

"I never found a girl before I felt like I do about you. I'm just crazy about you, and you'll feel the same way about me, I know. A lot of girls have fallen for me, but I never really fell before. I just couldn't see them. But now I have. Don't you worry that you haven't thought about me before. I like you all the better for that, and I just know we're going to be crazy about each other. You'll love me all right. I'll *make* you love me!"

Amorelle drew a little frightened breath. Could he? Would he? Did she want him to if he could? She couldn't understand herself.

"You know, Amorelle, they don't treat you the way they should at your uncle's house. They don't know what a good thing they've got in you. You aren't happy a bit there. I've seen it. Don't you want to get away? Don't you want a home of your own where you can do as you please, with no one to find fault and kick up a fuss all the time? A home and a man to love you and care for you?"

It was that way he talked, block after block, as they walked down the winter street under the great white winter moon. Her hand was warm in his, his footsteps set to keep pace with hers, the wooing light in his eyes, all his faults hidden under a great overwhelming love that had just struck his fancy and brought the best of him to shine in his handsome eyes.

And it stirred her. It did stir her in spite of all her resolves and preconceived notions of lovers and wooing. When he described that little home that could be theirs, her hand, resting in his big warm one, relaxed and almost nestled there for an instant. All her alarm was forgotten. So much can happen under the moon with a good-looking man suddenly become tender for a love he thinks he has discovered. It was so that Amorelle's judgment faltered, and she listened to his plea, till almost she felt his love was sincere, and her reasons fled and left her without excuse.

Yet she would not give in to him that night. She kept affirming that such sudden love could not be real, that they were not fitted for one another. She tried to remember her father's good advice and the rules he had given for a perfect marriage. That first one about being unequally yoked together with unbelievers.

"Are you a Christian, George?" she falteringly asked when he had gotten her to the point that she had promised to think about his proposal.

"A Christian? I? Oh, *sure!*" he answered with assurance. "Is that the thing that's sticking in your crop? Why, I joined church when I was fourteen, along with a whole bunch of kids, and I been working in church work ever since. They made me Christian Endeavor president when I was sixteen, and before

I was twenty, I was secretary of the West Branch Union. Christian, I should say! I've sung at almost every meeting of the Branch for the last six years, and I been chairman of the Exec. For all the semi-annual conferences since I was knee-high to a grasshopper. Why, sure, you and I would just hang together on those subjects. Oh, I know I've been strolling around with this bunch for a while, but I never really belonged. I useta sort of admire Louise, but she's getting too sporty for me. She's lazy, too. Take the way she always makes you do the work. And she's selfish. When I marry, I want a girl that thinks of her home and her husband and wants to make it pleasant for a man when he comes home tired. Oh, sure I'm a *Christian*. You and I would just be pals on that. I admire a girl that's religious."

This was a long speech and seemed to leave something still to be desired in the way of Christian comradeship, but there was no fault about it that Amorelle knew how to put into words. As far as he was enlightened, he seemed to be in sympathy. Perhaps it was her work to enlighten him. Perhaps that was what the Lord wanted her to do. Of course it might not be his fault that he had not been better taught.

They came back at length to the house—without any peanuts—not because George had exhausted his arguments, but because Amorelle was so tired and cold and trembling in every limb that she could scarcely walk another step. Shrinking back from the kiss he insisted on giving her at the door, she sped up to her room and dropped upon her knees beside her bed to try and think out and pray out this new problem which had come upon her so unawares.

She had promised him finally that she would think about the matter carefully, and she wondered, as she climbed wearily into her bed at last, why marriage in so many different forms had to be thrust upon her during this hard winter.

And yet when she thought about George's fervent words and his eager promises and that strong arm around her, those handsome lips upon hers, in spite of her best resolves there seemed to be something she did not understand drawing her almost against her will to him.

Oh, God, help me! Show me! Save me from doing the wrong thing! she prayed again and again and then began to go back over the question and try to tempt herself with all the advantages that might come to her from a marriage with George. She did not know that she was not really yielding herself to God's guidance but was rather considering her own advantages.

Her final thought as she dropped into a troubled sleep was, *Well, perhaps I've been romantic. Perhaps this is really all there is to love, and God has sent it. Perhaps I should not turn it away. It isn't unpleasant. It might be desirable. It may be I've expected too much of love. It may be this is God's plan for my life. Can I be content with this?*

Chapter 11

George didn't come to see Amorelle the next night, but he called her up on the telephone and called her "darling." It startled her, but it touched her, too. She had been deciding against him all that day, but when she heard he had to take the evening train for Chicago on business for his office, there came a feeling almost like disappointment. She found she had been looking forward to his coming. She wanted to see if some of her impressions of the night before still held. For instance, that beautiful light in his eyes, that sort of tenderness that had been almost unbelievable and had pled for him against her strongest arguments. If that was real, could she afford to throw it carelessly aside, even though in many ways his upbringing had not been like hers?

She turned away from the telephone with a lonely feeling, and then hugged herself that she had it. Perhaps she did care a little for him after all. Perhaps it was as he said, that she would learn to love him in that fervid way she had always thought lovers loved.

He sent her a big, elaborate box of candy from Chicago. Louise discovered it and kidded her about it. She was annoyed as she felt the color coming into her face, yet there was a strange satisfaction in having the family know that somebody cared enough to send her something.

She thought about that afterward, searched her heart, and told herself that was just pride; it was self-love, and it was a dangerous thing to have around when she had a question like this one to decide.

Sometimes she told herself she hadn't any question, that it was just ridiculous, that of course she couldn't even think of marrying a young man like George. She tried to think of George as having been a son-in-law of her scholarly father and shivered a little. She saw for an instant her father's clear, keen, kindly eyes resting on George as she had known him in these few short months, and somehow the thing seemed impossible to consider.

Yet her father had not been a snob about scholarship. This young man was in a business that was good and honorable. What was it about George that made her feel he didn't fit with herself? She still wasn't sure she could love him, but that would probably settle itself when she knew him a little better and had a chance to be with him and think of him in the light of a lover. Was it that there was something innately unrefined about him? She wasn't even sure of that. All young men and girls nowadays used impudent language that was not what she had been brought up to use, but perhaps these were things that a young man would outgrow, just customs of his environment.

So she reasoned with herself during his absence and found her mind distracted from her Bible study greatly. Well, there was a point. If he would go to her Bible school with her, surely then they would have a great point of contact and perhaps grow to think alike on the big things of life, which of course was the thing that mattered more than anything else.

The morning George got back from Chicago he sent her a box of lovely pink roses, and Amorelle felt almost happy about them for a few minutes. But Louise discovered them almost at once and cast jealous glances and made caustic remarks, and Amorelle perceived that she was not to be allowed to go her way in peace, no matter how things came out.

"Well, you certainly have got old George good and fast!" said Louise. "My word! I never knew him to let out shekels enough to buy roses for anybody before. He must have fallen good and hard. He's the most tight-fisted old wad I ever saw. I bet he got them at a bargain counter at that. That's the reason I threw him over. He was never willing to spend a little on a girl."

So Amorelle took her roses up to her room where their perfume spoke to her eloquently of the young man who had so surprisingly declared that he loved her, and sometimes the thought of his caresses was actually comforting to her. She wondered, could she really be falling in love with George Horton?

That morning there came a letter from Miss Landon that gave her thoughts a little interval and took her back to Rivington and her other proposals of marriage.

Dear Amorelle:

Mr. Lemuel Pike was here this morning and wanted my permission to go through your boxes of books and your father's desk in search of a paper he had dropped when he called upon your father the last time. He said he had not wanted to trouble you those first few days, and then he suddenly found you were leaving so soon that he only had time to get your permission to go through your things and find his property.

I thought it was very strange that he had waited all these months to come if the paper was so important, but he said he hated to bother me, and he wouldn't have come now only he found he had to have the paper at once to verify a title. I told him I had no authority to let anyone go through your things; he would have to get a written order from you. He said he had lost your address, so I told him to write to the Rivington post office and it would be forwarded. I wasn't sure you would want him to know your address. I wouldn't. I don't trust him.

It may be all right, of course, but I thought you ought to know about it. I told Johnny Brewster, and he said he was the worst kind of crook and I better not let him in. He says people all distrust him only they can't catch him at anything. But maybe you know what it is he wants and can straighten it all out. I hope you can.

I haven't been so well the last two months. It's been colder here than usual. A lot of skating on the old pond back of my woods. I see them go by and think how you used to go

*skating with your little red cap and mittens on. I hope you
are having a happy winter. I miss you, and I miss your dear
father-minister a lot. I can't get to church much anymore.
I'm sort of giving out I guess.*

> *Very lovingly,*
> *Lavinia Landon*

Amorelle wrote a quick reply:

Dear Aunt Lavinia:

*Your letter just came, and I am very indignant that
Lemuel Pike should annoy you. I never told him he could
go through my things, and I can't understand what he
wants with them. I'm sure Father had no papers that
belonged to him. There is something peculiar about it all.
You know I told you somebody got into the manse just
before I left? I haven't told anybody else, but I was almost
sure it was Lemuel Pike. I saw him in the light of his own
flashlight. He was hunting around under the study rug. I
can't understand it at all. I didn't tell the policeman who
it was because I didn't want to get mixed up with him in
anything. I never trusted him at all. But it certainly is very
odd why he should tell you that. Perhaps he thinks Father
had some evidence against him somehow. He used to come
to the house occasionally, and Father always looked troubled
afterward. I do hope he won't trouble you again, but if
he does, just tell him I never gave him permission to go
through anything of mine and I never will. I am quite sure*

my father had nothing of his. If he makes a fuss, send for
Johnny Brewster, or the police if necessary.

If he keeps on bothering you, just tell me and I'll have
the things moved to a storage house. I can't have you
bothered when you are sick.

I have been having a busy winter. It's not so happy.
No one can take the place of my dear father, you know
that. But I'm going to Bible school, which I love, and I'm
studying bookkeeping, which is also interesting. I seem to
find plenty to do, but I do miss all my old friends, especially
you, dear Miss Lavinia. Sometimes I'm just hungry to see
you. Perhaps I can find a way to visit you next summer
somehow, I'm not sure. I do hope you'll be better. I would
love to come and help you and nurse you if you are sick.
If I were only nearer to you I would run right over today.

> Very lovingly,
> Amorelle Dean

After she had mailed the letter, she had a comforted feeling
of having visited Glenellen, and she wished she could run in
on Miss Landon and tell her all her perplexities. She had never
been married, but undoubtedly there had been admirers. Miss
Landon was too attractive a woman not to have had proposals of
marriage. Her advice would be good she was sure. But somehow
she could not write her problems out and make them plain for
her friend to judge. She just had to face her own perplexities
herself.

Her heart was very heavy, her thoughts troubled. She was drifting more and more toward yielding to George. His golden eyelashes and his merry ways lingered attractively in her mind, and she was so tired of glum looks, cold orders, and a feeling that she did not belong.

Nightly she prayed that she might be shown, but daily she carried her burden herself, not realizing that she was not relying on God but relying on her own judgment to solve her problem.

Then George appeared one night with a gorgeous ring, confessing that he had borrowed her glove to get the right size.

She was not a connoisseur of diamonds, but even an ignoramus could not help but see the depth of light in its clear facets, the beauty of workmanship in its setting. And it was really a regal stone in size, too, quite a little larger than the ring Aunt Clara was wearing.

Amorelle caught her breath in admiration.

"George! What a gorgeous diamond!"

"Yes," said George with satisfaction. "It is! It's especially fine. I took a real judge of diamonds to help me pick it out. Put out your hand and let's see if it fits."

"But, George! That's not for me! Why—I—haven't—given you my answer yet."

"No, but you're going to tonight!" said George with confidence. "That's why I haven't been bothering you for a few days back. I was waiting till the ring got done. I wanted to put it on and get you marked with my mark the minute you said yes. Come over here on the couch where we can talk without any snoopers coming by in the hall."

George had come in a half hour before dinnertime, the only time when one could be sure of a few minutes privacy in the house. The rest of the family was usually in their rooms then getting ready for dinner.

George drew her over on the couch and put a possessive arm around her. He stooped and almost reverentially looked deep into her eyes, then laid his lips so gently on hers, so tenderly, that she somehow could not make herself draw back. His physical attraction was getting a hold over her so she could not resist, and it came to her that it would be so much easier and happier to yield and let his love, which seemed to be so genuine and almost rare, take possession of her soul. Perhaps it was because she had resisted that she had not experienced that thrill of joy of which she read when love came to others.

This doubt that she had been feeling about the fineness of his nature seemed almost to be set at nought by the beautiful ring he had brought. The rareness of its beauty surely showed that he himself was rare, and that his love was overwhelming toward her for him to spare no money to get her the finest and the best.

Suddenly she let her lips yield to his for the first time, and he crushed her softly to himself, pressing his lips upon hers. There was a tumult of something strange and almost frightening through her being. Was it rapture? Ecstacy? Was this love? It must be. Suddenly into the wonder of yielding herself there broke a hard, cold, tantalizing voice.

"Well, *really*! Is this the way you two carry on behind my back? So you're *that* kind of a huzzy, are you, with all our soft prating about Bible study?"

It was Aunt Clara, stiff as a ramrod, her eyes like cold steel, looking through her lorgnette at them from the threshold of the hall door.

Amorelle came down from her poor little dream of ecstasy into depths of shame, her cheeks flaming crimson, her startled eyes staring at her aunt wildly, her lips speechless. Oh, what a terrible situation she had allowed herself to be drawn into! What unspeakable things was Aunt Clara thinking about her, and how was she ever to explain?

But George, undaunted by the situation, sprang up and drew her to her feet with him.

"We've just been getting engaged, Aunt Clara," he chirped blithely. "Congratulations, please, and Amorelle wants to show you her ring. Pretty little bit of ice, what?" And he led her unwilling feet close to the irate lady.

"Engaged?" said Aunt Clara with a snort. "Really engaged? *You* two! You don't *say*! Well, I'm sure Amorelle is very fortunate!" And she bent her head condescendingly to look at the ring on Amorelle's reluctant hand that George held out for her inspection.

Engaged! thought Amorelle with a strange new dismay and clutched for the joy that had filled her only a moment before. Had it really been joy or just a sort of fantasy in which she had lost her head for a moment? Oh, and there was no turning back now, not after what Aunt Clara had said!

But Aunt Clara was inspecting the ring carefully and lifting accusing eyes to George's face.

"George, that's real!"

"Of course!" swelled George proudly.

"But it's very *valuable!*"

"Yes," said George with growing pride, "that's what I was just telling Amorelle. I wanted to do the thing right when I did it! Especially for a girl like Amorelle."

"But how in the world could you, a young man just starting in business, *afford* to spend the money for a ring like that?"

"Oh, I have money saved up," boasted George with a swagger, "and diamonds are always a good investment. In these times when banks aren't so certain it isn't bad to have a few dimes invested in a diamond. You can always turn 'em into money."

"That's quite true, of course," said the lady with a sudden respect for George. "Amorelle, you'll have to be *awfully* careful of that ring. You shouldn't wear it working around the house, and you should *never* wear it when you go off alone at night to those strange classes of yours."

"Yes, I was just going to tell her about that," said George. "You can't be too careful when you wear valuable jewels. But then, of course, mostly I'll be with her when she goes out at night anyway."

Aunt Clara got that, gave George a thoughtful stare, and then looked at Amorelle, as if suddenly her stock had gone up a point or two.

"Oh!" she said. "Of course! Well!"

"What's 'Oh, well'?" snapped in Louise, suddenly tripping down the stairs. Then her sharp eyes lit on the diamond, still held forth in George's proud hand, and she fairly pounced on it.

"Oh, how gorgeous! George, you don't mean, not *really*—

that—you and *Amorelle*! Why you sly brutes you! And you bought that ring for her? Not *bought* it out and out? You didn't get it on the installment plan? Oh, *George*! How simply beatific! Why, George, *darling*! If I'd known you would have loosened up enough to get me a ring like that I'd have taken you myself! Enoch!" she called to her stepfather, who at that moment came in the front door, "Just gaze on that sparkler!"

She grabbed Amorelle's hand and pulled her forward so that he could see. Uncle Enoch looked down at the ring and then up at his niece, a piercing look, an almost pitiful look, a look that had a likeness of her father's glance in it. Then he looked keenly, challengingly, at the young man and back to Amorelle, as much as to say, "Is this *really* what you want? Is *this* all you want?" The look wrung Amorelle's heart. It searched her soul, and it left her miserable and undone.

The dinner bell rang and they went into the dining room. Aunt Clara rose to the occasion and invited George to stay for dinner. George often used to be invited there to dinner, but of late, since the advent of Sam, he had not been there so often. But George was all ready to stay. If they hadn't asked him he would have stayed anyway. He went to the cabinet and got himself a plate; he opened the drawer of the sideboard and found knife and fork and spoons. He brought up a chair and settled himself beside Amorelle, giving her hand a squeeze now and then under the tablecloth and touching her foot surreptitiously under the table; but he talked to Louise as if that were his main interest that evening, and Louise chattered and laughed back and had a grand time while Amorelle sat silent and miserable, trying to cloak her misery behind a wan little smile.

Now and then she felt her uncle's eyes upon her, with that look like her father, and her soul sank lower. What had she done? Engaged herself to a man she knew so little, and engaged so openly that there was now no way to draw back without making Aunt Clara's dreadful accusation seem to be true! But why, why did George act that way with Louise? He was actually flirting with Louise!

She tried to excuse his hilarity by saying that he was happy and that now he looked upon Louise as his cousin and therefore could treat her in a more intimate way. But in spite of herself, it troubled her. It did not seem the fine, true way to act, if he cared as he had seemed to care when he put the ring upon her finger.

Then she told herself that she was jealous, and that was ridiculous. If he had wanted Louise he might have had her. He had declared himself for herself, and therefore she need not be annoyed with his foolishness. Likely it was just a bit of fun.

Then suddenly George began to talk about buying a house and asked Uncle Enoch quite respectfully what he thought of property values in certain parts of the city.

Uncle Enoch answered his questions in monosyllables. Louise relapsed into sullen silence, alternately looking at the diamond on Amorelle's hands. Suddenly Amorelle had an impulsive wish that the diamond were on Louise's hand instead of hers and that she were out of this strange engagement that had come upon her so unawares that she was not even sure how much she was to blame for its culmination.

She had to sit and listen to Aunt Clara take up the theme

of a house and tell just what it should be and where it should be, and she had a sudden vision of Aunt Clara trying to run their household and Louise breezing in whenever she chose and sitting on the arm of George's chair and calling him "Dolling Cousin George" as she kept doing all during dinner. Somehow the little home that had held out such allurements to her weary, homesick soul began to grow drab in contemplation in the light of such possibilities.

It was the evening for her Bible school, and suddenly, to her surprise, as she rose from the table and looked toward the door to slip away as she usually did, she found that George was going with her. Her heart gave a sudden rebound. Was he really going to throw his interests with hers and be a true comrade? A little, just a little, of the elation that had enwrapt her when he put the ring upon her finger swept back over her now, and a sweet color flooded her troubled face. Uncle Enoch saw it and studied her keenly again. Was his little girl perhaps happy after all with this strange, giddy, too-good-looking young man?

They went away into the starlit night—George carrying her Bible under his arm; George lifting her up off her feet occasionally, just to show that she was his own and he could lift her if he chose. And Amorelle caught again for a little time a flame of that joy she had felt in such a tumult before dinner. It was going to be nice to have a comrade like this who loved her and cared for her and protected her. She forgot the little episodes at dinner that had troubled her. She forgot Louise and Aunt Clara's cold eyes—she even forgot Uncle Enoch's troubled gaze—and just let herself be happy.

It was nice to have George escort her into the Bible school and take his place beside her. She saw many admiring eyes turn toward him and look at her in question. She experienced a little thrill of pride in him and was glad. That surely meant that she loved him, didn't it?

George held her Bible for her, though most of the time she had to find the places for him. He didn't seem to be acquainted with the book. But he would get interested, and they would study together. That would be wonderful! And they would have sweet conversations. That would be thrilling!

But the class was only half over before George began to fidget, to touch his fingers to hers under the cover of the Bible, to whisper to her how pretty she was during a wonderful exposition by the teacher, and finally to yawn covertly. Her heart sank, though she tried to tell herself that this was only his first time, and he had not gotten the thread of the study yet.

Out in the street, he suggested they get some ice cream.

"I've got to get something to wake me up," he declared. "That room was hotter than seven furnaces. Are those classes always so long? It seemed to me that guy never would get done. He said things over in seven different ways."

"That's to help us remember, to get the thought thoroughly across to us," said Amorelle eagerly. "He is considered a wonderful teacher."

"Well, maybe he is," admitted George good-naturedly, "but me, I was more eager to get you out and away where we could be by ourselves. Say, whatever made you go into this Bible thing anyway, Amorelle?"

"Because I love it," she said eagerly. "I've always studied a great deal with my father, and this was an opportunity to get what some of the great writers and thinkers and Bible students have found out today. It will help me so much in private study and in teaching others."

"Well, you don't need to consider teaching others now," said George, taking a large spoonful of ice cream. "My wife won't need to teach. I can support her all right!"

"Oh, but every Christian should teach as well as they can to give out the good news."

"Oh why not leave that to ministers and missionaries? If you get married you'll find your hands full without trying to teach the nation. I guess you know enough Bible now for all the teaching you'll need to do. Why don't you quit this thing now we're engaged? I'd liketa take you out. We could go to the rink one night a week and skate. Wouldn't you like to skate?"

"Yes, I love to skate," said Amorelle with a troubled look, "but I love this Bible study more. Couldn't we do both? I thought it was so nice to have us both studying together. I wouldn't like to stop my course so near the end. It's only about six weeks more, you know. By the time it is up, you will love it as much as I do. I know, for I've seen it tried."

"Not me," said George decidedly. "I've had plenty tonight. If I tried to keep that up one night a week I'd disgrace you by falling asleep. I'm no student, and I learned all the Bible I need to know when I was a kid and went to Sunday school."

"But I thought you said you were a Christian," said Amorelle. "Surely if you love the Lord you want to get to know His will."

"Good night! I learned the Ten Commandments! What more do you want? Isn't that enough to get one to heaven?"

"No," said Amorelle gently. "Knowing the Ten Commandments won't ever get anyone to heaven any more than knowing the law would keep a criminal out of jail. Not even trying to keep the Ten Commandments will either, because no one can keep them perfectly, and if one least little bit of a one is broken then they all are broken. The Bible says so."

"Great Scott, if being good and keeping the Ten Commandments don't save you, how do you ever get to heaven?" asked George.

"Accept Christ's atoning sacrifice on the cross in our place. It is the only way!" Amorelle's voice was soft and earnest. "Nothing that we can do makes us good enough. We must be accepted through Christ, and through His righteousness."

He looked at her through his long, curly, golden lashes and whistled softly.

"You're too deep for me, beautiful," he said indolently, "but you certainly do look lovely with your eyes big like that and your face all so earnest. I could kiss you right here in the store."

Amorelle drew back, annoyed.

"Oh, George! You turn everything into ridicule," she said sadly. "I do so want you to get interested in this. It's wonderful!"

"I'll take your word for it, girl," he said, touching her check playfully. "Finish out your class if you want to, but count me out. I've got my business to attend to, you know, and I can't spare so many evenings for childish things. I'll take you there and come for you when I can, and that ought to be enough. If keeping the Ten Commandments isn't enough for me to get to heaven on, I'm afraid I'll have to try the other place. Or perhaps they'll let me in on your record; how about it?" He laughed cheerfully, threw down his money with a swagger on the tiled table beside the check, and rose, pulling out her chair for her.

"Let's go!" he said.

Amorelle felt as if she had suddenly run up against a wall and was blinded by the blow. What was there about this man she had so suddenly acquired that made her always so uncertain? There must be something wrong somewhere. But perhaps she ought not to expect too much of him all at once. He had been going with a crowd who joked about sacred things every hour of their lives. He would not know how it hurt her to hear him talk that way. Someday she would tell him, and then he wouldn't do it. Surely if he loved her so tenderly he would not want to hurt her. And she in turn must not hurry him too fast. He seemed to know so little about heavenly things, why should he want to know more when he didn't understand how important and wonderful it was? She must be patient and be willing to go slow. She would pray for him, and all would come right. He was a Christian at least. He said he was. She hugged that thought to her heart.

Of course, all these questions ought to have been settled before their engagement, to say nothing of before it was announced so fully. If only Aunt Clara had not appeared with her terrible voice and awful suggestions and precipitated the affair! But it was too late to recall that now. The engagement was on record in full force and she must make the best of things as they were. Oh, why had she let him take her in his arms that way and kiss her so intimately, so tenderly, before she was *sure* beyond the shadow of a doubt? Or—was she sure? Her mind was so tortured that she could not tell, and she was glad when he finally said good-night and left her to go to her quiet room and think; glad that there were a lot of young folks present and he could not be so very free in his farewells. Oh, God, what was the matter with her? Why didn't she know her own mind? What would her father say to it all? If he were *only* here to help her.

Chapter 12

*B*ut the days went on and Amorelle's mind was not at rest.

There were times when everything was lovely and she forgot her fears. George bought her a pair of fine skates and took her down on the creek to skate. He was delighted that she was so accomplished in the art in spite of the fact that she came from a climate where the skating days were comparatively limited. But Amorelle had used well those rare occasions when there was skating and was graceful as a feather on the ice. Once she gave up her Bible school evening to skate with him, and he in turn suffered through another Bible class with her. That cheered her, and she hoped against hope that she might be able to lead him little by little to be interested in what was so vital to her.

Often she told him bits of what had been said in class, and always he would listen and seemed interested and then when she had finished would say, "That's the way I want your picture, beautiful! Just like that with your eyes so big and earnest." And she would turn away in despair and try to smile patiently. She knew she must not nag him.

But sometimes he seemed so utterly trifling that she wondered if she ever could love him.

By this time she had fully convinced herself that she did love him, although she told herself again and again that it was a great mistake that she had become engaged until she had settled several questions with him, and she felt that a day of reckoning must come before long. Certainly before they were married.

As spring drew on Amorelle was very busy, and there was little time to consider problems. Both her schools were nearing examinations, and she had extra studying to do.

Also, George was involved in what he called "invoicing" and demanded her help. He told her several times what a good thing it was that she took that business course; she could be such a help to him in his business when he got to be utterly on his own. Once she half playfully suggested that he might feel even more glad sometime that she had taken the Bible course and could help him. "Because," said she, looking up at him shyly, "you know when it comes to getting ready to go to another world, we all have to be 'on our own.' "

He gave her a half-annoyed look and said, "Amorelle, I'm surprised at you joking about a thing like that!" and went on with his work.

When he was absorbed in something, he seemed to forget all the nice things he had said to her. Sometimes he even found fault with her now, and his tone was growing almost alarmingly possessive. He talked about being married in June and said they must go out and find a house pretty soon, and Amorelle's heartbeats quickened. Was she ready to go so soon to live with him, with him and nobody else? Not that it was any pleasanter at her uncle's house, for even Uncle Enoch had grown silent and tactiturn since her engagement, especially since that one day when he said just as he was leaving for the day, "I don't see what you see in that empty-headed dolt! Are you sure you want him?" He had not waited for an answer and had never since given her an opportunity to answer, but his question had lingered and tormented her whenever she had time to think. It seemed almost as if it might have been the echo of her father's voice asking her.

George took her down to his office several evenings to help him. Sometimes she was weary when she went and dreaded the long evening shut up in the office, just when it was getting toward spring. But she always went patiently and sometimes rather enjoyed the time straightening out snarls that a blundering new assistant had made.

George was always good natured at such times and kept telling her how much she was helping and how she was saving him money. He might have had to get in an expert accountant if she hadn't found out what was the matter. At such times she went home partly satisfied, feeling that she was doing her best and things would work out in time. Nevertheless, her heart found no real rest. Often at night she would think of what her father and mother's marriage had been and face the truth that her own was not going to be like that. Then she would tell herself that no two people were just like any other two, and she must not expect such an ideal marriage. George was steady and loved her. She ought to be satisfied with that.

Only sometimes when he got impatient with her and spoke harshly, almost roughly, she wondered if he really loved her. Perhaps it had only been a fancy that would wear off. Then at other times, he would be gentle and cheerful with her, and she reminded herself that all people had nerves and tempers. She must not expect perfection.

So the days went by, and there seemed nothing that she could do but struggle on with her problem and seek to do her best.

Aunt Clara had complicated matters by having a dressmaker in the house and asking Amorelle to work along with her every day, and then to finish up what the dressmaker left unfinished. This was in addition to her other work and just as she was studying for her examinations. It became necessary for her to sit up very late sometimes to make up for her loss of the usual study time in the daytime. This was especially hard on the days when George demanded her assistance.

"I don't see why you don't give up that silly Bible school," said Aunt Clara one evening at dinner when Amorelle was hurrying to get off, and her uncle noticed that she was looking pale and had dark circles under her eyes.

"I am almost done now," she answered patiently. "I have only one more examination besides tonight."

"Examinations!" snorted Aunt Clara. "How ridiculous! For a girl who expects to be married in June! I think it's high time you were doing something about your trousseau. You ought to be hemming napkins and tablecloths and saving your money to buy them. It isn't decent for a girl to get married without some kind of an outfitting. You'll find George is very practical. I was talking to him about it the other day."

"I have plenty of household linen, Aunt Clara," answered Amorelle patiently.

"You have? Where did you get it?"

"It was my mother's," answered the girl. "We always kept it nice and used it only on rare occasions. Father insisted that he wanted it kept for me because it was Mother's, and he had me buy inexpensive things to use every day."

"H'm!" said Aunt Clara. "Well, I'm glad to see he had a little forethought for you."

Amorelle answered nothing. She had learned that that was the quickest way to end a discussion.

Nevertheless, Aunt Clara kept nagging on, insisting that Amorelle begin to make house dresses, even giving her a few cast-offs to make over.

Then, as the days grew more springlike, George decided it was time to go house hunting. Amorelle shrank from that. It seemed to make the matter so final. And all the time she was praying, "Dear God, show me please!" and going right on, not waiting for God to show her. Then one day she read in a book she picked up at the Bible school, "When in doubt as to God's leading, wait. Do nothing until He leads the way. Do not go ahead of God."

This greatly troubled her and stayed with her all that day. And that very evening George came after her with a borrowed car and wanted her to go and look at a house in the suburbs.

It was a charming house, with porches and bay windows and a pussy willow tree in the yard. It filled her with joy to think of living there, having a home of her own and doing as she pleased.

The house had a white-tiled bathroom, and a blue-tiled kitchen with a lovely white sink with porcelain drain boards running across one end. There were low windows looking on a little grassy backyard, and the neighborhood was lovely; nice, neat homes all around and crocuses coming up in the flower beds. In her mind's eye she saw pretty muslin curtains at the windows and her own furniture placed here and there. For a few minutes her fears and problems vanished, and she rose to enthusiasm and told George it was the very thing and she was delighted.

"The price is pretty high," he said, shaking his head. "I don't know as we ought to buy it, not right off at the start. Still, it's a peach, of course. We could look around and see if we find anything just as good cheaper."

But on the way home George talked as if the little house was a settled thing.

"I'll go see the owner," he said. "Maybe we can haggle him down a little if we kid him along. He might make a lower price if we paid a year's rent in advance."

Several days passed before George had time to see the owner, and he came one evening with a grouch.

"Couldn't do a thing with that man," he announced when he got Amorelle alone. "I talked to him for two hours, and he just set his jaw and said that was his price. Couldn't tempt him with even a year and a half in advance, though that would scarcely pay, reckoning up the interest and all. He says he has a rule never to change his price. Well, let him keep his old house. He'll learn. I've got on the track of two or three others; one especially I think'll be fine, and the price is fifteen dollars less than the first one. That one was in a snobbish district anyway. We'd have to put on a lot of dog if we lived there. And we just can't afford to go out a lot or do much entertaining the first two or three years. Especially if we had to pay that much for a house. We'd have to live up to the house, see?"

Amorelle's heart sank. She had fallen in love with the little house at first sight, and it somehow seemed to make her approaching marriage a happier affair and not nearly so fearsome and uncertain.

They went to see the other house the next day. George did not bring a car. They had to take a trolley.

"There's another good thing about this house today besides being cheaper," he orated on the way. "It's more accessible. Trolleys and trains not far away and no need to have a car right away. Although there's a garage if I found I needed one for business," he added. "Here, here we are! This is the corner where we get off."

Amorelle stepped from the trolley expectantly and looked around her with growing dismay. She had envisioned a suburb, and here were diverging rows of tiny two-story brick houses in every direction, glaring back the sunshine to the simmering red of the brick pavements.

George walked ahead of her up the curb, talking eagerly.

"It's only a block and a half from here, right down the middle of the next row. Handy for the trolley. I sha'nt have to get up so early as I do now—"

Amorelle halted and looked around a bit, as if by taking a fresh start the impression might somehow be better. She spoke slowly, gently, reluctantly.

"But—I thought it was a suburb. You said—"

"Well, it is," snapped George brusquely. "This is 'the annex' they talk so much about in the papers. 'North Harrington'; it's only just become a part of the city. It's practically a suburb. See those trees up there, only four blocks away? That's Lemon Park. Have band concerts there every now and then. Over to the right is the dump, and out that street is the cemetery, only five blocks away. You see, we're practically in the country. And only twenty-five a month! Think how we can save. Fifteen less than the house you're so crazy about."

Amorelle fell into step silently, her troubled gaze searching the surroundings, studying anxiously the little children playing hopscotch on the sidewalk.

"Do you know anything about the neighborhood?" she asked, as George paused in the middle of the block and looked up at the number.

"Oh, good enough neighborhood. Doesn't matter, does it? We sha'n't be entertaining much for a couple of years yet, I tell you, not till I get my promotion, and think how we can save on clothes! We don't need to have anything to do with our neighbors, you know, not till we get ready to move up into swell society. Here's our house. All right, eh? Needs a little painting around the porch, but I can do that evenings, or maybe you'll amuse yourself doing it when you haven't anything else to do."

George was too occupied unlocking the door to notice Amorelle's silence as she hesitated on the step, looking down the dreary line of sordid porches stretching from corner to corner like stalls in a market. Halfway down the street two children were fighting over a wagon; and a brawling mother shot out of the door untidily, administered a common punishment, and hastened back with a furtive glance toward the strangers.

Amorelle's slender grace stood out noticeably in the sordid neighborhood. Always her sweet gentleness sat upon her like a pleasant garment and put her apart from the common run. And now, even in her simple dress, she was something rare and out of place standing on that cheap little porch. Her wistful brown eyes were full of sudden distress. But George, all unaware, strode on into the house.

"That's the parlor. Wallpaper's all right, not scratched up much. We can set a chair in front of that spot. Agent said it had been recently papered. We sha'n't have to bother about that."

Amorelle took in the tawdry gold background with flaring baskets of roses at intervals on endless knots of bright blue ribbon, and she shuddered.

"Oh, George! This paper would be awful to live with."

"Now, Amorelle, don't go to getting fussy. I'm not a millionaire yet! It isn't good for you living so long in luxury at your aunt's. You'll get notions. We've got to economize, you know. Besides, I'm thinking of getting a car. It'll save carfare and make a good impression down at the office."

George walked jauntily through the archway into the speck of a dining room papered in greasy magenta, with finger marks, and gloomily lighted by a single window opening darkly on a dusky brick-lined passageway to the seven-by-nine backyard. The floor was thick with dust, showing the weave of a coarse ingrain rug that had lain and left its aged imprint. The wood was "grained." There was a closet in one corner, a dirty shelf with a bit of slobbery candle, eloquent of the former occupant, and the opposite door opened into a dim kitchen with one high window over a grim iron sink. A rusty gas range with its door gone completed the desolation.

Amorelle stood in the kitchen aghast an instant and looked around her with sudden perception of a long line of desolate days looming beside that awful sink.

"Oh, George! We *can't* take it! This is a terrible kitchen! Think of that nice white sink in the little bungalow. It is worth the extra money."

"Nonsense!" George's voice was harsh and sharp. "Spend money just for a sink! Amorelle, you're crazy! We can't afford trifles. You might just as well give up notions first as last. What difference does a kitchen make? A place to wash dishes! I don't care what kind of a kitchen we have. This is plenty good enough."

"You wouldn't have to stay in it." Amorelle's gentle voice was shaking with distress. She was not used to standing up to George.

"Amorelle! I never thought you were a *selfish* woman! You surely don't mean you want me to spend fifteen dollars more a month just for *a sink*! Why, if it came to that, we could paint this one. Come on upstairs."

George strode back to the staircase and mounted two steps at a time. The subject was dismissed.

Amorelle did not follow at once. She stood by the little high window over the kitchen sink and struggled with tears that suddenly threatened to overwhelm her. It wasn't that she could not put aside her desire and help save if it were necessary. But George was getting a good salary. He was able to give her conveniences and comfort, and he didn't seem to care. It was his lack of tenderness that hurt her.

"Amorelle!" he called peremptorily. "Come on upstairs."

She wiped her eyes and went slowly up the steep little flight.

There were two rooms and a bit of a bathroom, with a tiny square of a hall accommodating a ladder to the tin roof. It was stiflingly hot up there. The walls were unpapered and illustrated crudely with penciled sketches in caricature, jokes, and crossed-out names. The plumbing was old-fashioned with a boarded-in tin bathtub.

"We can whitewash up here," said George. "We'll take this front room for ours, and I'll have the back one prepared for a den where I can take men when they come to see me on business."

Amorelle's troubled gaze rested on the one shallow closet with its sparse row of hooks and then traveled out the window, where across the street a heavy neighbor, with her sleeves rolled high and her straggling gray locks stuffed into a soiled pink satin boudoir cap, lolled from the opposite window, gazing up and down the street. A baby's sudden cry rang out, followed by a resounding slap and another yell. A radio whined next door, and a blatant hand organ suddenly piped up far down the street.

George had not noticed that she was not attending to his words. But now he came back to where she stood, and suddenly, almost roughly, he caught her in his arms with an air of possession that started her.

It was the first time they had been absolutely alone together except in her aunt's living room, where they were constantly liable to interruption, or on the street. It was as though George had just realized this and was taking advantage of it, as if a box of sweets had been left alone with him and he meant to eat them all himself, not even sharing them with her. There was something almost unholy about the fierceness of his embrace that frightened her, as if he would devour her. His kisses burned upon her lips and rained hotly upon her face. There was nothing like tender love in them. Involuntarily she struggled away from him, pushing against his chest with her slim, young hands and turning her face away. He held her tightly, almost fiercely, for a moment; but she struggled from his arms, her back against the wall, her eyes wide, her face distressed. Then he backed off and glared at her thunderously. For a blond-eyed man, he could grow exceedingly dark.

"What is the meaning of this, Amorelle? Is it possible you are going to be childish about a kitchen sink?"

Amorelle covered her face with her hands and drooped. She felt herself trembling. She could feel through her closed eyes the coldness of his glance. The silence when his voice ceased hurt her like a lashing.

When he spoke again, it was with the cold voice of a stranger.

"I guess we'd better go back. You don't seem to be in a very pleasant mood."

He went downstairs without waiting for her. She shivered in the heat of the room and followed slowly.

He did not speak a word all the way back to the trolley. She had a feeling that she ought in some way to explain or apologize, but she could not find the words. She did not quite understand herself. A glance into his stern face made her sure he would not accept it if she did apologize.

She was thankful that the car came along almost immediately and that it was crowded, so that she had to sit at the farther end and conversation was impossible.

He spoke no word, even when he left her at the door with just a lifting of his hat. As he turned away, she stole a glance at him, with that recurring thought of his being a stranger—a stern, offended stranger.

She hurried into the house. It was Ida's day out, and she was expected to prepare the evening meal for the family.

The kitchen was hot and full of flies. The washer-woman had been there laundering the curtains and had left the screen door open. Amorelle was glad to get into her work dress and go to work. It seemed to quiet the wild, frightened throb of her heart. She drove the flies out and went about her duties with quick, skillful fingers—mincing parsley for the creamed potatoes, seasoning the peas that she had shelled before going out with George, arranging the salad on the plates, broiling the chops, cutting the cherry pie, making the coffee, setting the table. She did everything deliberately, trying to convince herself that nothing had happened, that everything was as it had been before she went to see that awful brick house—before George—Oh, what had been the matter with George? Or was the matter with herself?

But she must not think about it now or her trouble would show in her face. Her aunt and Louise would ask what was the matter, and she never could explain. They would not understand if she should. They would probably side with George, anyway. They approved of George thoroughly. And perhaps she had been unfair to him, but every time she thought of the way he held her in his arms in that hot little upstairs room, it made her shudder. There was something wrong somewhere, but now she must put it away. Her present business was to have dinner ready on time.

It was while they were eating the cherry pie that her uncle remarked that Amorelle looked pale.

"Better take her along on your picnic tomorrow, Louise," he suggested, for the talk all through the meal had been about that picnic—who was going, what they were taking, and what to wear. "It seems to me she doesn't have enough young company and outings."

"She has George," said Louise coldly. "Isn't that enough for an engaged girl?"

"Why, yes," blustered in Aunt Clara. "She was just out with George this afternoon, Mr. Dean. You're talking about something you don't know anything about, as you usually do!"

Amorelle flushed at the unusual notice and hastened to protest.

"I'm quite all right, Uncle Enoch," she said with a forced smile. "I guess it's the unusual hot weather so early that makes me look pale. But I don't really need an outing."

"Better take her along!" commanded the uncle in the stern tone that was used so rarely that it was generally obeyed by his family.

"Why, of course if she *wants* to go," drawled Louise. "They're not exactly her crowd! I *guess* there'll be room, though I've invited that nephew of Dr. Garrison's who is visiting. He's been abroad, and they say he's perfectly stunning! Intellectual type, I hear. I should not like it to look as if we were a big mob—but of course. . ." Her voice trailed off disagreeably.

"Better take her along, honey," cooed her mother. "Amorelle can make such good coffee, and you know all young men like coffee. She really will be a help to you. You know you're not very fond of cooking."

"Well, perhaps that's an idea," admitted the lazy Louise. "All right, Amorelle, you're elected. I guess we can stow you somewhere. And say, Amorelle, would you mind stirring up some of those little cakes you make and frosting them this evening? They'll bake while you wash the dishes, and George can talk to you while you frost them."

Now Amorelle had no intention whatever of going to that picnic. Moreover she was deadly tired, for she had canned cherries all the morning and then washed windows till George came for her to go and see the house. But she did not want the discussion to go on over her any longer, and she did not want Uncle Enoch to look troubled about her, so she answered with a tired smile that she would make the cakes.

She stayed in the kitchen all that evening, washing dishes and baking dozens and dozens of little cakes and then frosting them.

George did not come to talk to her while she did it. She had not expected him. She knew he would be punishing her for daring to disagree with him about the house. By this time she had grown to know about what reaction to expect of George in any given circumstance. Somehow it seemed a dreary prospect, long years of life with a George who sulked if you suggested anything he had not himself proposed.

Amorelle was quite glad that she was sure George would not come that evening. She wanted time to think things out. Somehow she *had* to get this matter straight. If the trouble was in herself—if she was being selfish—then she must realize and change, but if it was George then *something* had to be done about it. She was getting to be afraid of George and his moods, and she couldn't marry a man she was afraid of. Also, why was it that she had been so indignant, so fairly outraged at the way he had seized her and hugged her, kissing her as if she were something to devour, not as if he loved her tenderly as he used to at first? She didn't understand it. Once she put her head down in her hands while she was waiting for the last batch of cakes to finish baking and cried a few tears. Oh, why was life so terribly complicated? If only she had a father or a mother to guide her. If only God didn't seem so terribly far away.

The telephone rang just as she finished her work and was about to go up to bed. Her aunt called to her to answer it, and to her surprise it was George. He spoke in such a jaunty tone of condescending forgiveness that it stirred a faint resentment in her heart.

"That you, Amorelle? I couldn't get down tonight. Jim Price wanted me to take a little spin with him in the park. He was trying out a new car. Say, Amorelle, we'll have to give up our trip to the country tomorrow. I've got a lot of extra work and I can't possibly get away. Besides, I've had to let my secretary go to her grandmother's funeral, so I thought you might come down and take her place. It was a lucky thing you took that business course. I'd have to hire a temporary stenographer today. And say, how about asking your aunt to let you off early in the morning, say around half past seven or quarter to eight? I'd like to get started in the office before the rest of the force comes. And I'll need you all day. We can get a snack at the pie shop downstairs, or you might bring some sandwiches. How about it? The records from the whole district have come in, and we've just got word they have to be turned in tomorrow. I doubt if we get through before late in the evening. It's all up to me, see, and I had to take the responsibility of letting that stenog off. But I knew I could count on you. We'd sort of saved that day for a run to the lake anyway, you know."

Something seemed to rise up in Amorelle's heart—or soul or temper or something—and snap. Was this then the love that was to protect her through life? Iron sinks, working after hours, continually giving up things?

For several weeks George had been planning to take her on a trip to the lake and had set apart his day, saying he felt sure he could get off, and now he had not only failed to get away himself but was planning for her to spend the day and evening slaving in a hot office!

Ordinarily Amorelle would have excused the whole thing, knowing that a man cannot always control the actions of his office and sure that sometime soon he would plan to make it up to her, but now she was not so sure. Would he? He seemed of late to be thinking more about himself than what they should do together. Here he had been riding all the evening in a luxurious automobile in the cool park, and she knew well enough Jim Price would have been glad enough to have taken her along, if he had suggested it. But he was punishing her for daring to suggest that that ugly little brick house in that sordid neighborhood was not good enough for their home. And now she was not even to have her long-promised trip in a trolley car! And he did not even suggest that it would come later. He was not sorry a bit. He was making her a convenience.

It was not like Amorelle's gentle nature to be bitter, and ordinarily she would have hastened to assure George that she was at his service most willingly. But somehow the heat and her weariness and, most of all, her disappointment in George, whom she had been doing her best for weeks to put on a pedestal, had gotten her nerve. The ugly brick house and iron sink but, most of all, the task that her man had set for her tomorrow loomed before her impossibly.

But what would he say if she declined? Was she ready to bear his gloom and grouch? Was she ready to break with him finally?

George was headstrong and overbearing. He would stand no trifling. She hesitated with the receiver in her hand, and she heard him impatiently tapping the desk at the other end of the line.

"Well?" he said sharply.

What would she say? Oh, had she no backbone at all? Sometime there must be an adjustment of things or there would be disaster.

Then suddenly she remembered the picnic for which she had been toiling all the evening without the slightest intention of going. It held no attraction for her, for she well knew Louise would manage it so that she would have no part in anything; but why not go for once? It would serve as an excuse, and at least she would have the day in the woods to think this thing out and try to understand herself. Impulsively she decided.

Her voice sounded cool and even as she answered him.

"I can't come, George. I'm sorry to disappoint you, but I'm going away for the whole day with Louise. She needs me. I'm not sure we'll be back till very late in the evening."

Astonishment, incredulity, indignation were undisguised in George's voice.

"You're going away with *Louise*? What right has she to ask you to give up the only day in the week you have for recreation? Besides, Amorelle, I *need* you."

If he had not said that about recreation, she might have yielded, for it was not her nature to refuse nor to hold malice— and she was already repentant for what she had done—but the mention of a holiday in that connection, which he was intending to turn into a day of toil for his own profit, stung her deeply.

"Oh, you're mistaken," she said with spirit. "This *is* to be recreation. A lovely ride in a big car and a whole day in the woods. I haven't been in the woods since I came from Glenellen. My uncle was anxious I should go. He said he thought I needed it."

"*Oh!*" said George with significant emphasis. "If you look at it that way, of course! I can *hire* a secretary. There are plenty to jump at the chance. I supposed you would *enjoy* a day in the office with me! But it seems you *prefer* other society. Well, I hope you have a wonderful time! Good-bye!"

He hung up with a click, and Amorelle dropped into a chair.

What had she done? Had she thrown away her last chance of happiness? Had she angered him forever? Oh, would things ever be right?

Chapter 13

When morning came, however, the picnic looked to her impossible, and she came downstairs determined to call up George and say she would go down to the office after all.

But it developed that Louise was depending upon her for so many things during the day that there would be a scene if she stayed away from the picnic. So there seemed no way but to acquiesce, but it was with anything but pleasure that she did so.

The merry chatter of the gathering party filled her with dismay as the girls in pretty organdie dresses fluttered into the dining room to assist in the last rites of packing the hampers, and the young men carried the big ice cream freezer out and stowed things away in the three cars that were to convey the party.

No one paid the slightest attention to Amorelle, except to ask her where she had put the lemon squeezer and to send her out to the car with a forgotten package of sandwiches. But Amorelle was used to such treatment from Louise's friends and had schooled herself to be strictly an outsider. She meant to get her pleasure somehow from the trees and sky and a quiet nook in which to think after her duties had been performed.

Louise introduced the guest, Russell Garrison, to her friends, ending with, "That's all of us, I believe. Now shall we start?"

"I think you've missed one," said the young man, his eyes resting pleasantly on Amorelle.

A wave of annoyance passed over Louise's face, but she answered with a careless laugh. "Oh, didn't I introduce Amorelle? She's just my cousin, Amorelle Dean. Come, Mr. Garrison, you're to sit with me in the front seat."

Amorelle found herself presently in the little middle seat just behind Louise with a good view of the stranger, who kept turning back to include her in the merry conversation.

The backseat held two girls and a man, the other man of the quartet being seated in the mate to Amorelle's seat with his back toward her and his attention concentrated on the girl in pink on the backseat. Amorelle was as isolated—save for the friendly glances of young Garrison—as if she had been at home in her own room; and presently, the beauty of the way as they wound out of the city among green fields and wooded hills crept into her soul and made her forget herself and her troubles. Her starved eyes drank in the scenery—the fences covered with wild roses, the little homes smothered in hedges and vines, the curve of the road as it wound ahead into deeper foliage, an old stile by the wayside, the velvet furrows in a brown field all ready for planting, the fringe of fern along the bank, the swift flight of a startled bird, the poise of its wings in the air. Her eyes glowed, and her cheeks grew faintly pink with the delight of it, though she spoke never a word.

More than once Russell Garrison glanced back at the sweet face and followed the direction of her eyes, quietly enjoying the scene with her and wishing he might know her thoughts.

Several miles from the city, they crossed a bridge over a swift, bright stream that leaped out and wound away silverly in a parting of trees to disappear into a vista of loveliness under drooping, dripping branches, where sunshine played with ripples among wide stepping stones and waving branches cast alluring shadows. He saw her catch her breath with appreciation and great wistfulness grow in her eyes. As she turned back suddenly, their glances met, and he smiled understandingly. The little rippling stream seemed a pleasant secret between them that none of the others had noticed.

Just a few paces beyond this bridge, in front of a small country tavern, all three cars came to an abrupt halt. Something had happened to the car ahead. The young men all got out to help, but it was soon discovered that the trouble was serious, and the car would have to go to a repair shop. The girls all began to talk at once, suggesting ways and means, all except Amorelle, who sat gazing across the daisy field at her right. In her lap she held a big white box containing the little frosted cakes and some special sandwiches made of chicken breast that Louise had charged her to give to her and Mr. Garrison when the lunch should be served.

Young Garrison suggested that he telephone for his car, which had been at the repair shop when he started but must surely be done by this time. But Louise, fearful of losing her distinguished escort if he had a car of his own to drive, insisted she could manage it more expeditiously. So while Harry Sackett and Sam went into the tavern to telephone for a man from the garage to come out for Sackett's crippled car, Louise hurried back to her cousin.

"Say, Amorelle, you wouldn't mind waiting here on this patio till Emily Archer comes along, would you? It won't likely be more than an hour. Emily will have lots of room; there are only Tom and Minnie coming with her. If you'll do that, we can get all the girls in the two cars, and the men can ride on the running boards. You won't mind, will you? That's a dear! I knew you wouldn't. Now perhaps you'd better go and telephone Emily, to make sure she's on the watch for you."

Amorelle got out of the car, feeling as if Fate were playing battledore and shuttlecock with her day but not caring much. It was just as interesting to sit here and look out across that daisy field, and Emily Archer was always pleasant. No, she didn't mind.

Harry and Sam had come back from telephoning, and they were moving the crippled car to the side of the road. They did not hear Louise's triumphant announcement, "It's all fixed, girls. Amorelle has offered to wait for Emily. You know she doesn't belong to our set anyway, so it won't matter to her where she rides. Now, girls, pile in. Nina, you and Carol and Mabel on the backseat. Boys, tie that freezer on behind; now, the men on the running board of Louise's machine," just as she threw in the clutch to start.

Russell Garrison gave a quick glance over the car, wondering where they had stowed the quiet girl with the seeing eyes. Had she been put into the other car? He glanced back and caught a glimpse of a yellow gown disappearing into the door of the tavern. Something about the set of her head made him sure who it was. He frowned and touched Sackett on the shoulder.

"Haven't they forgotten one of the girls?"

"Oh, that's only Amorelle. Louise says she offered to stay and wait for the Archers; they are coming later."

"But that's no place for a girl to wait. You saw the condition of those men."

"Oh, Amorelle can take care of herself," laughed Sackett easily, and he turned back to talk with Louise.

Amorelle was a little startled when she saw the men and noticed that they had been drinking. She hurried into the tavern to find the telephone. Perhaps there would be a woman inside. She would ask Emily to come as soon as possible.

It took some minutes to get the number, and then it was the maid who answered. She said Emily Archer had suddenly decided to go to New York with her brother, and that Tom and Minnie were not going to the picnic at all.

Amorelle turned away from the telephone with a startled feeling, realizing that she had used the only dime she had with her to telephone. She had not expected to need money on a picnic. Now what was she to do?

A loud guffaw from the patio caused her to shrink still more, but a sudden faint hope that the picnickers had not yet started sent her flying out to see.

They were gone!

The white road stretched brightly in the sun in either direction, and not a soul in sight.

The blank look on her face brought more laughter and loud comments from the group on the patio.

"Better come and have a drink with us, kiddo! Your frien's all gone an' lef' you! Hot day! Have a drink!"

She almost flew down those steps, not even glancing toward the crippled car as a possible refuge. It was too near the tavern. Straight as a die she walked down the road over which she had come in the car a few minutes before, holding her head up and her shoulders squared, clutching the big white box as though her life depended on it, her heart beating wildly, her eyes scarcely seeing where she was going.

Suppose they should follow her. Their harsh laughter sounded out again. All her life she had had a horror of a drunken man, but she must not run nor let them see she was frightened.

Then she heard rapid footsteps, and her heart almost stood still. They had started after her! What should she do? Run, or stand and face them? She quickened her pace but did not look behind. Her knees were trembling, and there was a catch of terror in her throat.

"Miss Dean!"

The sudden relief was so great she felt like sinking down, but she managed to stop and turn around. Russell Garrison came striding up to her.

"You certainly can walk," he declared, mopping his hot face and fanning himself with his hat. "Say, what's the idea, dropping you out by the roadside this way?"

Amorelle broke into a hysterical little laugh and suddenly found two tears standing before her vision.

"Oh!" she said with relief, "have they come back?"

"No," said he, "but *I* have. Do you mind? I couldn't see leaving you here with those bums. They're all tanked up!"

The tears suddenly flew out and down her cheeks, clearing her vision but making her feel like a frightened child. She flashed him an apologetic smile and brushed them away with the back of her hand.

"Why, I'm crying!" she said with another laugh. "I didn't know I was so silly. But, you see, I've just discovered that the people I was to wait for have gone to New York, and I spent my last dime to telephone to them. I didn't quite know what to do. Those men—"

"I should say!" said Garrison indignantly. "You poor kid. I certainly am glad I followed my impulse for once and dropped off."

"Oh," cried Amorelle in dismay, "but your day will be spoiled, and Louise will be furious."

"Well, I shouldn't say she was the one to be furious. As for the day, are you keen about that picnic? They're all strangers to me, you know. I'd a lot rather explore that creek with you that we passed awhile back. To tell the truth, I've been wanting a chance to talk to you ever since we started; and you know you're just crazy to see where that creek starts. You can't deny it. I saw it in your eye. Couldn't we?"

"Mercy!" exclaimed Amorelle, thinking of Louise's face if she could have heard him. Then her eyes lighted up with the joy of his understanding. "It would be wonderful, of course," she said wistfully. "It was beautiful of you to think about it, but you don't understand. This picnic was really gotten up for you. I don't belong to their crowd, of course, but I've heard them talking, and you are *the* guest of honor. It won't do for you not to be there. Besides, they'll come back for you just as soon as they discover your absence. My cousin would never forgive me if I let you go off where they can't find you. What we must do is to go back and sit in that car until they come."

"They won't come back," said the young man, smiling wisely. "Sackett will take care of that. He saw me drop off, and he doesn't intend your cousin shall find it out till they get there. He wants her all to himself. I could see that from the start. When she discovers I'm not there, he'll tell her I'm in the other car. And when she finds out I'm not, he'll explain that he meant the car that is coming for you. They won't miss me till they get to the stopping place, wherever that is; do you know?"

"Not exactly. It's somewhere on Ross Mountain at a place called Giant Rocks. How about the man who's coming for the car? Wouldn't he take us?"

"He's not coming till late in the afternoon. Sackett just phoned him. If you think it's going to make any difference, I'll go back and telephone for my car. My uncle's man can bring it out. But you're not going back to that dump. Here, you sit down under this tree till I get back."

He took off his coat and flung it down for a cushion; and

she sank down relieved, suddenly finding her limbs more than unsteady.

It was cool and quiet on the shady bank where she sat, and the sounds of bees humming in the clover across the road mingled with the voice of a meadowlark in the distance. The sweetness of the morning stole upon her, steadying her. Things were going to be all right, after all. He would get his car, they would explain to Louise, and then afterward she would keep absolutely in the background. Louise would forget that he had been with her part of the morning and would only see how splendid he had been to her cousin. He couldn't be expected to know how little Louise cared what became of her cousin.

It wasn't long before he came striding back, looking worried.

"I'm awfully sorry," he said anxiously, "but my car isn't back yet. The chauffeur just phoned my aunt that it wasn't quite finished, and he wouldn't be home till half past twelve for lunch. He can't possibly get here before half past one or two. Would you like me to phone to the city for a taxi?"

"Mercy no!" said Amorelle, aghast. "That would be ridiculous and cost a fortune. No, we must just wait here. I think they'll come back."

He dropped down on the bank beside her, smiling.

"Well, we shall soon see. If they don't come in half an hour, I think we might go and explore that stream, don't you? It'll be cooler there and not so dusty."

"Oh, but they will surely come," said Amorelle, looking worriedly up the long, bright road and wondering what Louise and George would say if they could see her now. Louise would blame her, even if it was her own fault. George would blame her because she hadn't stayed at home with him.

The young man watched her changing face, saw the shade of anxiety tinged with bitterness that passed over the brightness of her spirit, and wondered what caused it. He set himself to dispel the trouble in her eyes.

Suddenly he took out his watch and showed her. It was a quarter past eleven. She had to admit that there was not little likelihood of the picnickers' returning, and there was no reason why they should not walk into the woods and explore the little stream.

"Let me carry that box," he said, taking it from her as he lifted her to her feet. "You don't mean to tell me the glad news that this is *lunch*, do you? How fortunate! I'm hungry already, aren't you? Let's find a nice place and spread the feast as soon as we get into the woods."

"Oh!" exclaimed Amorelle in new dismay. "I forgot. What will Louise say? This was her special box."

"Well, I fancy there'll be enough else for her to eat," remarked the young man, smiling. "I saw several hampers of goodies being stowed away. She needn't begrudge us this."

"But these were some special things she had made for—" Amorelle suddenly stopped her thinking aloud and began to laugh. The young man looked into her eyes with merry understanding.

"You don't mean to tell me they were made for *Sackett*?" he challenged merrily. "If they were, I shall take pleasure in eating them up. He has the young lady all to himself; he will not miss the food."

"No," laughed Amorelle. "Oh, I oughtn't to tell you, but it

is very funny. They were prepared especially for *you*. Louise put them in my charge, so they wouldn't get mixed with the rest."

"Good work! I'll see that they are appreciated. I'm sure you've fulfilled your charge. Did she make them with her own fair hands?"

A flush passed over Amorelle's honest face, and while she hesitated he read her true eyes.

"*You* made them! You can't deny it! All the better. Then we shall not have to thank the lady. But don't look so troubled, please. We'll make her think she's thanked. Trust me for that. Now come on. The next two hours are ours. Let's enjoy them to the fullest. Here's our stream. Take this path. I knew we should find it lurking here somewhere, waiting for us. Look ahead. Did you ever see a prettier group of beech trees in your life? And there are rocks around that bend. We'll spread our table on that rock. Be careful there; that path is slippery. Let me take your hand."

They stepped into a tiny beaten path that wound away between the beeches and down to the bank of the gurgling stream.

The sun reached down between lacy leaf awnings and pierced the water with sudden bright stars of light that danced into their eyes and shot back to the water. Little, narrow, dart-shaped leaves floated lazily into groups and sailed away to a braided center, where more little leaves had made a tiny island, like a small fleet of boats. A blue dragonfly flitted silently over a pool that had somehow been detained by a scattering of stones, and a large frog suddenly brought out a "thug" of greeting as they passed.

The little path was thickly fringed with lush, broad blades

of grass and deep blue three-leaved waxen flowers. Farther on, where a tiny spring bubbled in, a tangle of watercress and forget-me-not spread across the way.

"We'll have some cress for our lunch," said Garrison, stooping to gather a handful and wash it in the spring. Then, laying it carefully on a large maple leaf, he gathered some sprays of forget-me-not and handed them to Amorelle.

Amorelle fastened the blossoms in the belt of her yellow dress and went joyously on up to the cool heights, where a large rock crowned with pines held out alluring promise and waved delicate branches of dark green against the lighter setting of the beeches and maples.

They sat down on the big rock and looked up, up through the hemlock branches, between the shifting light and shadow. Heaven seemed so high and wide and all the world full of gracious air to breathe. "Oh!" said Amorelle wonderingly. "I had forgotten how wonderful it was. I have not been in the woods since I left Glenellen four months ago."

"Glenellen. That's not any relation to Ellen's Isle, is it? You didn't come from Scotland, did you?"

Amorelle's eyes lit up with instant understanding.

"No." She shook her head, smiling. "But I'd love to go there sometime."

"Well, I hope you can. It certainly is a wonderful place."

"You've been there? Oh!"

"Yes. Three years ago. I have an old aunt living near there, and I went over and spent a summer with her while I was still in college. But where is your Glenellen? Tell me about it."

So Amorelle told about her childhood in the quaint little town of Rivington where her father and mother had lived. The young man watched her vivid, changing face and felt that he had not been deceived in his first estimate of her character.

There is much in having a good listener when one tells a beloved tale. Garrison knew how to listen and how to make her forget herself. The present life dropped away from her as she talked—Louise and her uncle and aunt; even George and the ugly red-brick house were things of the far away. She was the little girl of Glenellen going to school in the old schoolhouse, taking long walks with her beloved father around the lake and into the glen that had given the spot its name. She described to her companion the tall rocks with their curtain of fern hung down over the dripping sides; the little, darting fishes in the clear water; the high look of the sky as one lay on the moss below and gazed up. She made him see it all and her longing to go back to the dear old days. He seemed to know the child she had been, before trouble and this shy isolation fell upon her. He felt as he listened that he had entered a sacred sanctuary of a soul which, once entering, one can never forget.

Then something—was it the memory of the city? Her uncle's house? Louise? *George?*—brought Amorelle suddenly back to herself and the present. What was she doing? Monopolizing Louise's special guest! And what would George think if he could see her? Her guilty heart gave a bound of astonishment. She was having a *good time! Such* a good time! Was it right to feel so happy sitting here just talking with a stranger, when George was back in the office working hard?

Chapter 14

$\mathcal{B}$ut the stranger gave her no time to think disturbing thoughts. Perhaps he saw the shade gathering in her eyes. Some fine intuition taught him that she had a background of unpleasantness somewhere, and his first impulse was to make her forget it, to bring back the happy look that made her eyes so beautiful.

"Look up there!" he said suddenly. "No—farther on—on the branch of that old chestnut. Don't you see a splash of scarlet? Yes, now you've got him. That's a scarlet tanager. Isn't he a gem? Just see the gleam of the sun on his back. He's a shy fellow. You couldn't often get such a good look at one."

They were off again on birds, just reveling in all they knew about them; and Amorelle forgot again who and what she was, till suddenly her companion reached a bold hand for the box.

"I'm hungry as ten bears," he said, "and it's twelve o'clock.

Whoever heard of waiting longer than that for lunch on a picnic? Are you going to open that box, or shall I?"

"Oh!" said Amorelle, a small cloud of anxiety growing in her eyes again. "I suppose—we—must."

"We certainly must," said the young man cheerfully. "I'll take all the responsibility. Just wait and see how admirably I put all the blame over on Miss Louise when we find her and make her eat humble pie all the afternoon. Don't worry! This is *our* day. We are going to have a good time. Oh boy! Isn't this some box?"

He lifted the coverings of wax paper and disclosed dainty sandwiches and many little cakes, all wrapped separately, with two glass containers of potato salad, a glimpse of salted almonds, olives, and some choice bits of celery in between. It was a perfect little lunch for two, prepared with an eye to effect, and as he surveyed it with satisfaction, Garrison could not keep a twinkle of amusement out of his eyes. He looked up to the troubled, comprehending eyes of the girl, and they burst into merry laughter, which lasted several minutes and would have seemed to a mere observer out of all proportion to the cause.

"No, but really," said Amorelle, suddenly sobering down, "this is going to be a terrible blow to Louise not to be present when that box is opened. She won't like it at all for me to be the one to eat it with you."

"Well, *I* do," said Russell Garrison frankly, "and as she is the one who arranged it that way there's nothing for us to do but fall in line, is there? Here, have a napkin, and don't look so sober. Isn't this our picnic? We're stranded on a desert island. You know it wasn't our fault they didn't have room for us."

"They had room for *you*," said Amorelle with a troubled look in her eyes.

"But not for you?" he questioned, eyeing her keenly.

"Oh, they really thought I was coming with the others, but they have changed their minds and gone to New York instead."

"And were you starting to *walk* home?" He watched her changing, lovely face.

"I don't know what I was going to do." She gave a little nervous laugh. "I certainly was glad you came, though I thought at first you were one of those awful men coming after me. But I'm so sorry you felt you had to stay for me. I'd have gotten home somehow."

"I'm not sorry," he said with a pleasant grin. "I picked you out right off as the nicest one of the bunch. I hope you don't mind me. Here, have a sandwich and forget everybody else for a little while. You look to me like the kind of girl who is always thinking of what other people want and never has time to get what she wants herself. Aren't these wonderful sandwiches? Say, I'm glad I came."

Amorelle felt that the first bite of forbidden food would stick in her throat, but her companion was so merry, and beguiled her into the joy of the day so fully, that she ate and forgot that she was only the little Cinderella cousin who ought at that minute to be burning her fingers and broiling the chops for the picnickers on Giant Rocks, instead of sitting on a rock of her own under a hemlock canopy, eating the food prepared for the favored few.

And George! In the office with his hired secretary! Taking her out to lunch, perhaps! Making a date to take her riding when he should try his new car for the first time? Ah! George was utterly forgotten for the moment while she sat and enjoyed the day and held sweet conversation with one who had read all the books she loved, had seen the great places she had longed to visit, who seemed to think her very thoughts sometimes, even before she dared to speak, and understood just what she meant.

When they had eaten as many of the chicken sandwiches and little cakes as they could swallow, they went down to the brook to wash their hands. He caught her hand and helped her down the slippery, piney way till her feet were firm on the mossy, vine-broidered bank. They sat there awhile and watched the water bugs racing back and forth in the netted sunbeams and listened to the song of a meadowlark high above. There were yellow, starry flowers across the stream and tall cattails blowing reedy in the wind. The humming of a bee came drowsily across the music of the wind in the hemlock boughs that dipped in the water, and over the fields the sound of the whetting of the scythe rang cheerily as the day droned on.

"It seems just like a bit of heaven here," said Amorelle dreamily. "A world without sin or wrong or sorrow in it."

"Doesn't it!" said Garrison eagerly. "I was just reading about that this morning."

He put his hand in his pocket and drew out a thin little Testament and fluttered the leaves over accustomedly.

Amorelle's face lit up.

"Oh," she said eagerly, "I have mine with me, too." She opened her handbag and took out a very small pocket Testament.

He glanced at her with delight.

"So you're that kind of a girl," he said eagerly. "I knew there was something about you different from all the rest that made me pick you out as the only one worthwhile, but I didn't hope it would be as good as this. You know the Lord Jesus then, I'm sure, and you love the Book?"

"Oh yes!" Amorelle drew a deep breath of pleasure. Here then was one with whom she might have fellowship for a little while. "I don't know what I should do without it," she added wistfully. "Everything, everyone else seems so disappointing."

"Isn't that the truth!" said the young man fervently, watching the shadows and lights play across her speaking face. "Everyone except the Lord Jesus Christ. He is not a disappointment."

Seeing the answering light in Amorelle's eyes, he went on. "Do you know, I've discovered a new verse in the Bible. Of course it was there all the time"—he laughed—"but the fullness of its meaning is new to me."

Garrison turned the leaves of his little book. "Here it is, Colossians 2:10. 'And ye are complete in Him.' I looked up that word *complete* and it means 'fully equipped.' I was astounded at the truth that opens up. For instance, take a house, a home. When it is fully equipped that means that it has everything that a home could possibly need. Beside a mere four walls and a roof, it has rooms for every purpose, heat for cold weather, air-conditioning for hot weather, up-to-date furniture for every use—"

Amorelle, large-eyed, was listening intently. She almost exclaimed as he went on. She was thinking of the brick house with the iron sink that could not by any stretch of the imagination be called fully equipped. It almost seemed as if he must somehow have known about it. Her alert mind, even as she listened, was comparing its old-fashioned, musty atmosphere to Christians who try to live on last year's experience of Christ, or last Sunday's Bible reading. She suddenly saw how unnecessary and inefficient it is to live a stunted, dreary life when there is plenty for every need in Christ. Just as there was plenty in George's bank account to get her everything to make a pleasant home.

All at once she realized that the young man had ceased talking and was looking at her, and she came to herself with a start.

"You're not listening," he accused her playfully. "Am I boring you, or are you worried about something?"

Her face grew crimson with embarrassment over her seeming rudeness.

"Oh, I *was* listening," she protested, "and of course you're not boring me. I'm intensely interested. I was thinking—about what you were saying—"

She looked down, embarrassed again. How could she explain to this earnest young man without telling him all about George and the iron sink?

"I really was thinking—about what you were saying," she pleaded. "It was wonderful. Please go on."

"Well, I'd give a good many pennies to know what those thoughts were," he said, smiling wistfully. She knew that he sensed that there was more in her heart than she told, and she was grateful that he respected her reserve and went on.

"But it was a wonderful thought to me, too," he said. "I studied over it quite a while and found here and there in the Bible so many needs already supplied in Christ. There is our need of salvation first of all, and there it is in Colossians 1:14: 'In whom we have redemption through his blood, even the forgiveness of sins.' Then we need to be delivered from the power of sin in our lives after we are saved. That is in the thirteenth verse, 'Who hath delivered us from the power of darkness.' That's the same thought as in Romans 8:2, you know. 'For the law of the Spirit of life in Christ Jesus hath made me free from the law of sin and death.' "

Their heads were close together now, hunting out the verses.

"How wonderfully clear you make it all," said Amorelle. "I never thought of it this way before."

"Then we need to get near to God," he went on, "instead of worshipping Him far off somewhere on a throne. That is already accomplished for us, too. Ephesians 2:13. 'But now in Christ Jesus ye who sometimes were far off are made nigh by the blood of Christ.' I suppose you are familiar with the same thought in the tenth chapter of Hebrews."

He looked up and found her nodding eagerly as she began to quote the words reverently.

" 'Having therefore, brethren, boldness to enter into the holiest by the blood of Jesus. . . .' "

A look of utmost delight came into Garrison's face as he recognized how truly they spoke the same language.

"Please go on," she urged, her face aglow with eagerness. He turned back again to Colossians.

"Here is wisdom and knowledge for us," he said, "and it's like every other need; it's all 'in Him.' "

"Why!" said Amorelle, her eager eyes starry. "I've needed wisdom and knowledge *so* badly, and I didn't know where to find it. How blind I have been! Why, these things *are* just like the equipment of an up-to-date house, aren't they? It's all there if you only know where to find it. Now I have the key— 'in Christ.' I'll never mourn for lack of anything again. Oh, why is it we don't *believe* more what God says? I've heard people say so often that they don't believe in prayer because they have asked God for something and He didn't send it."

"Well, don't you think that we sometimes confuse our *needs* with our *wants*? God has never said He would give us all our selfish, foolish desires. They might be as dangerous to us as a motorcycle would be to a five-year-old. But better than that, He said He would supply all our needs. It's wonderfully true, though, that He throws in extra surprises now and then."

There was deep meaning in the glance that Amorelle caught in his eyes just then, and she found herself blushing intensely. Now why did she have to do such a childish thing as that? What would he think of her? What would he think she thought he meant? Of course he meant nothing at all more than what he actually was saying. How could he know what a beautiful surprise God had sent to her in this wonderful day and this delightful conversation about her Lord?

Embarrassed over her own shyness, she blushed again till her cheeks were a gorgeous scarlet. What on earth was happening to her? she wondered excitedly. She must get control of herself.

"Oh," she gasped, trying to explain herself to him, "you can't possibly know what this day has been to me. I was in deep perplexity and trouble, and you've given me a key to solve all my problems. I cannot thank you enough. I needed just this to show me my way."

"Thank the Lord for that," said Garrison. "That's very precious to know. I'm so glad you told me."

Then suddenly the horn of a motor car wafted faintly, distantly, through the woods like the hint of a forgotten dream, and Garrison sat up with a start and looked at his watch.

"Great Scott!" he said disappointedly. "What do you think of that? It's five minutes of two. We'd better be hustling if we want to connect with the other half of this picnic. You're sure we must?"

But Amorelle was already on her feet, springing up the slippery way, suddenly aware of Louise and the immediate future.

"Oh—yes—indeed!" she called back breathlessly.

"Oh, look here, partner! That's no way to treat me," called the young man, and with three strides he was beside her again, catching her hand and helping her upward.

Laughing and happy, they hurried forward; only now Amorelle was thoroughly awake to everything that was going on. This young man was a perfect gentleman, more courteous than George had ever been, seeming to anticipate her every need—touching her hand, lifting her whenever it was necessary—yet always with that impersonal, matter-of-course manner as a brother might have done, and it made her feel honored, somehow set apart in the world of women as something precious to be cared for, as assistance from George had never done. Why was it? What was the matter? It was something to be tucked away in her mind and thought out afterward. Of course it might be a mere glamour of a stranger's unexpected attention; but there seemed to be something deeper in it than that, as if a picture had been shown to her of what life at its best should be, that she might know what a mistake she was making.

Of course this young man was not in her life, nor ever would be. He would go on his way come evening and likely never cross her path even distantly again, but his character, his personality as a representative of a Christian gentleman, would never go from her; and she felt instinctively that there was before her a great crisis in her life. She had a big question to decide. Did she want to be missing this sort of thing always? Was George enough to her to make up for what a man like this one, a good comrade who understood, could be? It was not likely that another man such as this would come near her life again, but would it perhaps not be better to walk her way alone than to throw her life in with one who could not understand her innermost thoughts? She recalled some of her father's advice: "It is infinitely better to walk your way alone through the world than be tied to one who can never be your mate."

These thoughts were only faintly shadowed in a flicker of foreboding as she climbed breathlessly back to the road, supported pleasantly and helpfully over every rock and turn of the path and kept from falling over the tangled grass or being torn by a casual briar that reached wanton hands for her garments.

They emerged from the woods, and with a throb of regret she

saw a large blue car parked on the bridge. The beautiful interlude was finished. But she realized gratefully that thoughtfulness had arranged that the men at the roadside tavern should not come again into their plans.

The chauffeur, it appeared, knew exactly where Ross Mountain and Giant Rocks were and gave minute directions. They took him to the nearest trolley line and went on their way. Amorelle, sitting beside Garrison in the front seat and beginning to see Louise's face just as it would be when they arrived, longed to borrow the carfare and go home with the chauffeur; only she knew that would be cowardly. But all the beautiful way, as they wound among the hills and while she was listening to his merry talk, her mind was busy in an undercurrent, setting itself in order for what was to come. There would be Louise, and there would probably be George to deal with afterward. Louise would see to that. And what a fool she had been to come at all! She was being well punished. If George knew he would surely be satisfied.

"My friend, you are troubled," said Russell Garrison, suddenly looking down at her with a glance almost tender, as if she were a worried child.

She flashed him a look of gratitude and tried to smile.

"I am beginning to realize how all this has spoiled Louise's day," she said.

"Please don't think of that. I don't believe it has been spoiled; and if it has, we will try to make that last part of it so pleasant that she will forget that there were any hitches in the morning. Come, brighten up, little girl. I've had a beautiful morning, and

I hope you've not had a dismal time."

"Oh, *I*—" breathed Amorelle with a starry look, and then stopped, unable to say what she had in her heart. "But—you have helped me *so much*. More than I can ever tell you," she finished.

"I somehow think this was all intended, don't you? I can't help feeling we were meant to be friends, and this is only the beginning," said Garrison, giving her another of those searching glances. "I mean to take you someday to another glen I know and see if you don't think it is almost as beautiful as your Glenellen. Will you go? Promise me you'll go. When shall it be?"

"Oh, but I—but you *mustn't*—" she began in trepidation.

Then suddenly they swept around a curve and came full upon the picnic party established behind a big rock, with an amazing view of valley and mountain spread out before them and the mangled remains of a feast at their feet.

Russell Garrison stopped his car quite suddenly with a surprised exclamation not at all so joyously spoken as might have been expected from a returned wanderer.

Louise arose stiffly, haughtily, from her place on the other side of the picnic blanket and gave her cousin an imperious look.

But Garrison was quick to read a situation. Indeed, he had read it already in anticipation. He sprang out with an assumed joyousness and proceeded to absorb the attention of the whole company for the moment, giving Amorelle the opportunity to slip gratefully into the background. He went straight to Louise, made a graceful apology, and somehow succeeded in putting the whole situation right. To her amazement Amorelle perceived that they were all ashamed of having left her alone and unprotected. She threw aside her hat and went quietly to work picking up dirty napkins and rescuing plates of sandwiches from an army of ants that was threatening them, and while she worked, one and another of the company came slipping up to her quietly and almost apologetically, with a really friendly attitude. She glanced at her cousin, and instead of the scorn which had met her when she arrived, Louise was looking over with a smile.

When her work drew her nearer to where they were, Louise said condescendingly, "I certainly am glad you kept the box with you, Amorelle. Poor Mr. Garrison would have starved if you hadn't had it. Say, Amorelle, I reversed the order of things and left the chops till evening so you could cook them. You'll find them in the little icebox. And the coffee is in the smallest basket. Make it good and strong. Now hurry and get this place cleared up. We are going to have the games after a bit, and I'll leave the supper in your hands. Thank goodness you're here! Now come on, Mr. Garrison, I've got the loveliest little nook to show you."

Garrison glanced back to his companion of the morning with amused indignation. Was this then what she had to bear? He half hesitated, as if about to stop and help her, but something in the attitude of her slim shoulders and the set of her shining brown head made him understand that she did not wish it. He followed Louise reluctantly, silently, down the path, without even offering to help her in the slippery places.

But Louise was gifted with a voluble tongue and covered the silence admirably. But he reflected that he could do Amorelle only harm by his absorption, so he roused himself to be entertaining and succeeded so well that Louise kept him talking long after the time agreed upon for the games.

When they returned to the rest of the company, a good fire was burning away down in a hollow, and Amorelle, on her knees before it, turned the chops, her delicate face etched clearly against the firelight in the early evening as she bent earnestly to her work, apparently unaware of the presence of others. He wished he might go and help her, wished he might have gathered the sticks for that fire. Who made that fire for her, anyway? He frowned. Or did she make it herself? He frowned again and turned deliberately away. He knew it would please her better so, but it went hard with him.

It was late in the evening when they were gathering up their belongings to go home, for because of his late arrival the day had been prolonged beyond the time first set. Louise, as usual, was dominating the company, ordering where everybody should ride.

In the dusky shade of a big rock, Garrison came upon Amorelle packing cups in a hamper.

"You're to go in my car," he said in an undertone that the others could not hear.

"Oh, please no!" said Amorelle in almost a whisper. "I thank you, but I wish you would let it go just as it happens. It really will be better so."

"Well, if you wish it; but remember, I'm coming to get you. You can't go back on our day, you know. How will tomorrow do?"

"Oh, it will be impossible!" said Amorelle in alarm. She had had time for reflection and the dream of the morning was fading in the reality of the present. "Please, I want to thank you for the beautiful time—"

"Mr. Garrison!" called Louise sharply. "I'm going to let Harry Sackett drive my car, and I'm going to ride with you. Come quick now, and let me show you the moon from the point of the rock before we go. It's perfectly wonderful!"

Garrison turned wistfully to look at Amorelle, but she had disappeared into the shadows and was absorbed in setting fire to the rubbish she had gathered. Perhaps it was a good thing that Louise could not see her companion's face as he followed her over the slippery trail. Louise had gotten her way, and Garrison let her have it for Amorelle's sake, but he inwardly resolved that the like should never happen again.

One glimpse of Amorelle he caught as he and Louise were returning. Amorelle was standing alone on a point of rock that jutted over the valley, her face lifted to the silver moon, her delicate profile clear-cut, like a cameo against the darkness of the night. Then she was called and stowed away in the backseat of the Sackett-driven car by order of Louise, and he had to listen to Louise's chatter as he drove down the mountain in the silver moonlight, wondering what Amorelle would have said about the night with its silver mists, piny-blue shadows, and that winding ribbon of a stream laid gleaming in the velvet blackness of the valley. He thought he could see her eyes glow as they watched it all, and he laid away every scene to talk it over with her someday. She was some girl! What was the matter with them all that they did not see it? And how could he manage to get a word with her when they reached the house without letting that foolish Louise see?

But Amorelle disappeared as soon as they got home and did not reappear, though he lingered after all the rest, much to the joy of pretty, flattered Louise. He heard Louise's mother call Amorelle, and Amorelle's voice answer from upstairs—"Yes, Aunt Clara, they're all put away. Yes, I counted them. Nothing was missing"—and then a door upstairs closed gently, and he knew that Amorelle did not intend to come downstairs again that night.

He was wondering as he drove home just how he should manage seeing her again. Should he telephone or write a note, or just call and ask for her? For he meant to see her somehow very soon. He liked her. She was a real girl. Then he happened to remember her handkerchief that he had taken to carry after she had wiped her hands at the brook. It was rolled up in a little wet wad in his pocket. That was it. He could return it. That would be an excuse without calling attention to her. Of course he must manage it just right or Louise would spoil his play, but he would manage somehow.

Chapter 15

Amorelle, lying wide awake in her bed in her hot, little third-story room under the eaves, was wondering how she was going to avoid Russell Garrison, and thinking what a little fool she had been to step so easily into a day's paradise and expect to come back to earth and live again. For suddenly she saw with that clear, revealing vision that comes to us sometimes in a swift flash in the watches of the night that she could never, never go back and be content in that little red-brick house and wash dishes day after day, even for only two years, at that awful black-iron sink under that high little blank window, all alone. Not for George Horton! And if she wasn't willing to do that for him, she didn't love him enough to marry him, did she? *No!* She *didn't!* It was appalling, but she didn't. It was her only chance, probably, all her life to have a home of her own, a hope of little children to love, and a right to order her own life, but it wasn't possible. She didn't love George, and she mustn't marry him.

That was probably the reason, too, why she had shuddered when he took her in his arms so roughly. That was why she shrank from his touch. There had been something so possessive about him. And if she had loved him, really loved him, she would have wanted to be possessed. She would have loved it.

The astounding truths broke upon her excited senses one by one and left her almost exhausted as they poured out their clear assertions of the future. There would be a scene with George. Not right away, for he would be offended and would stay away to punish her, but by and by when it really came over him that she meant to break with him. He would be outraged and would say she had deceived him. But she couldn't help that. Then he would tell her she didn't understand herself and that she would get over this. Well, perhaps she didn't understand herself. Perhaps she was just excited now. She would wait. She would be gentle. She would be willing to be shown, but she was *sure*, now, in the depths of her heart.

Then there would be the scene with her aunt and the questions from her uncle. How clearly she could foresee them all! How was it she seemed to know just what they would say, as if she had gone through it once before? Oh, if she could just go away somewhere and think it out sanely, quietly, and then write back to George! How blessed that would be. She would escape the scorn of aunt and cousin, get away from the prying, all the exclamation, and just be herself. Her father used to tell her that was the way to settle big questions, to get away from things that might bias and try to take a look at the subject as

God looked at it. If she only could! She had but one little life to live, and it had been lonely enough already. She didn't want to make any mistakes.

But where could she go?

"There isn't anywhere in the world," she said aloud sadly to the four sloping walls of her hot, little room. And then, dropping back to her pillow, she whispered into its depths, "Oh, God, You have shown me the truth; now please show me what to do! Please make it plain and unmistakable so I shall not be in doubt. Open a way for me out of this situation. I want to do whatever You have planned for my life. And I know You have already made provision for my every need. Now I am just going to count on that and trust You." With the lightest heart she had had in months, Amorelle fell sound asleep.

A letter lay beside Amorelle's plate the next morning when she hurried down a trifle late to breakfast, having overslept after her midnight vigil. It bore the postmark of Glenellen and brought a flush to her face and a quick throb to her heart, though she did not recognize the cramped writing.

Her aunt had come down early that morning, and she and Uncle Enoch were busy with their mail, so Amorelle opened her letter and read it.

Dear Miss Dean:

Yoo wont remember me but I'm taken the libertie of writin to you to say thet I just cum from Miss Landons house where I ben nursing her. She is bettur now but keeps wishin she cud see yoo. I thot yoo wud lik to kno. Mebbe yoo cud cum visit her. I done all I cud fer her. She hasn't enny of her own yoo kno. Hopin yoo can cum.

Yoors respectfully,
Henrietta Bonsall

P.S. We found Lem Pike tryin to git in the kitchum chamber winder where yoor furnitoor is. He clum up to the winder and got his head an sholders inside. The winder ketch give way ad the pollise got him.

Amorelle did remember Henrietta Bonsall. She was the old nurse that always went to everybody in Glenellen when there was sickness. They called her "Bonny," and everybody loved her. Bonny had cared for Amorelle's mother in her last sickness. Though it had been long years ago, and she only a little girl then, Amorelle remembered it well. And now Miss Landon was sick and needed her. Her resolve was taken at once.

She stole a furtive glance at Aunt Clara's smug face.

"The Robertses have asked Louise for the weekend," remarked Aunt Clara complacently. "That's nice. Louise will like that."

This was as good a time to speak as any. Amorelle caught her breath and spoke.

"Aunt Clara, I'd like to go back to Genellen for a while. I've had a letter from an old friend of Mother's. She's sick and wants me. I'd like to go this morning, if you don't mind. The canning and cleaning are all done, and you are going away yourself pretty soon. I don't suppose you'll need me."

Aunt Clara's face hardened.

"I certainly don't see what call you have to go all the way to Glenellen to nurse some old hanger-on in your father's church," said Aunt Clara crisply, "and I certainly do need you here. There are Louise's things to do up for her weekend, and I want you to make those ruffles for the organdie dresses. You know, the dressmaker left that work for you. Besides, we need you to help pack up when we go to the shore. And who will stay in the house and look after things, I'd like to know? You just write her it's out of the question. You can't have people from Glenellen pestering the life out of you forever."

"But Aunt Clara," began Amorelle earnestly, "she isn't a hanger-on. She was Mother's dear friend. And I've always meant go back and visit her sometime. I'd like to go if you can arrange it. I made those ruffles last week, the two evenings you were away, and put them on the dresses. They are all ready to wear, and I'll gladly do up Louise's things this morning. Then I could take the afternoon train. Ida told me she was going to stay in town this summer, and I thought perhaps you could arrange with her to look after the house."

"It doesn't suit me at all," snapped Aunt Clara in one of her cold tones of anger that always reminded one of Louise. "I have a great many things I need you for. Besides, how are you to get your clothes ready for your marriage if you don't stay here and sew? You can have your time and the sewing machine and nothing to bother you. And what will George say? You, an engaged girl! Have you asked George if he is willing you should go? There is another thing you seem to have forgotten, too. Where will you get the money to go a long journey like that? It's a long way to Glenellen. I guess you hadn't thought of that."

There was a dry finality in her aunt's tone that brought a helpless lump to Amorelle's throat.

"I have enough money," she said in a quiet voice. "I thought it would really be cheaper for you if I was gone during the summer. You wouldn't have to keep the house open."

Her voice was choking but she tried to control the tremble in it.

"Nonsense!" said Uncle Enoch suddenly in a thunderous voice, throwing down his paper so violently that it made the coffee cup rattle. "As if my niece couldn't take a little trip to visit her friends if she wants to! Of course you can go, Amorelle. Your aunt can hire help to do anything she needs. I'm sure it isn't any consideration of money."

"Amorelle, the iceman is at the back door. Will you just step out and tell him I want to pay the bill? You will find my pocketbook on my bureau, and the bill is lying on top of my desk. Attend to it, please, before he goes."

Aunt Clara was that way. She always could switch things off at the right moment, and somehow the milkman or the iceman or somebody always happened along for a nice excuse when Uncle Enoch undertook to smooth anything out for Amorelle.

The girl hastened from the room to obey her aunt's behest with a heavy heart. As she came down the back stairs again, she heard Louise going down the front stairs, late, as usual, to her breakfast. Now she would be in the argument, too, and there would be a regular storm. She would know how to floor her father utterly, and there would be no way for Amorelle to go unless she actually ran away. Had she the nerve for that? Did she really want to make a break of that kind between herself and her relatives?

She paused in the butler's pantry a moment to dry the tears that had sprung unbidden to her eyes, and the excited voices of her aunt and uncle came to her ears.

"It's no way to treat a young girl, Clara," from her uncle; and then Louise's petulant voice breaking in, "I'm sure I don't see why you make such a fuss about it, Clara. Why not let her go? I'd be glad to get her out of the way just now while that Russell Garrison is staying on. He's to be here two weeks. He made a fool of himself over her yesterday, taking it into his head that he must look after her just like all the rest of the girls. And we'll have to have her tagging everywhere with us if she is here, or he will think it odd. He's that way, one of those old-fashioned funny kinds of men that thinks a girl has to be kept in pink cotton. But he's nice, and he has loads of money, they say, and he drives a peach of a car. Mother, let her go. I'm bored to death, always having her around in the way."

Amorelle beat a hasty retreat up the back stairs to her room, stung to the heart. It was not more than was to have been expected of the pretty, heartless cousin, perhaps. But somehow coming this morning on top of all her other perplexities, it hurt immeasureably. She locked her door and flung herself on her bed, weeping. She felt as if she never could go downstairs and face life among them again. She had not eaten a mouthful of breakfast, but what was breakfast in such a situation?

Presently she rose and bathed her eyes. She was not a girl given to weeping. She had not the opportunity if she had so desired, and self-control had been bred in her from childhood. Somehow she felt now that the die had been cast. She must go away. And if she were going, she wanted very much to go at once. She went about quietly picking up her possessions, folding her few dresses, taking things out of her bureau drawer, and packing them swiftly in the trunk that had been kept in her room always. She would not take with her any of the cast-off finery. It did not take long to pack. She worked as if the need of great haste was upon her and she must get this done before anyone stopped her. She found her breath coming in short, dry sobs as she stooped over the shabby trunk and stowed away her belongings.

Before this was finished, she heard her aunt's heavy, labored tread upon the stairs and her short, asthmatic breathing as she neared the top.

Amorelle closed the trunk noiselessly, gave a quick glance around the room, with one movement swept out of sight into the closet any objects that might show her recent occupation, and waited.

Her aunt tried the door and, finding it locked, knocked and called querulously, "Amorelle! Amorelle! What in the world have you got your door locked for in broad daylight?"

Amorelle stepped to the door quietly and opened it.

Her aunt stood panting from her climb with the petulant

querulousness still upon her lips and brow.

"Amorelle, your uncle thinks you ought to go on this trip if you are so set upon it—" She paused for breath. "And Louise is awfully sweet about it. She says she'll take over your work so you can go. She is a dear child. She wants you to have a little pleasure."

Amorelle swallowed hard and turned away, trying to put down the hurt and indignation.

"Thank you, Aunt Clara," she managed to say steadily.

"Yes," said the aunt, "she's taken the trouble to call up and find out about trains. There's one at half past eleven this morning, but I don't suppose you could possibly get ready by that time. Louise says if you can, she'll take you in the car to the station."

There was an eagerness about her tone that Amorelle could not help feeling, although she was relieved that she was to have no trouble about being allowed to go.

"Yes, Aunt Clara, if it won't inconvenience you, I think I can get ready. But Louise need not bother about the car. I'll walk down early, for I have one or two errands on the way. I'll just go down now and phone for the expressman to come for my trunk."

"Oh, are you going to take a trunk? You'll be back before long, won't you? I did think I'd have you make some of that plum conserve while we were away, the kind we liked so much last year, you know, with the nut meats and the lemon peel—"

But Amorelle had hurried down the stairs and did not seem to have heard. When she returned, her aunt was in Louise's room, and Amorelle could not help hearing what they said.

"Then she's going at once? What luck! She'll be out of the way entirely when Mr. Garrison comes. That's a great relief. I didn't know how I was to get rid of her. He's so strange about such things. Do I have to take her in the car?"

"No, she says she wants to walk."

"So much the better. Then I can have all my time to dress. Mother, do you think the blue gingham with white organdie is the prettiest, or shall I wear the lavender Swiss?"

Amorelle hurried up the stairs like a wraith, smiling bitterly. It was one thing to be able to go on her journey peaceably but quite another to be almost hustled out of the only home she had in the world.

Fortunately she was too busy for the next half hour to entertain such thoughts, and it was with a reasonably placid countenance that she came downstairs and paused at her aunt's door to say good-bye. She would have liked to go without further words with her cousin, but something fine in her would not let her act the coward. To her great relief, the expressman came just as she tapped on Louise's door, making prolonged leave-taking impossible, so she called a pleasant good-bye and hurried away to look after her trunk.

Her aunt came to the top of the stairs as she was leaving and called after her, "Better come back soon and get at your sewing. Then you'll have time to make that conserve before the plums are gone."

But Amorelle managed to smile and get downstairs without committing herself.

Outside the door, she found her uncle unexpectedly sitting

behind the vines on the porch, looking a bit nervous and flustered.

"Oh, is that you, Amorelle? Going now, are you? Well, take this, child, and have a good time. You deserve it. And if you need any more, just write to me—at the office, you know. Good-bye." And he hurried into the house without giving her opportunity to say more than "thank you." As she tucked the money away in her little handbag, she discovered that there were ten crisp ten-dollar notes in the roll, and a warm glow came round the chilly place in her heart. The kindness in her uncle's voice meant far more to her than money. It would help her greatly to forget Louise's heartless words.

She had written a hasty note to George to let him know she had been called away to Glenellen to see a sick friend of her mother's and promising to write him later. She hurried first to the post office to mail this.

Then she had a book to return to the library, some knitting needles to take to an old lady who had loaned them to her, and she wanted to get a minute to say good-bye to the lame seamstress who sometimes did embroidery for her aunt and to give a picture book to the little invalid girl who lived in the same building with the seamstress.

She was breathless when at last she was seated in the train, barely in time to secure a seat before it started. But when the wheels began to move, it suddenly came over her that she was free. A great wonder came upon her that it had all been accomplished so easily after all. She remembered her prayer of the night before and marveled. Was this the answer?

Chapter 16

$\mathcal{I}$t was a long ride because the train she had taken was a way train and went only to the junction, where she had to wait four hours for the evening express and take a sleeper, but Amorelle was glad she had started at once. If she had waited, George might have turned up and made objections.

Her mind was filled with pleasant thoughts. It was as if she had just acquired a beautiful book filled with delightful experiences and charming pictures, and this was her first leisure to examine it.

It was not until late in the afternoon that she fully realized that she had spent the day between enjoying the views she passed and reviewing the day before. Constantly there came to her mind interesting phrases, glimpses of Russell Garrison's views of life, incidents and quotations that had enriched the few hours she had spent in his company. She looked upon the experience as an uplifting one for which to be thankful. He was not in any sense her friend, though he had had been most friendly. Of course he had not understood that she did not belong to his sphere, for he was wealthy and traveled and belonged to a fine old family high in social realms, she understood. But he had been wonderful to her, and it was nice to know how it felt to be treated that way. Of course she would never see him again, and it was just as well that she should not. She grudged him not to whoever should be his future companion on the way of life, but if one saw too much of a man like that, it might be hard not to like him too much.

That was the way she explained it to herself when her conscience suddenly rose and asked her how George would like to have her thinking so much about what another man had said.

It had not occurred to her to let Garrison know that she was engaged. She wondered if she should have done so. She had not worn her ring because of George's constant warnings about it. He would have said it was a great risk to wear a diamond to the woods. Somehow the ring didn't seem to be really hers, anyhow. It was George's investment, and her hand merely displayed it.

As Glenellen drew nearer, she found she had a better understanding of her own feelings toward George Horton than ever before. She resolved to write him a frank letter just as soon as she arrived and get the matter entirely off her mind. She could not be at peace until her unfortunate engagement was at an end. She had talked with her Lord about it, and He had shown her. Oh, if she had only realized sooner what riches she had in Christ. Wisdom and knowledge! It was wonderful!

As Amorelle walked down the quiet street from the Glenellen station, she was remembering old scenes and precious happenings. Here was where she had fallen off her bicycle, and her father had picked her up and carried her home and her mother had bound up her bruises and comforted her. Oh, to have a father and mother to bind up and comfort now. Here was the same old tree encroaching upon the sidewalk, where she used to play hide-and-seek with her playmates when they took a walk to Glenellen. There was the spire of her father's church off in the distance with the ivy climbing thickly over it. Up there was the way home to the manse that wasn't home anymore.

They had called a young married man in her father's place, although he hadn't accepted the call yet. She wondered, in case he came, if she could bring herself to go to church and hear him preach in her father's pulpit without weeping.

She walked down the length of the street under the maples, their thick foliage yellow-green in the sunlight, past the clustering houses of people she remembered as if she were opening an old photograph album, until she came to the little cottage with moss etching its shingles in velvet-green lines behind tall lilac bushes. It was only one winter, yet it seemed so long since she went away.

The old gate sagged but still bore its chain and weight. She swung it back with a loving touch and hurried into the house.

The little white-haired woman lying like a frail flower on the old calico-covered couch did not look much like the alert Aunt Lavinia that Amorelle had left, but the same loving eyes and voice were there, and Amorelle flew into her arms.

"I just had a feeling something nice was going to happen," said Miss Landon joyously. "I made Henrietta put on this wrapper and let me up awhile. Amorelle, little girl, stand back and let me look at you. You've got tired eyes, but you're just the same. I knew you would be. Your mother's sweet, patient mouth. Your father's true eyes and wonderful smile. They haven't spoiled you yet."

Henrietta came breathlessly from a neighbor's where she had been for fresh eggs. Bonny! Dear old Bonny!

Bonny took her to a little white room. There was an old four-poster bed with homespun linen sheets, a blue-and-white homespun spread, and a long mirror over a chest of quaint drawers. Her father and mother smiled at her from two frames on the wall. A handful of blush roses in a gray-and-blue jar on the windowsill filled the air with fragrance. A thrush sang somewhere overhead, and a big blue and orange and black butterfly hovered over the bowl of roses. It was all wonderful. She took off her hat, washed her face in the funny little thick, white washbowl, and wiped it on the soft towel that smelled of geranium leaves. She smoothed her hair and rested her tired eyes with a long look out of the window into the thick green of the lilacs.

Downstairs there was the smell of fried chicken and strawberries. It all seemed so sweet and homey, it took her right back to her childhood and made it seem almost possible that if she should go down the street to Rivington, she might find her dear father in the parsonage again.

After the evening meal she sat beside Miss Landon and

talked while Henrietta Bonsall whisked the dishes away and went down to the post office on an errand.

"Now, Amorelle," said the old lady, "before we begin I want you to know the truth. I've got hardening of the arteries, and I'm not likely to live long. It's been going on for sometime back, and the doctor says I'm almost to the end. You needn't look sad, because I'm perfectly satisfied. I've lived my time, and it's often been a lonely way. I'm glad to go home to my Savior. My Lord is calling me home. I've had a yearning for many a year to go where all of my family and most of my friends are, so it'll be a happy ending. But I took a longing to see you before I go and tell you all about my affairs, and I'm glad you've come."

"Oh, and I'm glad I've come, too, Aunt Lavinia," breathed Amorelle, struggling with quick tears.

"There now, put away your tears and listen," said the old lady, smiling. "I'm feeling fairly well tonight, but it may not last till tomorrow, and I've a lot to say before Bonny gets back. Bonny's the salt of the earth, but I don't tell my affairs to anyone in this town unless I am willing the whole town should know them. So listen, and don't feel bad."

Amorelle smiled and grasped the withered old hand that felt like a crumpled rose leaf.

"You don't remember, of course, but your father and mother were wonderful to me when I was in great trouble once, and your father fixed my money affairs up so I had enough to keep me all my days. And now that I'm going away, I've nobody in the world to leave it to but you, child. You see, it rightly belongs to you, because if your father hadn't saved it for me, I wouldn't have had it to leave. I would have been in the poorhouse all these years, through a rascally man who had charge of my property."

"But, Aunt Lavinia—" broke in Amorelle with wonder in her voice.

"No, wait, child, I'm not quite through. You needn't feel it's anything great. It's only this old house, free from mortgage, and a bit of money well invested, thanks to your father. But after the funeral expenses are paid and a bit to Bonny for looking after me, there'll be enough to keep up the house and take care of you if you are ever in need. In case you have no need of the house, you can easily rent it or sell if you choose, though I'd like to feel I was leaving a place for you to come to if ever things went against you as they went against me."

Suddenly Amorelle's head went down on the couch beside her old friend, and the tears had their way. She had been able to bear the loneliness, the disappointment, the desolation of the years, in quietness and patience, but this sudden care for her overwhelmed her overwrought young soul.

Miss Landon laid her hand on the smooth brown head and let her cry for a minute; then she said gently, "There now, child, cheer up, and tell me all about you! I'm just hungry to know everything. Begin at the beginning and tell me just as you would your mother, won't you dear?"

"Oh, Aunt Lavinia," burst out the girl, "why didn't I understand? Why didn't I write oftener to you? It would have been so wonderful to have someone who cared like this. There wasn't anyone in the whole wide world—"

"Child," said Aunt Lavinia, clasping her hand earnestly

and peering at the young face in the twilight, "you don't mean nobody cared. Oh, you must be mistaken. Nobody could look at your dear, sweet face and not care."

"Oh, they cared—a little—but not really cared, you know. Aunt Clara was cold and hard; Louise was selfish. Only Uncle Enoch was really kind. He gave me some money when I came away, a hundred dollars, and seemed very much interested in my having a good time. And then of course *George*—I thought he cared, but I'm beginning to feel almost as if it was only because I was going to belong to him that he cared, not just because it was I more than any other girl."

Amorelle's cheek was lying against the gentle old hand, and she was speaking out of the inmost depths of her heart without realizing she had a listener, this dear friend seemed so like her own mother in her tenderness and understanding.

"But who is George?" asked the older woman quickly.

And there in the twilight, with the tree toads singing sleepily outside and a drowsy cricket chirping at the door, Amorelle told the simple, drab romance of her lonely, young life, showed her gorgeous ring, told how good-looking he was and how much he seemed to care sometimes, especially at first.

Aunt Lavinia listened, making no comment beyond the quick, warm pressure of her hand now and then until the story was finished, and Amorelle lifted her head with the question that had been going over and over in her mind in one form or another for days.

"Aunt Lavinia, what is the matter with me? Why didn't I want George to kiss me? Why did it make me feel lonelier than ever to think of going to live in that awful little house with him? Do you suppose I was just tired and cross, maybe? And shall I get over it? Or am I the one who is selfish? Oh, you don't know how wonderful it was to run off here and get away from it all. You don't know how dear and still it sounds, and how the air smells good enough to eat, and this house looks like a precious palace. I never want to leave! Tell me, what shall I do? I *can't* marry George feeling that way, can I?"

The frail arms came quickly around her, drawing her close, and Aunt Lavinia's gentle voice had a decisive, protective note. "No, indeed, child! You mustn't marry a man *ever* unless you can't be happy without him. That is what's the matter with half the marriages in the world; people were just in love with getting married and never calculated on the long, hard pull together through life. Marriage is the most intolerable thing on earth if there is no love, or not enough love, and I guess it's the nearest to heaven if the love is true and pure and unselfish. Of course, as you say, you may be simply tired out soul and body and need a rest to be able to look at things sanely and naturally. But it sounds to me as if that man"—there was something in the way in which Miss Landon said "that *man*" that expressed her utter dislike for George Horton—"well, it seems to me he is just a selfish creature that wants you because you are sweet and wholesome and will make a good wife in his home. He picked you out the way he did his house, because it was cheap and would help him to save money; the way he will his automobile, because it will give *him* pleasure, make a good showing at the office, and give the most wear for the money. I know that kind of man. That may seem harsh, but what you have been telling me convinces me he is like that. Now, if you really love him, you'll be red-hot mad at that."

There was silence a second while the tree toads chimed an antiphony; and then Amorelle lifted her head and said half-ashamedly, with almost a roguish sound in her voice, "I—am—not mad, Aunt Lavinia."

"Thank the Lord," said Miss Landon earnestly. "I think you'll see your way clear very soon. That man is not fit for you. If there's not somebody different in the world for you, you'd much better walk your way alone."

"I've been thinking that, too," said the girl softly, "but I wasn't sure it was fair to him when I let it go on so long. I was lonely, and it seemed a pleasant way out. I thought I loved him."

Miss Landon was still a minute then she burst out, "Amorelle, do you remember your father well?"

"Indeed I do, Aunt Lavinia."

"Well, do you know what a grand, unselfish man he was? Do you remember how he and your mother were like one big, beautiful human soul?"

"I do. Oh, I do!"

"Well, child, can you imagine this George being like him?"

"No," breathed Amorelle very softly.

"Don't you know any other young men? Didn't you ever meet one you thought could be grand and unselfish and brave and tender?"

Amorelle hesitated.

"Yes, I met one, just for a day. But he wasn't *my* friend. It was just a happening. I'll never see him again, of course. It was he that made me see the truth—about George. But of course he's nothing to me, nor I to him."

"Well, if there's one, there are others. Don't you worry, child. You don't ever know what good things your heavenly Father has in store for you. Just you lie back and trust Him, and don't take up with the first thing that comes along just to save you from being lonely. There are worse things than loneliness in this world. Worse things than being an old maid! Now, child, it's time to go to bed, and I hear Bonny coming. Kiss me, and forget all your troubles. You kneel down and pray when you get to your room, and you'll find our Father will straighten it all out for you. That was your father's way, and it's straightened many a trouble for me, too. 'Casting all your care upon Him, for He careth for you,' he used to say so often. Try it, child. Try it!"

Amorelle, on her knees in the moonlight beside the white bed, accepted the challenge and laid her troubles like a little child in the hands of a strong, loving parent, and then lay down to sweet sleep.

"There's something important I forgot to tell you last night," said Miss Landon when Amorelle went in to see her in the morning. "We had a burglar here a few days ago! Lemuel Pike! He tried to get into the kitchen chamber window where your things are stored."

"Oh yes, Bonny wrote a few words about it. I meant to ask you how it happened. What do you suppose he wanted?"

"Well, that's what we can't understand. There is nothing gone. In fact, he hadn't been in yet when he was caught, for they found nothing incriminating on him. You know the old-fashioned catches on those windows aren't very reliable, and he must have loosened the spring, for it fell down on him and caught, and he couldn't stir or get away. It was really very funny. He was gasping and squealing and kicking around, hitting his toes against the clapboards, till he knocked the ladder out from under him and just hung there high and dry. Couldn't help himself, because the catch of the window held firmly, and he couldn't reach it."

"He must be crazy," said Amorelle thoughtfully.

"They say not," said Miss Landon. "One of the trustees of the bank, Mr. Aiken, was here yesterday just before you arrived. He went upstairs to look around as the police had done, but they found no evidence that he had been in there, and he *said* that he was only trying to measure the house for the tax estimate. You know they do that by the cubic feet in the house. I don't quite understand that, but it's some new method they have, and he's just been made tax assessor. How he ever got elected nobody knows, but he did. However nobody could quite see why he couldn't have done his measuring on the ground instead of taking a ladder and climbing up to the second story with his head inside a window that had been closed fast enough a few hours before, nor why he should come at midnight to do it either."

A startled look came over Amorelle's face as she remembered her own midnight intruder.

"Well, it seems," went on Miss Landon, "that the bank has something on this Pike man, something they're sure of but can't prove, and they have been trying for a long time to catch him in something red-handed. When Mr. Aiken found the furniture in the kitchen chamber was yours, he asked me if I could get in touch with you and get your permission for someone to look over things and see if they could find out what the man was after. He said it was very important. And I was just about to write to you when you arrived yesterday. The joy of your coming put it out of my head. My dear, do you know of anything among your papers, or in your father's desk, that that man could be after?"

"No," said Amorelle. "I don't. But I guess I ought to look and see. I didn't go over Father's papers in his desk before I went away. I was in such a hurry to get things out of the manse before the Ladies' Aid came in to tell me what to do." She could laugh over the memory now. "Also, I couldn't bear to do it just then," she added more soberly. "I've thought all winter I should have done it. But there is something strange about that man Pike. You know he came to see Father the night he died."

"He *did?*"

"Yes, just a few minutes before. And then, you remember, I told you I thought he was the one who broke into the manse the night after the funeral. He got away, you know, in spite of Hannah's throwing a can of paint over him on the back steps."

"Yes, I remember reading about it in the local paper," laughed Miss Landon. Then growing more serious, "But I guess you should have told somebody else, too, child. That may be pretty important. There is something behind all this, you may be sure."

"I'm afraid there is," said Amorelle, "though I can't imagine what. But there was a reason why I didn't want to say anything. You remember my telling you about Mrs. Brisbane and her hateful suggestions of husbands for me? Well, Lemuel Pike was one of the ones she suggested!"

"You poor child!" laughed Miss Landon. "What an utter fool that woman is! Why, nobody ever had any respect for Lemuel Pike!"

"Well," said Amorelle, "he wrote me a letter and proposed!"

"He *did?* It does look as if he must be crazy!"

"I never read the whole of the letter," confessed Amorelle. "I was too disgusted. It came after he had broken into the manse. But can't you see why I didn't want to get mixed up with Lemuel Pike's name in any way?"

"I surely can," said Miss Landon, looking troubled. "But now, dear, I'm not so sure in spite of that but you ought to tell Mr. Aiken all about it in confidence. Mr. Aiken was your father's friend and will keep the matter to himself if possible."

"Oh, I don't mind telling now," laughed Amorelle. "It seems ages ago and rather funny when I think back to it. I'll go right up and see what's in that desk. I ought to have done it long ago. I'm not altogether sure there wasn't something that Father wanted me to see after he was gone, but I didn't think about that till after I went away."

Just then there came a knock on the door, and Bonny ushered in a caller and appeared at Miss Landon's door.

"That same man is here again that came yesterday," she

said. "He says he heard Miss Amorelle was here and he wants to see her."

So it was in the company of her father's old friend and lawyer that Amorelle, after explaining to him what she had just told Miss Landon about Lemuel Pike, finally approached her father's desk and unlocked the secret drawer.

"I'm so glad you are here with me," she said to him as she turned the key. "I've dreaded this because I knew it would be so hard to go over Father's intimate papers."

"Well, I'm glad I'm here, too," said the man, patting her shoulder tenderly. "It is hard to do these things, I know, but it ought to be done at once, always. There might be something important."

"I know," sighed Amorelle, "but I didn't realize then."

Then she pulled out the secret drawer and set it on the desk under the light.

The first thing she took out was her father's book of receipt blanks, laid on the top of all the other papers as if it had been put there in a hurry, and suddenly Amorelle remembered seeing that book lying on her father's desk when she went to the door to let in Lemuel Pike.

"Oh," she said, taking up the book and opening it, and then started back. "Oh! What in the world can this mean?"

For there, lying smoothly in the little book, just fitting inside its long, narrow covers, was a pile of crisp bank bills.

"Why! Now I remember Father had money in his hand as I looked back when I went to let Lemuel Pike out!" she exclaimed. "And this book of blanks was lying on his desk when I let him in."

She held the money in one hand and the book in the other and stared at Mr. Aiken.

"Count it!" said the bank trustee with kindling eyes. "There is something behind all this, just as I suspected."

Amorelle counted it. There were five one-thousand-dollar bills, new and smooth as if they had never been folded.

"Five thousand dollars!" said Amorelle incredulously. "What can it mean?"

"Is there a record stub in that book? Is it made out?"

Amorelle looked at the book again.

"Yes, Father always made out stubs. It says 'Received of Lemuel Pike, five thousand dollars—payment loan.'"

"Ah," said Mr. Aiken soberly. "That shows what Lemuel was after. He figured that nobody would know about that money yet and he could get it back before you found it. But there's something strange about his having paid it in money and not a check. I wonder if your father would have left any record of that loan. When it was made and why. Wasn't it rather odd for Lemuel to borrow of your father? But perhaps he borrowed it long ago when he was a poor boy."

"Father always kept a diary," said Amorelle. "It's in his desk somewhere, I'm sure. He might have a record there. But here, what's this? A letter! No, a *copy* of a letter, to Lemuel Pike."

"Ah!" said Mr. Aiken.

Amorelle read the letter aloud. " 'My dear sir: May I recall to your memory that seven years ago at the above date you came to my study in deep distress and confessed to me that you had from time to time been taking certain sums from the Rivington

Bank—where you were then employed—for the purpose of investment, intending to replace them before their loss should be discovered. But your investment had failed and discovery was imminent. You begged me to help you and promised faithfully that the offense should never be repeated.

" 'For the sake of your old mother to whom your disgrace would have been crushing, you will recall that I borrowed on my life insurance the sum of five thousand dollars, the amount which you had embezzled from the bank, and loaned it to you. You knew that my life insurance represented my lifelong savings and was all that I had to keep me from poverty in my old age and to leave to my daughter if I should die. You gave me a written promise to pay this back from time to time as you were able and to clear off the entire sum at the end of five years.

" 'It is now seven years since I loaned you this money. In all that time you have given me only promises as interest and have never made but one payment on the principle, and that of only twenty-five dollars at my most urgent request. You have persistently excused yourself when I have suggested your paying a small sum every month or every quarter, although you have all the time been employed with reputable firms who have paid you good salaries.

" 'It has recently come to my knowledge that you are no longer a penniless man needing assistance but are rated one of the wealthiest men in Rivington.

" 'Since this is true, and since my health is precarious and I have been able to save almost nothing since loaning you this money, I feel that the time has come to demand my own again, and I feel thoroughly justified before God in what I am about to say to you.

" 'I am therefore serving you notice that if you do not return to me *all* that you owe me on or before eight o'clock Thursday evening of this week, I shall immediately place the facts and all papers connected with this matter, *together with a copy of this letter*, in the hands of my friend and attorney, H. T. Aiken, who, as you are aware, is one of the trustees of the Rivington Bank. Sincerely, Reuben L. Dean.' "

The face of the bank trustee was filled with satisfaction as Amorelle finished the reading of the letter.

"That is just what we need!" he said. "This will put a stop to the steady crimes in every direction, which have been going on for years and which we have been working on for a long time. Your father was not the only one on whom things of this sort have been practiced, and yet we could not get evidence because the victims, as a rule, were people whose sympathy and integrity prevented them from coming forward and giving information. He victimized only those he could trust to keep his confidence for him. I think this letter copy will be the key with which we shall be able to unlock a vast amount of evidence, which will put this man where he cannot do any more harm in Rivington. And the story you have told me concerning his proposal of marriage makes it plain that he feared you would come on this very letter. It may have been more the letter than the money he was after when he broke into both houses, though he is a miser, there is no doubt of that. A search of his house has been made for evidence, and already a number of secret hiding places have been discovered where he has been hoarding money. The great puzzle has been to understand how he always escaped by suddenly disappearing when he was almost caught. But this morning a small boy in his neighborhood casually made known that he had seen him many times at night disappearing up a tree. We are going to investigate that, and if he was the one who broke into the manse last fall, there ought to be some white paint in evidence to mark his going."

The bank trustee was laughing now, and Amorelle joined with him, though she was too bewildered to take it all in.

"There are other papers in the box. Perhaps you better see what they are before I leave," said Mr. Aiken, "although I think these are all I need for the Pike case."

Amorelle opened a long envelope and found it contained her father's life insurance papers, and being interpreted by Mr. Aiken, she discovered that there was still another five thousand dollars that was due her beside the money Lemuel Pike had paid back. Ten thousand dollars! Her father had saved all that out of his salary and yet had been so generous to everybody. Everybody except himself. She recalled how careful he was about personal expenditures, how he would not even buy clothes for himself until his were almost shabby. The tears gathered in her eyes.

"Well, I'm glad you've found that, and it ought to be applied for at once," said the lawyer. "If you'll just give me those papers, I'll take the necessary steps for you to secure it."

There were some government bonds, a few hundred dollars' worth, the deed to a little worthless property that had been taken over in payment for a debt, and nothing more except a letter from her father that he had written Amorelle a few weeks before his death. Precious letter! If she only could have had it for her comfort during the hard winter just past.

Mr. Aiken took his departure presently, and Amorelle, after reporting briefly to Miss Landon what they had found, went to her room to read her father's letter.

There was so much in that letter. She was amazed. When she read it the second time, and the third, she began to realize that it touched upon everything that had troubled her and perplexed her in the days that had followed his death. Yes, and in the whole winter. Here it had been stowed away in his desk all the time, full directions about how she should proceed, full details of his life insurance and everything financial. Advice that she had longed for! And he had even *told* her he was writing that letter, and yet she had so forgotten it that she hadn't opened his desk to find out.

That afternoon when she told Miss Landon about it, that sweet saint replied with a far-away look in her eyes, "Isn't that for all the world the way we do with our heavenly Father's letter? He has filled it with instructions, advice, sympathy, comfort, love, everything we need, including promises to supply all our needs, and we just get so busy trying to work out our own little problems that we don't take time to read it."

Amorelle smiled over that that night as she remembered her day in the woods with Garrison and what he had said along those same lines.

She took out her father's letter again to read it over, and suddenly one paragraph stood out from all the rest and claimed her attention.

*I've just one word to say about marriage, precious child,
more than I have already said to you by word of mouth.
Don't ever marry anyone unless you love him with all your
heart, and unless he and you are absolutely one in the matter
of spiritual things!*

Ah! Her father would never have favored her marriage with George. And she felt absolutely sure that, were he here this minute, he would say she must break with him at once, for she remembered his oft-repeated saying: "A bad promise is better broken than kept."

Chapter 17

The season was much more advanced here in Glenellen than in the west. For three days Amorelle basked in the quiet joy of Aunt Lavinia's home, sitting beside the dear invalid while she was awake and able to talk with her; hovering around the old nurse, Bonny, in the kitchen; sitting on the side porch behind the lilacs, shelling peas or just looking into the sweet, shimmering beauty of the little old-fashioned garden of pinks, phlox, and verbenas, with delphiniums and white Canterbury bells like tall steeples, and a bank of purple-and-gold pansies at the end of the porch. There were many bees and butterflies hovering in the sunshine around the quaint old house, and a hummingbird had built its nest in the honeysuckle vine. It was beautiful just to sit and dream and know that this was her own real home. If only the dear old lady could stay, too, and share it with her. How she loved it all! How good God had been to give it to her and make her free from further dependence!

She had put away the thought of George and of everything else connected with her life in the city. It was as if she were sheltered here to rest and wait to see what God would tell her to do.

Then on the fifth morning, as if a hand had been laid upon her, she awoke in the early dawn and immediately knew that she was to arise and write that letter to George. It was as clear as if she had received a direction from above, and she obeyed without hesitation. She had no need even to search for words. They were there, ready for her pen, waiting in the pearl-dewiness of the morning.

> *Dear George:*
>
> *I could not write you sooner because I had to get my bearings and understand myself. For a long time I have been knowing that there was something wrong about my feeling for you, and I wanted to get quiet and think it out. Now I feel that I have come to know the truth, and it is not kind to you to hide it from you any longer. I have come face to face with the fact that I do not love you enough to marry you, and I know I never will.*
>
> *I feel ashamed, George, that I did not know this before, but I truly thought I loved you in the right way, although you remember I was very uncertain about it for a long time at first. For some time now I have been troubled that some things were not as I had always supposed they would be, and I see now that it was because I did not care in the right*

way. It came with a sort of shock to me that day after we had been out to look at the house together, and I realized that if I really loved you as you thought I did, and as I hoped I did, I would not care what kind of a sink the house had, if you wanted it and liked it and it was better for you. So, you see, I had no right to marry you. I am afraid I have been thinking a great deal more about having a home the way I wanted it than about whether I would be making you happy, and you can see yourself that is not right.

I hope you will forgive me and bear me no hard feeling. Perhaps if my mother had lived, I would have been wiser about such things and not have made promises which I find I cannot fulfill. I am sending you in this same mail the ring you gave me, registered. I know you will find someone else far better suited to be your wife than I am and that you will someday thank me for not going any farther after I found out.

I shall always be your true friend and well-wisher.

Very sincerely,
Amorelle

After Amorelle had sent off the letter and the ring, she went around the house singing like a bird. Somehow it seemed that she had a new lease on life. The very air seemed sweeter, the day more bright. Aunt Lavinia, from her couch, watched her and smiled.

Three days later came a reply from George, written on business stationery.

Amorelle:

The ring and your letter just arrived. I thought you knew better than to trust anything so valuable as that ring to the mail! You remember I told you I got that diamond for an investment, and I thought you were sensible enough to take care of it, but it seems I was mistaken.

As for the letter, I see you still have your grouch on, but you are carrying things a little too far this time. I can easily have a new sink put in that kitchen, of course, and I probably should have done so, unnecessary as it seems, if you had gone about it in the right way. But it is the principle of the thing I can't stand. No one can bully me into anything by doing the spoiled-child act, and you might as well learn that now as any time.

Of course, I know that you don't mean any of this sentimental bosh you have written for a minute, and you haven't an idea of taking you seriously; but it is beneath the woman I expect to make my wife for her to descend to methods like this, and I warn you I will not stand for it.

However, I do not care to discuss this matter on paper. I insist that you come back to your aunt's house at once and put aside this childishness or I will not answer for the consequences. I will call on Friday evening, and we will straighten this thing out. But I am keeping the ring until you return, as I do not consider it safe to send such things by mail, and I want to be good and sure you know how to take care of it before I put it in your hands again. Be sure to be home Friday. I won't put up with any more tantrums.

George

When Amorelle read this letter, the color flew into her cheeks and her eyes grew hard and bright. Around her gentle, yielding lips that had worn patient lines so long, a firm determination grew. Then her face broke into a wondering smile. She let the letter drop to the floor and slipped down to her knees beside her chair.

"Father," she whispered, "I thank You for showing me."

Then she arose and wrote with swift pen:

Dear George:

You are mistaken. I am not in a grouch, and I mean every word I wrote in that letter. Please read it over again and try to understand. If I needed anything more to convince me that I was right in writing it, I have it in your letter, which came this morning.

I have nothing but kindly feeling toward you, and I regret that I did not know my own mind sooner, but I do not wish to discuss the matter further, and there is nothing to straighten out. There are just the facts as I wrote them in my letter.

I am not coming back at all. I have accepted a position in the bank here in Glenellen and am going to remain with my mother's friend, who is slowly dying and needs me.

Sincerely,
Amorelle

With a quick glance at her watch, Amorelle took both letters and hurried down to Miss Landon.

"Aunt Lavinia, please read these letters and see if you think George will understand now," she said, handing out the letters.

The old lady began to read, sniffing indignantly as she progressed and fairly sizzling with indignation as she finished.

"What a little pig of a soul that man must have!" she snorted.

But as she read Amorelle's answer, amused satisfaction came upon her face.

"No, child," she said with a twinkle, as she handed the letters back, "that man will never understand you because he isn't capable of doing so. He isn't big enough. But I think it will astonish him, and I certainly would like to be a fly on the wall when he reads it. You needn't worry any about that man's affections; he hasn't any, or if he has any, the seat of them is in his pocketbook. If he had cared the least little mite about the real you, he would have been down here on the first train. He would at least have telephoned or telegraphed. But no, I suspect that would have cost too much. Well Amorelle, child, run to the post office. You've just time to get this in the noon mail. I'm curious to see what the poor creature will do next."

Amorelle cast a frightened glance at her old friend.

"Do? You think he'll do anything *more*, do you?"

Miss Landon laughed.

"I don't think he's even begun yet. He evidently considers you so thoroughly his that nothing you say will matter. Wait till he really finds out that you mean it. Run along quick, child, or you'll miss the mail."

Amorelle hurried down the pleasant village street with a song in her heart. Somehow life had suddenly become good to live. She pushed the letter into the little post office window and then went over to the bank to tell them she would be ready to begin her work the next day.

The morning seemed to be pulsing in golden waves through her heart and making her feet move in rhythmic measure, as if some music of the spheres were directing all her movements. As she came in from the sunshine and stood in the door of the old lady's room, her hair seemed to be a halo around her face, and her eyes had taken on a starriness that made her very beautiful. Miss Landon, watching her, rejoiced in the sweet young life that had come to be with her in her last days. It was almost like having a daughter of her own.

Acting on her old friend's advice, Amorelle wrote to her uncle at his office a breezy, loving letter, thanking him for all he had done for her, telling him of Miss Landon's condition, saying she decided to stay with her while she lived and had taken a position in the Glenellen bank, which would enable her to be independent. She thanked him again for his kindness when she left and added at the end, "I think you may be glad to know I have broken my engagement with George."

Then she wrote a brief little note to her aunt.

Dear Aunt Clara:

I am writing to tell you that I have broken my engagement with George Horton. I felt that I did not care for him in the right way to marry him. I have a job here now in the bank and shall stay right here with Miss Landon while she lives. She has hardening of the arteries

*and has not long to live, the doctor says. She seems to want
me very much.*

Hoping you are all quite well and enjoying the summer.

Lovingly,
Amorelle

She read this letter over carefully, wondering whether she
had made it as pleasant as she possibly could, hoping that none
of her bitterness of soul had crept in, and feeling no ill will for
the days and nights of loneliness she had endured in her aunt's
house.

It was like cutting the last tie that bound her to another life
when she went down to mail those letters, and her heart was
filled with what was almost exultation as she dropped them into
the box, although she gave a little, wistful, lingering, affectionate
touch to Uncle Enoch's, for the old man who had given her so
much kindness as he had been allowed to give.

She never dreamed what a breeze she was stirring up back
in the West.

Promptly as the mail could carry, came a letter from Aunt
Clara:

Dear Amorelle:

*You must be crazy to think of such a thing as breaking
an engagement with so estimable a young man as George
Horton. Any girl in these days ought to be proud to have
caught such a man as he is. Your uncle says his business
prospects are fine. You can't expect ever to find another*

*who will look at you. You must know you are a plain, old-
fashioned girl. That is no matter, of course, if one is good,
and is sometimes a good thing, because one doesn't have to
bother so much about dressing up to her face, but it does
count with men, and you don't want to be an old maid do
you? Who will support you when you get old? You can't
expect your uncle to do it always, you know. And I'm sure I
don't see how a good girl, such as I've always supposed you
were, could do such a thing as break an engagement after it
has gone on so long. Why, you're almost the same as married.
It's not honorable, you know. If it should get out, it would
be a disgrace to the family. And it's utterly ungrateful in
you, after all we've done for you, to turn around and act this
way. I can't understand what's got into you. I suppose it's
that foolish old woman you're visiting who is influencing
you. But you're not doing right, and we won't have it,
your uncle and I. Haven't you any feeling for Louise? Poor
Louise, who was so lovely and unselfish about your going
away. I don't know what she'll say when she gets back from
Augusta Roberts's house party! And think how she sat up
half the night before she left sewing that pink gingham I
meant to have you put the bias bands on before you left!
It's very selfish of you. What will people say? What will
they think of Louise? You should think of Louise and not
disgrace her. She's younger than you and ought to have her
chance in life the same as you did.*

*Now, Amorelle, I'm speaking in place of your mother.
I want you to pack right up when you get this and come*

back on the next train. We'll send for George and patch this thing up. It's all nonsense about your not loving him. Girls don't know anything about love until they're married. It isn't delicate for them to. I'd be ashamed of Louise if she went around talking about whether she loved a man or not. Love comes afterward naturally. It isn't intended you should feel things like that before you're married. It isn't modest.

Your uncle says you have plenty of money for a return trip, so don't delay a minute. Mind! Take the first train. And we'll all forgive you and not say anything more about the unfortunate matter. I'll answer for George's coming round. I know how to manage him.

Indignantly, your aunt,

Clara

P.S. The plums are ripe, and we can get them put up before they are gone if you hurry.

When Amorelle read this letter she felt like a freed thing that had suddenly got tangled in a net again. Little trembly feelings came in all her joints, and the tears sprang to her eyes. She took it down to Miss Landon and let her read it. Was it possible she was wrong? Had she let her engagement go on too long, and was it dishonorable now to break it, the same as if she had married and must be true to her vows?

But Aunt Lavinia's voice was firm and decided.

"No, child! No! A thousand times. You would be dishonorable

indeed if you married a man you could not love. You don't realize what you are talking about. One cannot feign love through a long lifetime, and if you are tied to a wrong mate it is agony for both. This George might be so thick-skinned that he wouldn't recognize what was the matter. But he wouldn't be really happy any more than you would, because he would be merely having you as a chattel, like the furniture of his house, and you wouldn't be his in spirit at all, only in body. It is what is making so many wretched marriages today and so many divorces. And being engaged is *not* the same as marriage. It is not right to go on and take vows knowing you cannot keep them. That's no way to live. It's a desecration. God made the sacrament of marriage holy, a symbol of His relation with those who choose to be His own. That's what you father used to preach. Any who enter into marriage vows without giving the whole of themselves are desecrating it. There would be only wranglings and heartaches and no happiness for anybody. Isn't it worlds better for the body to be hungry and unsheltered sometimes than for the soul to go on shivering all its life? I tell you, child, you must be true to your own soul in spite of *any*body else. This is not a question where selfishness comes in. It is a question of holiness, of right and wrong. It would be a sin to marry a man whose soul cannot be a part of your soul."

Amorelle sat on the edge of the bed, looking out the open window where wooded hills rose mistily in the distance across a long stretch of sunlit meadow and the hummingbirds flitted past with a flash of purple and green and gold. Into her eyes there came a dreamy look. What would it be like to have a life companion like that? One who was a part of your own soul, who knew your very thoughts and anticipated them, who held sweet converse with you day by day and made life all a pleasant walk, even when the way was rough and dark? Then before her there came a vision of a man and sudden remembrance of his eyes as he called her "You poor kid!" and said, "I couldn't see leaving you with those bums." And again, when he gave her that warming smile and said, "This is *our* day!"

Something in her heart rose and grasped for unnamed joy, and then suddenly her conscience and her maidenhood arose in alarm. Her cheeks flushed, and she sat up very straight and took herself in hand. *Am I a fool?* she asked herself harshly. And the vision vanished mistily as she took her eyes sharply from the window, but not before the gold from the hummingbird's wing as he flashed by again had stabbed her heart with a sudden ache of joy.

"You are right, I know, Aunt Lavinia," she said. "Aunt Clara never was right unless it just happened to suit her. Now I'm going up to write to her. I'm sorry about the plums, but it can't be helped, and she can live without plum preserves, anyway."

"There will be plums in the backyard, child, if you feel that way about it. If you want to take the trouble, it may smooth her feelings. It's just as well to keep people happy, even those that do not understand."

"You dear thing," said Amorelle, stooping to kiss the soft old lips. "You are the youngest old lady I ever met. Thank you. If you don't mind, I'll make the jam."

So Amorelle went up and wrote to her aunt.

Dear Aunt Clara:

I'm sorry to go against your wishes, and I'm sorry to have you think I'm not maidenly and am disgracing you, but I think George understands. I feel in my heart that I would not be doing right to marry him. I am only sorry I did not understand myself sooner. But it was not until we began to hunt for a house that I began to realize that it was not a happy thing to me to think about going away with George, and then I knew something was wrong. That was why I wanted to accept the invitation and come off here to think about it. I'm sorry to have you all feel this way about me; but I think you will see later that I was right. Don't fret about my being an old maid. I shall be very happy. And I shall not expect you and Uncle Enoch to do anything for me. The bank is paying me a nice little salary, and I can lay up something every month for a rainy day. Besides all that, this dear old friend of mother's is giving me her little house and a small income to keep it going when she is gone, so I am all planned for, you see. Thank you again for all you and Uncle Enoch did for me. I'll try not to disgrace you again.

I'm sorry about the bias bands. If I had known about them I would have stayed another day and put them on. But we have plums here in the yard, great luscious ones, and I'm going to make two dozen jars of preserves when they are ripe and send them by express to you, so you won't miss them.

Now, if there are any other ruffles or bias bands or things you would like me to sew for you, just bundle them

*up with directions and send them on by parcel post. I'd
love to do them evenings, and there is a good little sewing
machine here. It won't be any trouble.*

Lovingly,
Amorelle

She brought the letter to Miss Landon, and the old lady's
eyes lighted as she read.

"I should say that was 'good measure, running over,'"
commented the old lady as she handed it back. "Amorelle Dean,
you're going to be just like your father. Now, run away to the
post office, and forget this and be happy."

Two days later Uncle Enoch arrived. Meantime, nothing
more had as yet been heard from George.

Chapter 18

Uncle Enoch had taken a surreptitious detour on his way from a New York business trip and was cross at the delays on way trains. He was stiff and sore from being up half the night, changing at little way stations, and terribly upset because he had gone some extra miles. But he took Amorelle in his arms and kissed her as if she were very dear to him.

Then he sat down, took off his glasses, wiped them carefully, put them on, and looked around at the neat, little shingled house with approval.

"Nice little place you've got here, Amorelle. Reminds me of my old home when I was a boy. We had a chain like that on the gate. Ever swing on it? I got strapped many a time for doing it. Nice vine over the porch. Honeysuckle? H'mmm! My mother used to love 'em. What's that? A hummingbird? You don't say! That's exciting! My! I'd like to be a boy again and stay a week.

Isn't that a trout brook down there in that meadow? Looks like it. Say! This is great!"

Uncle Enoch stayed all day and caught the midnight train home, telling Aunt Clara he was delayed by business. But he had a great day. He sat by Miss Landon's couch, learning wisdom and doing her honor. He ate chicken pot pie and applesauce cooked by the excited Bonny, and Amorelle got the day off from the bank and went with him down to the river fishing.

They sat a long time without speaking, the shimmering sunlight playing around them, no sound but the gentle ripple of the water.

Suddenly Uncle Enoch cleared his throat.

"I've missed you, Amorelle," he said hesitatingly. "I've missed you a lot."

He sounded so like a shy boy trying to express his feelings without betraying undue emotion that a sympathetic warmth came around Amorelle's heart. Sensing that he wanted to say more, she remained silent.

"You helped me," he went on. "I've thought a lot about those talks you used to give me about your Bible lessons."

He cleared his throat once more, evidently trying to get the courage to go on.

"I hunted up my Bible and read over some of those verses you talked about. They made me see—I guess—I'm not—what I ought to be."

His voice grew husky. "I *know* I'm not— I'm a great sinner! I used to think I had a tough time of things, and I was pretty good because I didn't break loose and go into—well, into the sins that most men commit," he broke off. "It's strange for me to be talking to you this way, but I thought you might sort of help. You seem to have what your father had. I used to watch you there at home, and you made me see there was something to all that your father used to talk about. But I haven't got it. I'm not right with God. I know I'm an awful sinner. Not because of what I've done. I've never done what the world would call great sin, but because of what I've not done. Why, I've *never paid any attention to God!*"

His voice almost broke with his intense earnestness.

Amorelle was more stirred by her uncle's confession than ever before in her life. But she felt so helpless in herself as she realized that the moment had come for which she and her father had prayed for years. *Oh, heavenly Father,* her heart cried, *I alone can't help this soul. Put Thy words into my mouth.*

When her uncle had ceased speaking, there came the words from the Book, and she repeated them softly, "'I came not to call the righteous, but sinners to repentance.' 'The Son of man is come to seek and to save that which was lost.' We're all sinners, Uncle Enoch, and there is no hope for anybody till he finds out that he is a sinner. Then all there is to do is to believe what God says, that He put *all* our sin on His own Son and gave us His life, His righteousness. 'All we like sheep have gone astray; we have turned every one to his own way; and the Lord hath laid on him the iniquity of us all.' Believe that, Uncle Enoch, and you are saved."

There was a long, long silence while the sunbeams danced across the stream, and the bees hummed drowsily in the clover blooms of the meadow on the other side. At last Uncle Enoch spoke again.

"I *do*," he said confidently, earnestly.

It was an afternoon long to be remembered, and Amorelle's heart was happy over the thought that her father's prayers through the years had been answered at last. Uncle Enoch would meet him in heaven, redeemed by the precious blood of the Lord Jesus.

When Glenellen's old jitney finally came for Uncle Enoch at eleven-fifteen to convey him to the midnight train, he bade them all good-bye with a tremble in his voice and a promise to come again someday. He hadn't had such a good time since he was a boy, he said. He took Amorelle into his arms again and kissed her tenderly, telling her twice that he should miss her very much. And then he gruffly whispered that she had done him a lot of good. She was just like her father.

There were tears in his eyes as he left her. Amorelle was deeply touched.

The very next morning there was a letter in the post office from George.

Amorelle!

I've bought a white enamel sink. It's a dandy—has two compartments, so you can use it for washing and rinsing dishes, and a sort of turntable faucet. It's worth seventy-five dollars new, they tell me, but I got it secondhand for twenty-eight fifty. It has just a little chip on the under edge, but you'd never notice it. I'm going to have it put in the house this week.

Now come home at once, and no more nonsense! We
won't say any more about it. I haven't any more time to
waste on such trivial things. See you Friday night. So long.

George

When Amorelle read this, she broke down laughing.

"Why didn't I see all this in him before?" she asked, suddenly sobering. "I've been going with George for months, and I never realized before. Of course he never gave me much of anything except the ring, which he bought for an investment, he said. And now I think of it, he was always telling me the price of things, but I thought it was just because he was thrifty! I didn't realize he was all for money. Why didn't I see it sooner?"

"You were under a glamour of youth, dear child. You put virtues upon him from your own ideal, and you hadn't probably seen him in circumstances to show his true character. Lots of girls marry on the strength of loving their own ideal and putting it on a man wholesale. When he takes it off in his own home, they break their hearts and think that marriage is a failure, when the truth is they were in too much of a hurry and tried to fit their ideal to the first man that came along."

"Well, I wish I'd had you to open my eyes, Aunt Lavinia. I'm afraid George is going to be rather a bother to get rid of."

There was not quite her usual sweetness in the letter she penned at once.

Dear George:
It isn't a matter of sinks at all. If I really loved you, I

wouldn't care what kind of a sink we had to have. Can't you see that?

I'm sorry you bought the sink, but you can probably sell it and make a little something on it. Or perhaps you'll keep it and use it yourself. I'm sure you'll find some nice girl, George, who is your real companion in life. I know I never could be.

Sincerely,
Amorelle

The reply to this was prompt and brief.

Amorelle:

I certainly am disappointed in your character. I didn't know you had it in you to be so persistently bullheaded and selfish about a house. But you won't make anything this way, I can tell you. I'm tired of this babyishness. You be home Monday night when I come, or I'm done. This is your last call, and I mean it. There are plenty of other girls in the world.

George

When Amorelle read this, she set her lips in a fine, firm line and burned the letter in the fireplace. She did not answer it.

The days shone on, each one like a shining crystal stone with many facets, each brighter than the day before, and the hummingbird flashed through the sunshine humming happily. Amorelle's heart was at rest. She liked her work; she loved Miss

Landon and was happier than she had been since she was a child.

Monday flew by and all that week, then came a letter from Aunt Clara at the seashore.

Dear Niece:

I am sending you some pieces of organdie I want hem-stitched. You will see where the first thread is drawn an inch or two. I want them all like that, and please get them back as soon as possible. I want them for my lavender gingham. The organdie ruffles all went to pieces in the wash.

George was at the house Monday night before we left. He seemed very much upset. He wanted your uncle to force you to come home. He said you weren't of age yet in this state and your uncle was your legal guardian, and he ought to force you to come home and behave yourself. Your uncle wasn't at home that night, and I don't know what he means to do about it. I told George I heartily agreed with him that you had lost your head and were acting very babyish, but of course, as I wasn't a real relative at all, I couldn't do anything. I think, if you want my advice, that the best thing you can do is to go quietly back in a week or two and just open up the house and begin to clean. You'll be tired of your notions by that time, and it will give George a little time to cool down. He'll come around all right. I suppose from what he told me he's been acting a little high-handed about a house, but he'll get over it. You have to manage men, you know.

Get these ruffles back by Thursday if you can. I need them.
Now think over my advice, and get back home next
week. The key is at Varney's store.

Your affectionate aunt,
Clara

Amorelle hemmed the ruffles and sent them Wednesday morning; but she did not write again. What was there to say?

One morning, the most crystal-clear Saturday of the whole summer, a big, shining blue car drew up at Miss Landon's door, and a young man stepped out and looked around him, took in with quick, appreciative eye the hidings of the lilacs, the moss etching of the roof, the honeysuckle drapery, and the dart of the golden-winged hummingbird. Then, with a light in his eye, he walked confidently up the path and knocked at the door. This was the place all right. He couldn't be mistaken. There was even the old gate chain where she used to swing.

He was there at noon when Amorelle came from the bank for her half holiday, sitting beside Miss Landon's couch, quite at home. They were apparently well acquainted.

Amorelle paused in the doorway, the sunlit halo around her head, and saw her dream come true. Her heart stood still and then gave a great leap. But after a second of surprise, she told it to be still and went forward quite naturally to meet him, though she could not quite keep the ring of delight out of her voice.

"Mr. Garrison! How did you come to be here?"

He rose and took her hand eagerly, looking down at her as if his eyes had been hungry for a sight of her, a rare smile on his lips.

"I—just came! Do you mind?" he said.

Then both of them laughed, for both remembered when he had said exactly the same thing before. Then they both remembered that he was still holding her hand, and they looked embarrassed and hurried to find chairs, he putting her carefully into the big stuffed rocker he had been occupying, while Miss Landon feasted loving eyes upon the two.

"Why, I—came to see Glenellen—your Glenellen. Will you show it to me?" he said.

Oh joy! Of course she would! What rare miracle brought a happiness like this to her? *Oh Father in heaven, I thank You,* her heart breathed, and then warned itself in the same breath not to presume too much on just a day's joy. Not to jump too far ahead and make herself think a day's joy was any more than—a day's joy. Of course not!

Bonny in the kitchen, listening, flew to work. Chicken! There was by some miracle a cold breast of chicken. What delectable sandwiches the fine, white, homemade bread made. Remarkable coincidence that there should have been breast of chicken. But the chicken was not for lunch.

There had been a delicious, creamy potato soup brewing for lunch before the guest had arrived, and raspberries from the bush in the backyard, red and yellow and black, with rich Jersey cream and velvety gingerbread as accessories. Bonny put a head of lettuce into the spring to cool while she sliced a few tomatoes and whisked together an omelet as an afterthought, and the lunch was ready.

"Now," she said, appearing at the dining room door, "lunch is ready, and if you two are going to the glen, I've got your supper all put up for you. There's apple turnovers just out of the oven. It's a hungry walk to the glen."

Two pairs of eyes met and smiled joyously. Amorelle wondered. Had such a thing really come into her life at last? Going off on a picnic with a friend just like other girls!

They left the big blue car parked among the lilacs and climbed the back fence to the way across the meadows, down by the trout brook, following it back to its source up through the beautiful glen.

If all the songs that were ever sung of fern-fringed, mossy glens and all the poems that were ever written to describe the cool, green depths where the water tinkles along over bright stones with strange, wandering sunbeams unexpectedly tangled in the midst of the feathery-fronded walls high overhead, had been combined into one exquisite bit of writing, it could not quite have come up to the song that sang itself in the hearts of those two that afternoon as they trailed down through the meadow, over the brook, and entered the dim hall of the glen.

Perhaps Glenellen is not so widely known as some other glens; perhaps its height and depth might not measure up to the size they put in the geographical part of the dictionary, but it is certain there is no more lovelier spot to be found anywhere than there.

As they entered the cool shadow of its green, rocky walls, the breath of the summer day beat softly on their cheeks as if the sun were bidding them adieu, and the cool breath of ferns struck sharp across their senses. A great silence reigned, as if all else kept still to hear the music of the little water as it tinkled over the stones in the midst, drenching the forget-me-nots and watercress and echoing up, far up, to blue sky fringed with ferns.

An awe came upon them as the silence made itself felt, and their voices hushed. Instinctively the man reached out his hand and took the hand of the girl. It might have been to detain her and prolong the first lovely glimpse or again to keep her from slipping, who shall say? And so they entered into the glen together.

"Isn't there something wonderful, almost holy, about it?" spoke Garrison at last in a low voice. "It seems a sacrilege to talk of ordinary things."

"Yes," said Amorelle in a hushed voice, her eyes filled with the dreamy look she so often wore. "I always feel when I first enter as if it was the outer court of God's house and I must wait until He comes and tells me I may go on." She spoke the words shyly, half frightened when she heard them herself. She was not used to speaking out her thoughts to other humans.

The young man looked down into her eyes with something good and beautiful within his own.

"How lovely!" he said gravely and after a pause. "So this was what you were thinking of that day when you saw the opening where the brook led away to the woods. That was what you were used to. No wonder you had that longing look in your eyes."

"Oh!" said Amorelle. "I hadn't been used to this for a long time. And this is the first time since I came back that I've been here. One doesn't go alone to the glen. There hasn't been anybody to go with—"

"And I have the first honor?" He gave her a look that set her heart in a tumult, and then suddenly he drew her down on a rock.

"Let's sit down here," he said. "I want to ask you something. They tried to tell me you were going to be married in a month or two. Is that true?"

Amorelle's cheeks grew rosy, and her lashes drooped. Then she lifted her eyes and tried to look natural; but somehow the flutter in her heart made it very hard to look into his eyes, and she dropped her own again.

"No," she said, trying to speak steadily but unable to keep a lilt out of her voice. "I was—*engaged*—but— It was a mistake. It is broken."

She lifted her face and smiled quietly.

"You are" —he hesitated, looking earnestly at her— "not sorry?" There was grave questioning in his voice.

Her face broke into sunshine.

"Oh, no!" she said happily. "Not in the least. It was a great mistake."

"Well, I'm glad. Now that's that, and we can go on. I like to know just how I stand with my friends. I hope you don't mind my asking. And you're at liberty to ask anything of me in turn, of course. One thing, I'm not engaged and never have been yet."

He sprang up and caught her hand, drawing her arm within his and walking so they went on into the heart of the lovely glen.

It was just about this time, so far as the sun in the sky was concerned, that a very new flivver drew up smartly in front of

Miss Landon's gate, and a big, blond young man with a "get-out-of-my-way-and-do-as-I-say" manner got out, smashed open the picket gate, and crunched boldly up the path, surveying the sweet, little old house with a look that uncovered all its defects and put it at his mercy.

While this young man waited impatiently for Henrietta Bonsall to come to the door, he had calculated fairly accurately how many feet, front and deep, the lot was and the probable price of land a foot in that part of town.

Chapter 19

Bonny had been lying down after the excitement of the morning and was trying to keep everything still so that Miss Landon would have a good nap. It took several minutes for her to struggle into her shoes, which she had removed from her tired feet for a little while, and to smooth her straggling gray hair. The young man at the front door grew impatient. He knocked loudly and continuously several times and then called, "Hello! Oh, I say! Isn't anybody at home? Amorelle!"

He looked quite injured when Bonny finally appeared and frowned blackly because Amorelle herself had not come.

"Isn't this where Miss Dean is visiting?" he demanded gruffly.

Bonny drew herself up with her sick-room air of competency and admitted frigidly that it was.

"Well, where is she? I want to see her," he said, walking unceremoniously through the door with an appraising look around the room.

Bonny backed up a step and surrounded him, as it were, her ample white apron held out a bit on either side, and so—amazingly and unceremoniously—drove him back on the porch again, sweeping the door shut behind her as she stepped out.

"We'll just talk here," she explained commandingly. "The lady of the house is an invalid, and she's asleep. You mustn't wake her up."

There was no perceptible lowering of the young man's voice as he again demanded Amorelle, but it was evident that he had perceived that he could not carry all before him in this high-handed way.

"Miss Dean ain't in," said Bonny quite collectedly. "She's away fer the day." Her voice was calm and dry. She eyed the stranger appraisingly. Her experience as nurse had taught her to read character remarkably well.

"Away!" frowned the young man, as though Miss Dean were deeply obligated to remain right there when he was coming. "Where?" He glanced the length of the little sunny street.

"Out of town," remarked Bonny placidly. The glen was at least a quarter of a mile away.

"Where?" insisted the dominant youth.

"I really couldn't say," answered Bonny, pulling out some tatting from her ample pocket and beginning to work on it as if she had wasted time enough.

"Well, go and ask at once, won't you? I'm in a hurry, and I've waited long enough already." He spoke in the tone of a manager dictating to a new secretary and struck a match on the porch pillar to light his cigarette, turning his back on Bonny as if he expected her at once to disappear and fulfill his command.

"There's nobody to ask," said Bonny, "not till Miss Landon wakes up, and that might be as late as five o'clock. She don't sleep so good, and she's not to be waked up when she dozes off. Them's the doctor's orders."

"This is ridiculous nonsense!" fumed the visitor. "I've already come a hundred miles out of my way, and gasoline is expensive. Woman, go and ask this Miss Landon you talk about at once where Miss Dean is to be found. I've got to see her on very important business, and I've got to start back to my city tonight. What are you waiting for? Oh, I suppose you're waiting to be tipped. Well, here."

He held out a quarter grudgingly with an ugly frown. Bonny gazed at it an instant. Then lifting her hand with a swift movement, she gave his hand a quick knock, which sent the quarter flying down the path, and stood facing him with ire in her eye.

"Now, young man," she said calmly with sickroom command in her voice. "You can go on your way rejoicin', or you can sit down in that rocker over there and wait till Miss Landon wakes up. It's all one to me, but you need not go offerin' me any of your dirty money. I'm nobody's servant ef I do wear aperns."

With that she went into the house and shut the front door.

Behind a vine-clad bedroom window off the porch, Miss Landon stifled a chuckle of delight. She had long ago decided who the visitor on the front porch must be.

George Horton, astounded, bewildered, gazed blankly at the door then thriftily retrieved his quarter. And after gazing speculatively up at the front windows, he walked slowly around the house, coming full upon the big blue automobile parked among the lilacs at one side. This he examined with car-wise eyes and much respect and then with quickened steps walked on to the back door.

Bonny was doing something at the kitchen stove and did not look up, but he boldly opened the screen door and stepped in.

"I say, my good woman," he began in what he meant to be a conciliatory tone, "you wholly misunderstood me. You don't know who I am."

"Well, no," said Bonny, turning slowly around and facing him. "I don't know as I do, and I don't know as I keer to. One thing I know, you ain't no gentleman, an' ef Miss Dean asts me, I'll tell her so. I've told you once, an' I'll tell you jest once more. She ain't here, and she ain't going to be till late t'night. She won't be home fer supper, an' I can't say any more."

Bonny stopped, lifted a delicately browned sponge cake out of the oven, and set some little brown cups of custard to cool in the window. The spicy aroma of cinnamon wafted fragrantly through the kitchen. George Horton sniffed. He was hungry. He eyed the woman belligerently. Then his eye traveled thoughtfully to the window. Golden custard against a shiny background of royal blue.

"Whose car is that out there?" he demanded savagely.

"Belongs to a visitor," said Bonny icily, "though I don't know's you've got any call to ast."

"Did Miss Dean go in a car?"

"Well," said Bonny slowly from the depths of the pantry

where she was putting the sponge cake on a plate to cool, "she didn't go on horseback, not that I saw." It was mortifyingly evident that Bonny had not noticed George Horton's fetching golden eyelashes yet, and George was not used to that.

"Is there any place around here where I can get something to eat?" he asked suddenly and hungrily, eyeing the custards once more.

"Oh yes," said Bonny cordially. "There's Sutton's, down by the bridge. They have chicken dinners for automobile parties. You'll find them on the right hand just after you pass the post office. They're real reasonable with their dinners, I've heard folks say. But if you don't want to pay that much"—lifting her eyelids with the most fleeting of glances—"you can get a ham sandwich at the bake shop and a glass of milk fer that quarter."

Bonny disappeared into the pantry again.

"Woman, look here!" said George Horton, thundering after her to the pantry door. "I've come a good many miles out of my way to see Miss Dean, and she ought to have been here. I want you to tell me about where you think I could find her. Did she go visiting or to the next town to buy something or what? And which direction did she take?"

"You've got no call to come in here," said Bonny, sweeping him sideways back into the kitchen. "This is private property. And I've told you before, I ain't in Miss Dean's confidence. She didn't come and ast me could she go, ner nothing. She might uv gone on business, and then again she might uv just gone for amusement. How should I know? The next town beyond to the north is Fowler's Corner. You might inquire at the post office how to find Spillard's. I heard Miss Landon tell her the other day she wanted to get Anne Spillard down to see her sometime. But land! She might notta gone there today, of course. Ef I was you, I'd take a room at Sutton's and wait till mornin'. 'Tain't likely noways she could see you b'fore then anyhow, fer it'll be late when she gets back. Now, my work's done, and I gotta go upstairs an' change my dress. Ef you don't mind, I'd like to lock up my kitchen 'fore I go. Yer welcome to set on the front porch an' rest a spell ef you prefer that to yer car, but I ain't got no more time to waste now."

George Horton, keeping one firm foot inside the screen door, hesitated.

"But you don't understand," said George with a puzzled, baffled expression not at home on his usually assured countenance. "I'm engaged to Miss Dean. I'm her fiancé."

"That's all right with me," said Bonny cheerfully, "jes' so you ain't got any engagement with me!"

"Could I write a note?" he asked, frowning.

"Well, I guess you know better'n I do whether you could or not," remarked Bonny sharply, taking firm hold of the door hook.

George's head gave a haughty toss, and he met her facetiousness with a withering scorn. Pulling out a small notebook and pencil, he began to write, leaning the book against the house. Bonny pulled the door shut and hooked it securely.

"You can just leave it on the winder-ledge," she said comfortably. "Put a stone on it so the wind won't blow it away, an' I'll see she gets it t'night sometime." She pulled down the green window shade and disappeared up the back stairs. And presently, peering through the slats of the shutters in the room above, she watched with satisfaction as the young man climbed into his flivver and rattled away down the road. He was not going in the direction of Sutton's. He was not going to stay all night! Bonny heaved a sigh of relief and went back to finish her work in the kitchen and investigate the note. If it had been written by Amorelle, she would have left it unread for years. But this person she considered an upstart and felt it her duty to find out what he was about, so she took it up gingerly and read.

Amorelle:

As you wouldn't come home, I have been at great expense and trouble to come to you on my way back from a business trip; but I find you gone, and this strange old woman doesn't know where, or won't tell, I don't know which. I think it's about time this funny business ends, but I haven't time to monkey around this way. I had something to tell you today that you would have wanted to hear, but I couldn't wait all night, so it's up to you to come home. See? I'll be down at your uncle's day after tomorrow night, and I want you there, no mistake this time! Understand? My business won't wait any longer, so take the first train and don't fail!

George

"H'm!" mused Bonny, folding the note carefully in its crease and laying it on the clock shelf. "I guess that'll wait till sometime tomorrow mornin' well enough. I'll jest ferget it tonight. I thought 'twas him all right! I sensed it right from the start!"

Nobody had told old Bonny about George Horton, but she had that sixth sense that felt everything connected with those she loved, and she knew how to keep her mouth closed on her knowledge.

Meantime the shadows began to grow deep in the glen, and the two who had wandered to its farthest end and explored its hidden beauties came slowly back and climbed to the big flat rock halfway up to the top of the glen to eat their supper.

As they opened Bonny's inviting lunchbox and spread the contents out on the white cloth that lay on the top of the box, neither of the two could help remembering another box they had opened together not so long ago.

"Chicken sandwiches! As I'm alive!" said Russell Garrison. "Isn't this a kind of coincidence? Wasn't that what we had before? I seem to remember they tasted better than any chicken sandwiches I had ever had before, but then you made those. These may be good, but those were the first we ever ate together. Perhaps that is the secret."

The color flew into Amorelle's cheeks, and she lifted glad eyes to meet his across the snowy cloth. This had been such a wonderful day, and he had been so much more delightful than she had even remembered. It hardly seemed possible, but it was true. And she knew there was going to be a terrible let-down when he was gone, maybe never to come back again. But she just would not let herself think about that. She would treasure every instant now while she had it, something to remember through the days to wipe out the memory of George Horton and her nightmare of an engagement with him. Just another beautiful day with a friend who felt as she did about all beautiful things, and who loved her Lord Jesus. She would not think of dull, drab days after he was gone. This day should be a beautiful jewel to deck the darkness of other days.

So her eyes answered to his eyes and took the sweet thrill at his words of praise as a gift from God to measure the poor counterfeit love she had discarded before it was too late.

All day these two had been growing more and more into a knowledge of one another. Like two children, hand in hand, they had started to explore a wonderland, and it had opened before their eager feet as the beautiful hours sped by, without a single disappointing episode.

And now, when the tempting little supper was laid out on the cloth, and while a wandering ray from the setting sun somehow penetrated down to their nook and touched Amorelle's hair, lighting it like a halo around her sweet face, Garrison bowed his head and gave thanks.

"Our Father, we thank Thee for this beautiful day Thou has given us together. We thank Thee that Thou has let our lives touch and brought us to this sweet fellowship. We thank Thee most of all for Thyself and that Thou hast saved us both and brought us to know Thee. We thank Thee that we both know Thee, which has made our fellowship so much the sweeter. And now we thank Thee for this evening meal, and wilt Thou let us feel Thy presence here with us, Thy love about us, Thy guidance in all our thoughts and actions. We ask it in the name of the Lord Jesus, our Savior."

Amorelle sat with bowed head, her heart thrilling. What a privilege to be one in a prayer like that! What a friend to have who could pray that way! How hallowed a friendship that could be cemented in praise to God! How utterly wonderful that God had a day like this in store for her all the time she was worrying and fretting and puzzling over how to make George Horton over to suit her own vague dreams of what a lover should be! She had tried to snatch eagerly after what she yearned for, when all the time God had this beautiful friendship waiting for her as a wonderful surprise. And when it came it did not come by any effort of her own. Why, one day of a friendship with a man like this was worth a whole lifetime filled with the rough courting of a man like George Horton, even though he was good-looking.

She lifted her eyes when the prayer was ended and saw that this man, too, was handsome, but in a very different way. He had fine features, but they were also strong, and there was nothing bold about the steady, gray eyes that met hers with such a wonderful smile. His smile did not rollick all over his face, but it was bright and tender and warm, and there was a peace in it that rested one just to look at it. Ah! She could not compare this rare man with George. She was done with George forever, and her heart sent up a glad thanksgiving that her eyes had been opened in time. So she met the smile that shone upon her like a benediction, with a smile as free and glad.

"There is something different about you," said the man, looking at her steadily, rejoicingly. "I noticed it the minute I saw you today. The shadow is gone from your eyes."

"It's gone from my heart, too," said Amorelle softly. "I'd been going through an awful experience for several weeks, trying to find out what was the matter, not knowing what was the right thing to do about it, and I never realized that God would give me all the wisdom and knowledge I needed until you told me. Then what a load rolled away from my shoulders. You don't know what you did for me that day."

The glad eyes searched deep into hers.

"And I like a fool tried to stay away from that picnic that day." he said. "I thought of every excuse I could, but finally I saw that my relatives were terribly pleased that they had got up some young company and a little entertainment for me while I was visiting them. So I went, but it was the last thing I wanted to do; and when I saw the crowd I felt still more aversion, until I saw you. I just couldn't understand how a girl like you had happened among those others. But then I found out that nothing happens, that God had brought you there and that He had brought me to find you. At least that's the way I felt about it."

They were eating the sandwiches now and drinking the bottle of orange juice that Bonny had prepared. Delicate bits of celery and tiny sweet pickles were vanishing, but the two didn't know what they were eating. It was all nectar and ambrosia. Apple turnovers and cream cheese, they ate every crumb. But they were more interested in their sweet conversation, and they sat talking until the twilight began to deepen in the glen.

Then hastily they gathered up the cloth and napkins, made their way down to the little spring below them to wash their hands, and turned to climb up to the top again to be in time for the moonrise.

They were standing close together looking up the fern-fringed wall toward the luminous evening sky with its opal-tinted clouds, loath to leave the dim, quiet seclusion.

Garrison suddenly took his gaze from the top of the embankment and brought it to Amorelle's face. How dear, how lovely she was, there in the dimness beside him, her face like a delicate cameo etched against the dark greenness.

Softly he laid his arm around her and drew her gently close to himself.

"Amorelle," he said reverently, "I love you. Is it too soon to tell you so?"

Amorelle turned to him a face filled with deep wonder and dawning joy.

"Too soon?" she breathed. "Oh, too soon! How could it be, when I've been wondering how I could bear to have you go away and I to never see you anymore!"

Then both his arms came around her and drew her close, his lips were on hers, and heaven seemed to come down in the dim, sweet darkness and envelop them. And suddenly Amorelle knew what *real* love meant. Knew beyond a shadow of a doubt. Remembered what her father had said, "When there's doubt, there's no doubt!" And then she knew that it was true.

They came out of their trance, presently, to realize that it was getting dark and climbing on a glenside would be difficult with only starlight. But first, before they started, they knelt beside the little spring and prayed together, consecrating their lives anew together to the Lord who had died for them.

Then his arm around her, her hand in his, they climbed to the top of the fern-rimmed wall, feeling their way along the narrow, precipitous path that was sometimes slippery with pine needles and often with cool drippings from the trickling springlets, slowly, joyously, close to one another. They reached the top at last and found a rock in a high, lovely place where they could look out across the rim of the glen that yawned below them, cool and dim, with night sounds hauntingly lovely like music that has never been written.

There they sat close, sheltered by a group of hemlocks, his arm around her, her head on his chest, and watched the rim of silver that amazingly became a great moon and flooded the earth with silver as it came slowly up and sailed over the sky. Amorelle felt that she had never seen a real moonrise before. They would never forget the thrill of it, the feeling that God had given them that great display as a sort of celebration of their joy.

Late as it was when they got back to the cottage, Miss Landon was on her couch in the sitting room awaiting them, and they went in, hand in hand, and told her of their great joy.

The old saint turned her eyes, bright with happiness, upon them and fairly beamed.

"I'm so glad for you, so glad for you *both*," she said with a bit of tremble in her voice. She put up her arms and pulled both faces down till she could place a warm little trembly kiss on each one.

"I knew the Lord had something precious in store for my little girl," she said softly with shining eyes.

"Perhaps," said Garrison suddenly, as if he had forgotten a very important matter, "I ought to have given you some credentials. You don't know me or my family at all, of course. Perhaps that ought to have come first."

"You don't need to tell me or give me credentials, young man," said Miss Landon lovingly. "I can see it in your eyes. Your eyes look like the little girl's father's eyes, and you don't see such true eyes on a young man's face very often today. As for your family, I'm hearing you belong to the family of the King. What more could I desire?"

"Now," said Garrison, when the hour had grown so late that he knew he must take his leave, "what are we going to do next Saturday afternoon? Can we go to the glen some more, or is that too soon for me to come again?"

"Oh, can you come next week again?" said Amorelle in great delight. "How *wonderful!*"

"Why, certainly; New York is only ninety miles away. Why shouldn't I come where my heart is the minute I get a chance? Besides, I have a ring to bring you to take the place of the one I never saw." He smiled and lifted her hand to his lips as they stood out on the doorstep. "It may not be as gorgeous as the one you used to have, and it never was an 'investment.' But it's been in our family a long time, and there is a story connected with it. It belonged to my great-great-grandmother. It was her engagement ring. My mother has always loved it, and I fell heir to it. It was made by a great artist in jewels. It has a sapphire, a diamond, and a pearl curiously wrought together."

"Oh," breathed Amorelle, starry-eyed, "I'm so glad it is not in the least like the other one. I would not want to be reminded of that."

His glance twinkled happily as he kissed her good-bye.

"Well, I'm glad you told me all about everything," he said. "Now we shall have no skeletons in the closet. Good-bye, darling, I'll see you next week."

The big blue car shot out at last in the moonlight and started back to the city. About fifty miles farther on the highway, it passed a little flivver, standing darkly in the shadow of a roadside inn. Its owner had succumbed to hunger and weariness and gone inside for rest and refreshment.

But the driver of the big blue car had no need for rest. He carried with him a joy so great that he felt as if he should never be weary again.

And back in the little cottage he had left, a girl in the moonlight knelt beside her bed and thanked God for the way He had saved her from sorrow and given her this so great joy instead.

Chapter 20

In the little roadside inn, George Horton slept the sleep of the baffled and disappointed. He slept so hard that he was late in starting home the next morning and late all along the way. He went home cross to find everything out of joint in the office, and he blamed it all on Amorelle. He resolved that now, *now*, if she did not turn up at her uncle's house the very next night as he had ordered her to, he was *done*. He would have no more nonsense! He would go after *another girl*.

There were plenty of other girls, of course, and how pleased they would be to see him coming!

The next night he went to the Dean house to find it utterly dark, with no response to his repeated rings. At last he turned on his heel and walked away, angry, furious, determined to get even with a girl who dared stand out against him so long. Who would ever have dreamed that that quiet, meek, little Amorelle had it in her to be so bullheaded?

So instead of going home, he went to see a girl with yellow bobbed hair and very red painted lips and plucked eyebrows.

Before the evening was over, she had made him take her to the movies and buy her a five-pound box of chocolates and treat her to ice cream in the most expensive place in town. It was *awful* to think how much money he had spent as he walked home, and all just to spite Amorelle. But she would see! In time she would come around, he thought. He would keep this up until she understood. She would miss having attention now she was used to it, and when she saw he was keeping his word, she would write a humble apology. He felt he knew Amorelle. She would find out that she couldn't sit around visiting friends hundreds of miles away and keep him racing all over the United States after her and expect, finally, to bring him around and make him rent that expensive house for her. She couldn't do it! He would maybe get to think as much of this Gloria Gladwyn as ever he did of Amorelle, or maybe more, and that would serve Amorelle exactly right!

He looked in the mirror when he went to his room and noticed how handsome he was looking that night and was convinced that he was right. He knew what he could do with those curly eyelashes, and Amorelle would find out what it was to do without them!

So he went to bed with vengeance in his heart.

~~~

Amorelle liked her work in the bank, and when she went home it was wonderful to find her old friend waiting for her on the couch with that sweet mother-smile on her face and Bonny with a nice meal ready to serve. It was going to be so hard to have this all slip away pretty soon when Miss Landon was called Home.

But there was that other great, deep joy in her heart, that new love that had come, that seemed too wonderful to be true. And there were the Saturdays to look for and plan for. Sometimes Amorelle just longed to tell her father all about this new happiness that had come to her, and often she got out that last letter he had written to her and read over and over the advice he had given to her about marriage. Why, it seemed just as though he must have known how God was preparing a mate for her. And perhaps he already knew about it all. What a beautiful talk they would have about it when they got together in heaven!

But life wasn't all just waiting for Saturdays either. There were letters—with parts that were meant to be read aloud to Miss Landon—and sometimes Amorelle read a line or two that were her own special property, just to let her old friend know what a wonderful lover she had.

When such letters were read, Bonny would always manage to have the kitchen door open so that she could hear and would hover hungrily and noiselessly at the doorway, polishing a plate or a cup till she almost wore the flowers off, so anxious was she to know every precious thing about this lovely romance that was happening right before her love-starved eyes.

Amorelle had never answered George Horton's note that he left under the stone on the windowsill. She had read it in Bonny's presence and had delighted the soul of that old rebel by tearing it up, then and there, and stuffing it in the incinerator outside the back door that was then blazing up with the trash Bonny was burning. Bonny had stood behind the door and watched through the crack and chuckled to herself while it burned. And so now she took her joy and entertainment getting what crumbs she could from this real romance that had come to the girl she so loved.

And when Garrison brought the beautiful old ring with its three gorgeous jewels in their quaint, rare setting, she rejoiced to see it gleaming on the girl's finger.

It was on Saturday afternoon, just after the holidays, that Amorelle took a letter from the post office as she passed on her way home from the bank. But before she had had time to identify its writer, Garrison's car drew up to the curb and his smile drove everything else from her mind. She stuffed the letter in her handbag and did not think of it again until later in the afternoon when she went to her bag to get some papers she had brought up for Miss Landon to sign.

Miss Landon was growing daily weaker, like the fading of a lovely frail flower, and the two young people had been giving her as much of their Saturday afternoons as she would let them, for they felt they would not have her with them long. So the days of her lingering were made very sweet to her after the long, hard toil of her lonesome life.

Amorelle took out the papers, and the letter came out with them.

"Oh, here's a letter," she said. "I forgot all about it. Oh!"

The two who watched her look at the letter saw pain and annoyance flash over her face.

"What is it?" said Miss Landon with her mischievous twinkle that they hadn't seen so much lately. "Has George come to life again?"

"Oh yes," sighed Amorelle with annoyance. "I won't read it!"

"Oh yes," said Miss Landon, "read it. Perhaps he's announcing his engagement! I'm curious to see what stage he has reached. Read it aloud. Russell will enjoy it, I'm sure."

"I'm not sure that *I* shall," said Amorelle with a grimace as she glanced over the letter. "I'm beginning to realize that I was terribly blind that I didn't see sooner what kind of a man he was."

This was the letter:

Dear Amorelle:

Well, I've come to it at last. I'm going to take the house you like so much!

I'll have to own I can't find any girl who fits into my life quite so well as you do. You're so sensible. I've tried a lot of them, and it's cost me some money, but I consider the expense worthwhile because how else should I have known? There's nothing like being satisfied, you know.

So now I've come back to you, Amorelle, and decided to let you have your own way. I'm going up tomorrow evening and sign the lease with the privilege of purchase within a month if I choose. It may be a better investment to own, because then we can get out and rent it any time if rents go up and we need to save money.

Say, Amorelle, why didn't you let me know there was money in this business of you staying away off there so long?

I've been up to talk to your uncle, and he says you're to get that house and quite a bit of money. He also says your father left you well fixed. Of course, in that case you did the right thing by sticking by the old woman. I wouldn't have made a fuss if I'd known.

But say, how long is it going to be before the poor gink croaks? This business of having you away forever is getting on my nerves. How much is in it anyway? Enough to pay us?

Say, if I telegraph you I've got pneumonia or something, can't you get off for a few days and come up and look at the house again? I think it's high time we got this thing patched up, don't you? I'm perfectly willing to forgive you everything, and I've got the house you asked for. What more do you want?

Yours as ever,
George

Amorelle read only a few sentences aloud; then scanning the rest, she suddenly flung the letter on the floor and burst into tears.

"You can read it if you like," she managed to sob out. "I can't. Oh, what a fool I was to think I ever cared for him!"

Garrison came and gathered her into his arms and wiped her tears away gently, but she sobbed out, "I'm not fit for a man like you when I could be such a blind fool as to think I loved a man like that!"

"There, don't cry!" he soothed with a twinkle in his eyes. "Can't you be a little sorry for the poor geezer? At least he had sense enough at last to appreciate you."

"No," said Amorelle, breaking into hysterical laughter now, "it's only that he thinks I'm more economical than the other girls he tried to get, and I've come into money."

Then they all joined in a hearty laugh.

Quite soon after that, Lavinia Landon slipped away quietly in her sleep and left them, and they smiled through their tears to see the joy on her sweet, quiet face.

It was several weeks later that a noisy, mud-splashed flivver, driven by a determined young man with grim set lips, clattered into Glenellen late one afternoon.

Somehow he had taken the wrong road and got turned around, entering the town from the wrong direction. He stopped at the railroad station for directions. It always irritated him to waste anything, even time. It did not spell *efficiency*, and he ruled his life by that word. But in this case, he could not seem to help it.

So, much against his will, he condescended to ask of some men who were lounging around the station if they knew where Miss Amorelle Dean lived.

An original settler who had known Amorelle almost ever since she was born looked at him in mild curiosity and drew himself to something like an alert attitude, opening his mouth to answer. But before he could speak, a small boy with freckles and red hair broke in.

"She *ain't*! You're too late! She's married! She went away in a twelve-cylinder car. She's goin' ta Europe on her weddin' trip.

You can't possibly ketch her now. Her boat sailed at noon!"

George sat speechless in his flivver and stared at the attentive group of onlookers while the small boy added a few more details, which only filled him with a finer fury. Then he stepped on his starter and got himself out of that town as fast as he could, shaking the dust, as it were, from his feet.

But as the roofs and spires of Glenellen faded from his mortified gaze, and he collected his scattered faculties somewhat, he remarked aloud to the passing landscape, "Well, I'm glad I had forethought enough not to sign that lease yet! There's so much saved anyway! What a fool she's made of me! Maybe I'm lucky after all."

Then as he reflected on the various remarks that had drifted to him about the house that had been left to Amorelle and the "tidy bit of money," he added under his breath with something almost like a sigh, "What a fool I've been, though! I'm afraid I won't find another girl like Amorelle!"

But that very evening, celebrating his disappointment in a comfortable hotel dinner, he looked through his curly golden lashes at the black-eyed, dashing waitress and remembered that he still had his looks.

GRACE LIVINGSTON HILL (1865–1947) is known as the pioneer of Christian romance. Grace wrote over one hundred faith-inspired books during her lifetime. When her first husband died, leaving her with two daughters to raise, writing became a way to make a living, but she always recognized storytelling as a way to share her faith in God. She has touched countless lives through the years and continues to touch lives today. Her books feature moving stories, delightful characters, and love in its purest form.

Love Endures
Grace Livingston Hill Classics

Also available in series. . .

The Beloved Stranger
The Prodigal Girl
A New Name
Re-Creations
Tomorrow About This Time
Crimson Roses
Blue Ruin
Coming Through the Rye
The Christmas Bride
Ariel Custer
Not Under the Law
Job's Niece
The White Flower
Duskin
Matched Pearls
April Gold
Amorelle
Rainbow Cottage
Ladybird
The Gold Shoe
The Substitute Guest
Kerry
Crimson Mountain
Beauty for Ashes